-TEARS OF DARKNESS-
THE WALLS OF JERICHO

2

SOPHIA LIDDELL

TEARS OF DARKNESS
        Volume 2: The Walls of Jericho

TEARS OF DARKNESS

VOLUME 2: THE WALLS OF JERICHO

SOPHIA LIDDELL

TEARS OF DARKNESS, Volume 2: The Walls of Jericho
SOPHIA LIDDELL

Artwork by
VERONICA LIDDELL

This book is a work of fiction.
Names, characters, places, and incidents are
the product of the author's imagination or are
used fictitiously. Any resemblance to actual
events, locales, or persons, living or dead, is coincidental.

TEARS OF DARKNESS, Volume 2: The Walls of Jericho
© SOPHIA LIDDELL 2018

Check out my blog and get updates @
sophialiddellbooks.webs.com

Join me on Crunchyroll @
www.crunchyroll.com/user/SophiaLiddell

First Edition

Paperback Cover ISBN#
978-1-7323049-2-5

TEARS OF DARKNESS

CHAPTER
04
WHAT YOU LEAVE BEHIND

Sarah and Valerie sat on the couch in their pajamas. Sarah wore her white and blue pajama shirt that extended to her knees. Valerie wore a matching white and pink pajama top and bottom shirt and pants. A pink silhouetted butterfly was stitched on the breast pocket. She had a slight bruise on her cheek where Sarah had slapped her the day before. They held hands together as they watched the latest episode of Magical Girl Squad. They watched it in honor of Mary, who never got to see it, nor would she ever get to see it again.

Lieutenant Michael, who had no interest in the show, sat in one of the recliner chairs and watched it anyway for Mary's sake. He also knew that it would make Sarah and Valerie happy to have him join them. He sat there in a tan colored t-shirt and his olive green pajama pants.

Earlier that day, Lieutenant Michael completed the transfer request forms that would allow Jennifer Gonzalez to be transferred to his unit. It would be much easier this time since Jennifer was not only already trained, but, also because she was already in Sacramento sector. According to the report, Jennifer was being treated at the military's hospital facility at the base down the street.

The poor girl was the lone survivor of the Leviathan Company. The World Government was scrambling as fast as they could to rebuild the destroyed unit. He had heard that they would likely move the Leviathan Headquarters from

Los Angeles to the San Diego Sector. Los Angeles was nothing but radioactive scorched earth now. Until Leviathan Company could be rebuilt, tensions would remain high for the surviving Wielder Companies in the region.

Lieutenant Michael kept reviewing in his mind the memory of Jennifer being carried out of the helicopter on the roof. Even in her paralyzed state, she continued to grip onto the severed hand of her former Lieutenant. Losing all your friends to death would certainly break a person. It was, no doubt, even worse for her since she was still only nine years old. He had no doubt that she was suffering from mental trauma. He would have to help her through it.

The show was boring to him so his mind kept drifting randomly. He began to think about the memories he had with Mary again. He began to think about the last things she said to him. He could still feel the memory of her warm hands on his cheeks, the sensation on his lips. It still shocked him. Suddenly, the ending theme music began to play, and Lieutenant Michael's mind was forced back to the present. He returned his attention to the television.

Valerie looked up at Sarah and said, "That was a really good episode. I ... I think Mary would have really liked it."

Sarah nodded and gave a depressed smile, saying, "Yeah, I think so too. The girls finally found the fortress of the evil king in the mountains. I think we're going to get to see the final battle soon."

Lieutenant Michael groaned as he pulled himself out of the chair. He said, "Okay, girls. It's Friday, so, you know what that means." He went into the kitchen, opened a cabinet, and pulled out the small black case that contained their weekly injections.

Sarah sighed and began to roll her right sleeve up as Lieutenant Michael walked back over to them. He opened the black case and pulled the injector unit out. He stuck a small vial of liquid into it and then pressed it on the base of her right bicep. There was a slight click and Sarah winced from the prick.

Lieutenant Michael then lifted the injector unit back up and pulled out the now empty vial. He stuck a new vial inside the injector unit and then pressed it to Valerie's right arm, just below her bicep. Valerie closed her eyes and braced for the slight prick of the injector needle. There was a small click and the weekly injection was done.

Valerie opened her eyes and rubbed the spot on her arm. No matter how many times she received the injection, she would always close her eyes and then rub the spot where he injected her.

Lieutenant Michael put the injector unit back in the case and said, "Well, girls, I've received the okay to go get Jennifer tomorrow. After breakfast, I'll go get her and bring her here. I want you girls to make her feel at home. Remember that she's lost all her friends so we are going to have to help her to make new ones."

Sarah nodded and shook her fists in excitement, saying, "You can count on me, Lieutenant. I'm the big sister now, like Mary and Susan were to me so I'll definitely help her out like they helped me."

Valerie clasped her hands together and said, "Don't worry, Lieutenant. I'll do my best to be her friend and we'll watch Magical Girl Squad together."

Lieutenant Michael rubbed both of their heads with his hands and said, "I know you two will. I can always count on you for stuff like this. It's bed time now so off you go."

Sarah and Valerie jumped off the couch. Together they wrapped their arms around Lieutenant Michael's torso and said in unison, "Good night, Lieutenant!"

Lieutenant Michael put his arms over their backs and said, "Good night, girls. I hope you have a good night's sleep."

Sarah and Valerie let him go and then walked toward their rooms. Lieutenant Michael sighed and returned the black case to the cabinet. He poured some water in a kettle and put it on the stove to boil. He put his own herbal blend mix together in a teapot and waited for the kettle to whistle.

Lieutenant Michael took out a serving tray and put the tea pot on it with two tea cups. The kettle finally began to whistle so he poured the water into the tea pot. He then picked up the tray in one hand and walked through the doorway of his apartment to the door on the other side of the hall.

He softly knocked on the door and waited. Hopefully Rachel had not gone to sleep yet. The door opened and Lieutenant Rachel stood there smiling at him in the doorway. She was still in her uniform with the black stripes. She said, "I thought you might be coming tonight."

Lieutenant Michael said, "Well, you know me. I didn't really want to be alone by myself this evening. I brought my famous herbal tea to share. I was hoping you would sit with me and have some again."

Lieutenant Rachel opened the door all the way and stepped aside with a look that he knew meant that she felt sorry for him. Michael came in and put the tray on the dinner table. He sat down and began pouring the herbal tea into the cups. Lieutenant Rachel sat down next to him.

He blew on top of his hot tea and then took a sip. Rachel watched him and waited for him to speak but he said nothing. He just stared into his cup of herbal tea and rotated it in his hand. She said, "How are you doing?"

He shrugged his shoulders and said, "I'm miserable. I keep waiting for Mary to make one of her stupid jokes that I hate so much but then I remember that she's gone. She's gone."

Lieutenant Rachel put her hand on his arm and said, "What can I do to help you feel better?"

Lieutenant Michael said, "Just being with me is enough."

Lieutenant Rachel gently said, "Did you want to sleep with me in my bed tonight?"

Lieutenant Michael chuckled and said, "Well, it might just come to that, but if one of my girls couldn't find me in the middle of the night, they might get even more scared."

Lieutenant Rachel said, "I think you worry about them too much sometimes. You should make sure to take care of yourself too."

Lieutenant Michael took another sip of his herbal tea and said, "Well, you're probably right, but they're all I have and I'm all they've got."

Lieutenant Rachel said, "That's not true, Michael. You got me too. I'm there for you whenever you want."

Lieutenant Michael put his cup of tea down and took Rachel's hand into his own and smiled at her. Suddenly there was a soft, almost inaudible noise. Lieutenant Michael let go of Rachel's hand and looked toward the hallway, saying, "Okay, Giana. I know you are there. Come on out."

An embarrassed Giana slowly poked her head around the corner of the hallway and said, "Good evening, Lieutenant Michael. I was just trying to get a glass of water." She walked around the edge of the wall wearing a red and black plaid pajama set that looked almost identical to the one that Mary used to wear. She walked past them toward the kitchen. As she walked to the kitchen, she smiled at them with an exaggerated grin.

As Giana walked past them, she said, "Don't mind me. Keep doing what you're doing." She entered the kitchen, pulled out a glass, and filled it with water. She then walked back toward the hallway with the same exaggerated grin on her face, and disappeared beyond the wall.

Lieutenant Michael rolled his eyes and said, "Geez, the walls have ears."

Lieutenant Rachel said, "Well, we were being noisy I guess. So ... have you selected a new Wielder yet to fill Mary's position?"

Lieutenant Michael took another sip of his herbal tea and said, "Yeah, her name is Jenifer Gonzalez. She is actually that lone survivor from Leviathan Company."

Lieutenant Rachel said, "I see. Poor girl. I remember her just sitting there in the corner of the helicopter. She got on before we did."

Lieutenant Michael finished the herbal tea in his cup and said, "I haven't asked you yet about what happened in your section."

Lieutenant Rachel leaned back in her chair and sighed, saying, "I'd have to say that we got really lucky. The position that we were in had a buffer of Leviathan Company in between us and the main Harvester group. The poor souls on the left side of us got torn up by those new Harvester types."

Lieutenant Michael spoke up saying, "I hear they're calling the new Harvesters: Archer-class."

Lieutenant Rachel nodded her head and said, "Yeah, those Archer Harvesters completely tore up our fifth squad too. The fully-grown Harvesters over ran the Leviathan squad to the right of us. It was at that moment that we got the call to retreat so we all ran together before the Harvesters got close enough. I'm pretty sure that the only reason they didn't reach us was because they were too busy devouring that Leviathan squad. We could hear the screams as we fell back."

Lieutenant Michael said, "I'm glad you and your girls all made it back safely. It would have been even more devastating if I lost both Mary and you on the same day. Mary was so brave at the end. I ... I tried to make her fall back with us when we got the order, but she stood her ground. She helped me to see that if we had done that, none of us would have made it back, or, even worse, Mary would have been the only one to make it back. Honestly, I think that is the worst part of it. That's why I want to take Jennifer in now, because I think that it is worse to be the lone survivor."

Lieutenant Rachel nodded her head and said, "Yeah, I can agree with that."

Lieutenant Michael continued, saying, "That's the problem that the girls have. The Red Wielders are the ones most likely to survive. Us Lieutenants aren't worth a dime in this war. The blues are great but their abilities are primarily defensive. The yellows are just healers, without protection they're dead. The reds are strong enough to survive on their own. Mary understood that better than I did. Mary was filled with love for everybody. She never hesitated to put herself at risk to help anybody."

Suddenly from around the corner a girl started to cry. Lieutenant Michael and Rachel turned toward the hallway to see Giana coming out again. Giana stood there with tears in her eyes. She walked over to Lieutenant Rachel and buried her face on her shoulder.

Lieutenant Rachel said, "What's wrong Giana?"

Giana said, "The last thing I said to Mary was that if she died, I would kill her. She's dead now and I miss her so much."

Lieutenant Michael stood up and said, "Well, I can see that you got your hands full so maybe it's time that I get back to my place."

Giana reached out and grabbed onto the sleeve of Michael's shirt.

Lieutenant Michael stopped and looked at Giana, waiting for her to speak. She just stared at him. He said, "What's up, Giana?"

Giana looked up at him as tears continued to roll from her eyes. She said, "Mary told me that if she ever died to tell you that she left a letter for you under her pillow."

Lieutenant Michael nodded his head and said, "Yeah, I found it. Thanks."

Giana, still holding onto his sleeve, walked over next to him and leaned her forehead onto the side of his arm. He wrapped his arm around her back and said, "Thank you for being Mary's friend. I know you meant a lot to her."

Giana started to cry loudly again, saying, "She was one of my best friends."

Lieutenant Michael said, "I know. I hope that you can be friends with the girl that fills her position too."

Giana, calming herself, said, "I'll try." She then let go of his sleeve and straightened herself back up. Lieutenant Rachel got up and stood behind Giana.

Lieutenant Michael picked up his tea tray and said, "Well, guess I'll be going to bed myself now."

Lieutenant Rachel put an arm around his back and rested her head onto his shoulder saying, "Thanks for the tea. Try to have a good night."

Lieutenant Michael rested his head on top of her head and said, "Thanks for putting up with me tonight." He then turned to Giana and said, "I'm counting on you Giana."

Giana nodded and said, "Don't worry, Lieutenant. You can count on me." She tried to smile at him with her tear-reddened eyes.

Lieutenant Rachel opened the door for him and then gently shut it behind him as he left. She then turned to Giana and said, "Are you okay?"

Giana said, "I'm okay now. Listening to you talk about Mary just made me emotional. I'm sorry that I ruined your adult time. I didn't think that you had it in you to invite him into your bed so soon."

Lieutenant Rachel started to blush and she looked toward the ground. She awkwardly said, "I ... I didn't mean it like that." She then looked up and glared at Giana. She frowned at her and said, "Wait a minute, were you eavesdropping this whole time?"

Giana started to giggle and said, "Yes, I heard the whole thing. I can just see it now. You'd open the blankets for him and he would crawl into your bed. He is overcome by sadness as lay the covers over him, you would then pull his head into your chest and gently stroke his hair." Giana pretended to hold something against her chest and then waved her other hand back and forth, pretending to stroke something.

Giana continued, saying, "Then, after a few moments, being overwhelmed by grief, he would succumb to his animal urges and ravish you in the night."

Lieutenant Rachel stood there embarrassed, still blushing. She shook her head and said, "You need to drain your brain in the gutter. It's filled with too much perversion."

Giana shrugged her shoulders and said, "What else am I supposed to think? You're the one who invited Lieutenant Michael into your bed."

Lieutenant Rachel said, "I thought you wanted to help me?"

Giana said, "I do, that's why I'm happy that you had the courage to say it. Hopefully, he'll think about it. Maybe he might even sneak into your bed one of these nights. Eh?"

Lieutenant Rachel shook her head and said, "Okay, okay, that's enough of that. You are supposed to be in bed now."

Giana sighed and said, "Okay, I'm going. Geez. I hope you have sweet dreams tonight."

Lieutenant Rachel shook her head and said, "Good night, Giana." She watched Giana go back down the hallway. She then headed toward her own room herself after turning off the light in the apartment.

Lieutenant Michael walked back into his apartment and put the tea tray on the counter in the kitchen. He shut off the main light to the apartment and walked into his room. He walked over to his desk and picked up the personal file that was on it. On the thumb-tab was written the name Gonzalez, Jennifer.

He sat down on his bed and opened the file and began to read it again. He wanted to make sure that he had a good grasp on her basic profile to make the transition easier for her to adapt to her new unit.

Jennifer's previous Lieutenant was a woman name Sharon Thomas. Lieutenant Thomas wrote in her psychological profile that "Jennifer is a very nice girl who is easy to get along with. She is always smiling and looking to make friends. As to her combat abilities, I would say that she is average for her age group. She still requires some assistance but she does not hold herself back in fights. She is always willing to stand her ground against the Harvesters. She seems very dependent on me, which could be related to her level of trust in me. She gets along very well with her team mates. She is the youngest girl in the group and looks up to both of them. She does not seem to have any issues in trusting them."

Lieutenant Michael set the file back on his desk and said to himself, "Well, Jennifer, I hope that you can trust me like you did her." He then walked over to the door and turned off the light. He crawled into bed and went to sleep.

The alarm began to sound at six-thirty in the morning. He begrudgingly rolled over and turned off the alarm. Out of habit he then felt the area in his bed where Mary was prone to lie. Being half-asleep he was half-expecting Mary to sit up in his bed. He then remembered that she was dead and would no longer sneak into his bed again. A twinge of pain gnawed at his heart at the thought. He didn't want Mary to sneak into his bed, but he was used to it and she would never annoy him again with it. He then looked for either Sarah or Valerie but neither of them were there either.

Lieutenant Michael sat up and rubbed his eyes. Today he would get to meet the girl who he first saw on the transport helicopter. The memory of the severed hand was still imprinted on his mind. As he stood up, a knock came to the door. He walked over to the door and opened it. Valerie stood there in her pink and white pajamas. She had brought her thumb to her lips and looked embarrassed. He noticed that she would often do this when she wanted to say something but was too embarrassed to do so. He waited for her to speak, but she said nothing. He said, "Good morning, Valerie. How did you sleep?"

Valerie, still acting shyly, said, "Good morning, Lieutenant."

Lieutenant Michael looked at her confused and said, "What's up, Valerie? Did you need me?"

Valerie shook her head and shyly said, "I ... I just wanted to make sure you were okay."

Lieutenant Michael smiled at her and rubbed her on top of the head, saying, "There's no need to worry about me. I'm fine. Are you okay?"

Valerie said, "I dreamed that Mary was still alive."

Lieutenant Michael nodded in understanding. He put his hand on Valerie's shoulder and said, "Stuff like that is normal. To be honest, when I woke up, I thought Mary was going to be beside me. It just means that we both miss her. It will take a while to get used to the fact that she's gone now."

Valerie nodded and her face started to show her depression, "Yeah, I really miss her."

Lieutenant Michael thought she was going to cry again, he said, "Me too. We'll miss her for a while, but she still lives on in our hearts. It's not the same thing I know, but thinking that way helps me to feel closer to the ones we lose. Having Jennifer with us will help too. She can't replace Mary, but she'll be a friend who we can put in our hearts too. Okay."

Valerie didn't start to cry but instead she nodded and said, "Okay, I think I understand, Lieutenant." She turned around and went back into her room. Lieutenant Michael shut the door, locked it, and then got dressed for the day.

Valerie went back into her room and began to dress into her uniform. The hair band that she had taken from among Mary's possessions sat on the desk next to her bed. After she had put on her dress and jacket, she took the hair band and wrapped it twice around her wrist on her left hand.

Valerie turned off her light and left her room. As she shut the door behind her, Sarah opened the door in front of her. Sarah smiled at Valerie and said, "Good morning, Valerie!" Valerie smiled back at her and returned the greeting. Sarah walked over to her and hugged her. Valerie hugged her back.

Together they went into the bathroom and began to brush their hair. Valerie looked at her face in the mirror. The slight bruise that Sarah had inflicted on her appeared to be gone. She could also see Sarah watching her out of the corner of her eye. Valerie spoke up and said, "Don't worry, it's gone now."

Sarah nodded and said, "I'm glad. I didn't mean to hit you that hard."

Valerie said, "No, I deserved it. I'm just glad it's gone before Jennifer got here. I wouldn't want to explain what happened." Valerie put the butterfly clip in her hair over her right ear, pulling the hair on that side back behind her ear.

Sarah put her hair into a pony tail using the hair band that she also took from Mary's possessions. She looked at herself in the mirror and said, "My uniform is starting to feel a little tight again. I think my chest just got bigger again." She cupped her hands over her chest to measure them.

Valerie said, "Mary would be jealous."

Sarah said, "The only problem though, is that it means that I'll probably get my period sooner rather than later. It might even happen before I turn twelve. Guess I should tell the Lieutenant that I'm going to need new clothes again."

Valerie said, "I wonder if Mary felt any pain when she died."

Sarah looked into her own reflection in the mirror as if she was looking at someone else. A look of contemplation fell upon her. She said, "I don't think so. I didn't tell you this before because it was so horrible, but I watched Susan's body fall apart. The last thing she did was smile at me. Even as her body broke apart there was a look of peace on her face. Then, her body just exploded in a flash of yellow light. If it was painful, I don't think she would have that look on her face. I imagine that is what happened to Mary."

Valerie said, "I don't know if it would have been better if I watched her die or not. I'm glad I didn't see it but there's a part of me that wishes that I would have been with her to the end."

Sarah turned her head to Valerie and said, "I can't answer that for you. Maybe when it's my time to die, you can watch me, and then make that judgment. As for myself, I still don't know if I want to see or not, but I think once is enough for anybody."

Valerie reached out and took her hand, saying, "I hope that that won't happen for a long time."

Sarah smiled at her and said, "I hope so too. I want to be with you for as long as possible."

Valerie nodded her head and said, "Yeah, but I got to make myself stronger, or this might happen to us again."

Sarah said, "Yeah, I need to get stronger too."

Lieutenant Michael stood over the stove stirring a pot of oatmeal. As he continued to stir, Sarah and Valerie walked into the dining area, and sat down at the table. Sarah sniffed into the air and said, "Not oatmeal again, Lieutenant!"

Lieutenant Michael turned to her and said, "Good morning, Sarah."

Sarah replied, "Good morning, Lieutenant. How are you doing?"

Lieutenant Michael said, "I'm fine, just making your favorite breakfast right now."

Sarah stuck her tongue out at him. Lieutenant Michael chuckled and went back to watching the pot of oatmeal. Sarah got up out of her chair and walked around to the entrance of the kitchen area. She stood in the entrance way and clasped her hands together as they hung in front of her.

Lieutenant Michael noticed her and said, "What's up, Sarah?"

Sarah looked embarrassed, she started to blush a little and tried not to smile. She said, "Lieutenant ... I ... uh ... I think I need some new clothes. My chest is starting to feel too tight again."

Lieutenant Michael turned his head to look at her and said, "Really? Already? Didn't we just get you a new uniform like two or three months ago?"

Sarah nodded her head and said, "Yeah, it was right before Susan died."

Lieutenant Michael turned back to the pot of oatmeal and said, "Well, after I get Jennifer I suppose we'll have to visit the quartermaster and get you fitted with a new uniform."

Sarah, still embarrassed, said, "Can I get some new bras too?"

Lieutenant Michael turned off the stove and said, "Well, I suppose so since your uniform is too tight. Makes sense that your bras would be too small. Guess we're going to have a busy day after all."

Sarah stepped into the kitchen and grabbed some bowls and spoons. She began to place them on the table and then realized that she had pulled four bowls and spoons instead of just three. Sarah knocked herself on the head and said, "I accidently got one for Mary." She went back in the kitchen and put the bowl and spoon back in their place.

Sarah went back to her seat and quietly began to spoon oatmeal into her bowl. She picked up her spoon and plunged it into her bowl. As she stared at the oatmeal on her spoon, she started to cry. She put her spoon down back into her bowl and buried her face into her hands, leaning her elbows on the table.

Lieutenant Michael reached out to her and began to stroke her back, saying, "There, there, Sarah. Every thing's going to be alright."

Sarah said, "I miss Mary so much!"

Lieutenant Michael said, "I know, Sarah. We all do. You're not alone."

Valerie started to tear up too, though she was not crying like Sarah was. She said, "I miss her too."

Sarah began to compose herself. She wiped the tears from her eyes and said, "Sorry, Lieutenant. I'm okay now."

Lieutenant Michael said, "Don't worry, Sarah. If you need to cry, it's okay. Do it for as long as you need to. Don't hold it all in. Get it out."

Sarah said, "I'm okay now." She started to eat the oatmeal.

Lieutenant Michael turned to Valerie and said, "Are you okay, Valerie?"

Valerie nodded her head, saying, "Yeah, I'm okay."

Lieutenant Michael said, "That goes for you too, Valerie. If you still need to cry for Mary, don't hold yourself back. Do what you feel like doing. It's not good to hold it all in by yourself. We're going to get through this together."

Valerie nodded her head and said, "I'm okay, Lieutenant." She then bowed her head, brought her palms together, and said a silent prayer before she started to eat.

Lieutenant Michael said, "We get a week of bereavement leave so we won't be called to action unless there is an emergency. Next week, on Thursday, will be our start day. Since Jennifer is already trained we can get back in the field and pay back the Harvesters after that time. Actually, I've been thinking about asking to be put on hunting duty."

Valerie tilted her head and asked, saying, "What's hunting duty?"

Lieutenant Michael said, "Well, what we've been doing is called Defensive Duty. We go out and protect the walls and the people inside them. Hunting Duty is when we go outside the wall and hunt down Harvesters. We'll be attacking them instead of defending cities."

Valerie nodded her head and said, "Oh, that makes sense." She began to eat her oatmeal again.

Lieutenant Michael said, "After breakfast, we'll do the dishes. After that, I'll leave to get Jennifer."

Valerie said, "Can I come too?"

Lieutenant Michael shook his head and said, "I'm sorry, Valerie. It's a better idea for me to speak to her first. That's why I came to get you all by myself. This way, we don't put too much pressure on her at first. Trust me, Valerie. I know what I'm doing."

Valerie nodded her head and said, "I trust you, Lieutenant. I'll wait right here for Jennifer to come."

Lieutenant Michael nodded and smiled at her. He reached over and rubbed the top of her head and said, "Great! I'm counting on you to help Jennifer feel at home here."

Sarah said, "I'll wait here too."

Lieutenant Michael nodded and smiled at her again. He also reached over and rubbed the top of her head, saying, "I know that you already know what to do since I saw you help Valerie. I know you can do the same with Jennifer."

Together, they finished their breakfast and then did the dishes. Sarah stood in the place of Mary and scrubbed the dirty dishes, handing them to Valerie. Valerie rinsed the dish off with water and then handed it to Lieutenant Michael. He dried the dish and put it away in its rightful place. He watched Sarah scrub the dirty dishes, just a couple of days ago, it was Mary who was standing there in that place. A twinge of pain gnawed in his heart again as he watched Sarah take her place.

Lieutenant Michael stepped through the automatic door of the military hospital. The smell of antiseptic air offended his senses. An army clerk sat at the front desk wearing an olive drab dress uniform. Lieutenant Michael walked up to the clerk and said, "Hello."

The man looked up at him and said, "Hello, Lieutenant. What can I do for you today?"

Lieutenant Michael pulled the requisition notice out of his file and handed it to him, saying, "I'm here to pick up Jenifer Gonzalez."

The man looked at the paper and nodded his head, saying, "One moment, sir." The clerk picked up an older style phone and dialed three numbers on the keypad. He waited a moment and then began to discuss the situation with someone on the other end. The clerk then hung up the phone and said, "Feel free to have a seat over there, sir. Her doctor will be down here in a few moments." The clerk pointed toward some chairs in the lounge area.

Lieutenant Michael nodded and said, "Thanks." He turned and headed toward the chairs in the lounge area. He sat down in a padded chair and waited for the doctor to come. As he sat, he began to count the number of girls that he has had to pick up in the past. "Jenifer is the eighth girl I've had to pick up. I've had five girls die now."

As Michael was deep in thought, an older gentleman wearing a long white coat approached him. Underneath the coat, the man wore a tan-colored dress shirt with an olive drab tie. He also wore pants that matched the color of his tie. The man spoke as he approached, saying, "Good morning, Lieutenant Snyder. My name is Jordan Paulos. I am Jennifer's doctor."

Lieutenant Michael stood up and saluted the doctor, who was a higher rank then he was. The doctor acknowledged his salute and said, "Don't worry too much about that. We're pretty informal here. I just wanted to talk to you a little bit before you meet Jennifer in person. We can talk as we walk though so come on and take a walk with me."

Lieutenant Michael stood up and said, "Of course, Doctor Paulos."

Together, the two of them began to walk to the elevator. As they walked, Doctor Paulos began to speak saying, "To be honest, Mr. Snyder, I don't think Jennifer is fit for duty. She has suffered some serious emotional trauma and it shows."

Lieutenant Michael nodded his head and said, "I figured that would be the case. That's part of the reason why I wanted to take her in. I'm hoping that my team can help her through it."

Doctor Paulos nodded and said, "I'm glad to hear that. She definitely needs all the help that she can get. It's a difficult situation when a Wielder suffers this kind of trauma. I can't give her any anti-depressants because the injection she takes has been shown to increase the potential of harmful side effects dramatically. I suggested that she resign but then she won't have access to the weekly injection that will extend her life. I did talk to her about resigning anyway but she insists that she wants to remain in the Wielder Corp. I tried to put her on leave but the World Government is in a panic because of the loss of the Los Angeles Sector and they are demanding that she return to duty because we are short just one Wielder Company."

Doctor Paulos shook his head and said, "You won't believe what my superiors told me." As he said the word 'superiors' he held up his hands and made quotation marks with his fingers. He continued, saying, "They told me that she just has to get over it. I tried to fight it, but, since Jennifer is insisting on returning to duty, there is nothing more I can do. So, I'm really glad that you already have some idea of the situation."

Lieutenant Michael said, "Yeah, I was there in Los Angeles with her. I saw how she was when they removed her from the helicopter. I promise you that I'll do my best to help her through this. Is she still crying?"

Doctor Paulos shook his head and said, "That's part of the problem. She hasn't cried at all, which I would consider a normal reaction. She seems to be pretty emotionless. To me, and I'm no child psychologist, but to me that shows that something is broken inside her mind and she can't work it out. I'm hoping that time will help with that. You might want to get her to talk about her experiences. Talking will probably help her to get it out of her mind so she can heal emotionally. I know that, once I turn her over to you, she is no longer under my care. But, if you need any help, I'll be happy to be involved."

Lieutenant Michael nodded his head and said, "Thanks for letting me know about all your concerns, doctor. I'll definitely be sure to keep an eye on her and talk with her. If there's anything I think you can help with, I'll try to contact you. Do you know Doctor Lovecraft?"

Doctor Paulos nodded his head and said, "Yes, I know her. I'll try to contact her and let her know what I told you as well."

Lieutenant Michael began to remember the expressionless look on Jennifer's face when she was sitting in the corner of the transport helicopter. He said, "My squad was the last ones on the transport helicopter. I saw her sitting in the corner. I saw the broken look on her face."

Doctor Paulos nodded, saying, "Yes, she came out of her trance a few hours after they brought her in. The medics who brought her told me that she was clinging onto a severed hand."

Lieutenant Michael nodded and said, "Yeah, I saw that."

Doctor Paulos continued, "The medics had to pry the severed hand out of her grip. She refuses to talk about what happened out there, so I don't know her story. But, what I think happened is that they were holding hands as they tried to retreat. When they got caught in the onslaught, the only thing Jennifer could save was the hand of her Lieutenant. Even that is a lot more than what can be normally saved in this type of situation."

As Doctor Paulos spoke, the memory of Mary's face came back to him, her voice echoed in his memory, "You know that we can't out run these Harvesters. I'm not going to let you all die with me."

The doctor led Lieutenant Michael through the hallway to an office room in the back. The doctor knocked on the door and spoke loudly so that he could be heard inside, saying, "Jennifer, it's Doctor Paulos. I'm coming in, okay?" There was no answer and the doctor opened the door without intending to wait for a response from her.

Doctor Paulos stepped inside the office room and Lieutenant Michael followed behind him. Lieutenant Michael saw a little girl sitting in a chair next to the wall. He remembered her image from a few days ago. Her dark wavy hair had been caked in human blood and Harvester goo. It was now clean and well combed. She had pulled the hair on her temples back and held them together in a hair band in the back of her head. The rest of her hair hung freely over her back and shoulders. Her caramel skin, once covered in patches of mud and harvester goo, was now clean. She was slouched forward, looking downward. Her hands sat loosely on her lap.

Doctor Paulos walked up to her and said, "Jennifer, I've brought your assigned Lieutenant to meet you and take you to your new home."

Lieutenant Michael stepped forward as Doctor Paulos started to leave the room. He spoke to Lieutenant Michael as he was leaving, "I'll leave you to it, Mr. Snyder." He then closed the door behind himself.

Lieutenant Michael turned his attention back to Jennifer. He stepped closer to her and said, "Hello Jennifer. My name is Michael Snyder. I'm going to be your new Lieutenant."

Jennifer didn't seem to notice him. He knelt down beside her and tried to look up into her eyes. Underneath her eyes were dark circles, which made it look as if she had not gotten much sleep. He looked up at her and smiled, saying,

"I know you've been having a really hard time. I was there in the fight at Los Angeles. I lost one of my girls so I know what it's like to lose someone you care about."

Jennifer seemed to finally snap out of her trance. Her eyes moved to meet his gaze. She stared at him and said, "Would it be okay if I called you L.T.?"

Lieutenant Michael smiled and nodded his head, saying, "Sure. Nobody has called me that before but I know about it. What do you want me to call you?"

Jennifer replied, "Just call me Jennifer. Not Jenny, not Jen ... Jennifer."

Lieutenant Michael nodded and said, "Sure, Jennifer. I promise I won't shorten your name." He held up his right arm to the square as he said the word 'promise'. He then said, "The two other girls on your team are Sarah and Valerie. Sarah is blue and Valerie is yellow. They're looking forward to meeting you. I hope that you can all become good friends."

Jennifer looked back down toward her hands in her lap. She sneered and said coldly, "I'm not here to make friends, L.T. I'm here to kill Harvesters till I either die or am killed by them."

Lieutenant Michael was shocked by her statement. His happy face changed to a sullen one. He sighed, paused, and said, "Well ... I suppose that's true but it is good for a team to become friends. We have to trust one another so that ..."

Jennifer interrupted him and said, "My team trusted each other, now they're all dead. They betrayed me, how can I trust you then?" She suddenly grabbed her right wrist and squeezed it tightly. She closed her eyes and winced as if she was in pain.

Lieutenant Michael reached over and put his hand on top of her hand that gripped her own wrist. She immediately opened her eyes and forcefully pushed his hand away from herself. She spoke harshly, saying, "Don't ever touch me again!"

Lieutenant Michael withdrew his hand and said, "I'm sorry Jennifer I didn't mean to do something that would make you angry. Please, forgive me. I promise I won't do that again."

Jennifer looked back at him and said, "So, you still want to make me part of your team then?"

Lieutenant Michael nodded and said, "Yes, I do. I can tell that you are in a lot of pain right now. I want to help you through it. If you need to snap at me to help yourself feel better, I can take it."

Jennifer chuckled with a fake laugh and said, "Are you an idiot, L.T.?"

Lieutenant Michael shrugged his shoulders and said, "Well, I know several girls who've called me dense." He smiled at her and scratched the back of his head awkwardly.

Jennifer rolled her eyes and then stood up out of the chair.

Lieutenant Michael stood up and said, "Well, Jennifer, are you ready to go to your new home?"

Jennifer shrugged her shoulders and said, "I don't have a home, just a place where they keep me till they need me."

Lieutenant Michael opened his hand and started to extend it to her. He then closed his hand, withdrawing it, saying, "This is the part where I would offer to hold your hand but I guess you don't want that, right?"

Jennifer rolled her eyes and crossed her arms over her chest, saying, "I know how to walk, L.T."

Lieutenant Michael dropped his hands and sighed, saying, "I figured as much. Our headquarters is about a thirty minute walk from here so they wouldn't give me a car."

Jennifer rolled her eyes again and said, "Figures. I don't mind walking though. Lead the way, L.T."

Lieutenant Michael said, "Is there anything I can carry for you?"

Jennifer shook her head and said, "No, all my stuff got burnt to ash in the nuclear strike."

Lieutenant Michael nodded and rubbed the top of his head, saying, "I suppose you're right. That was careless of me. I'm sorry."

Jennifer shrugged her shoulders and said, "Eh, whatever."

Lieutenant Michael snapped his fingers and said, "Well, I have to take Sarah out shopping for new clothing today. If there's anything that you need or want, we can get it for you too."

Jennifer shrugged her shoulders and said, "Okay. I don't really need anything though."

Lieutenant Michael nodded and said, "Well, that was just a thought, but, if you do see something you want, just let me know and I'll try to get it for you. You ready to go?"

Jennifer dropped her arms to her side and said, "I've been ready this whole time."

Lieutenant Michael gave her a thumbs up and said, "Okay, let's go then." He walked toward the door and opened it. He then stepped aside and motioned for Jennifer to leave first. She crossed her arms across her chest again and walked out the door. She then stopped and waited for Lieutenant Michael to come out of the room.

Lieutenant Michael shut the door behind himself and then walked down the hallway toward the lounge area where he originally sat. Instead of walking beside him, Jennifer followed behind him at least five paces.

After they left the military hospital, Lieutenant Michael stopped and turned toward Jennifer. She stopped walking, her arms still crossed over her chest. She glared at him looking annoyed.

Lieutenant Michael sighed and said, "Are you going to stay behind me the whole time we walk home?"

Jennifer coldly said, "Is there a problem with that?"

Lieutenant Michael said, "A little bit. It's my job to keep you safe and that is hard to do if you keep your distance behind me the whole time like that."

Jennifer rolled her eyes and said, "How are you supposed to keep me safe when you don't have any special powers?"

Lieutenant Michael's shoulders drooped and he rubbed his forehead. He sighed and said, "Look, I know you have been through a lot and that you are in a lot of pain right now. Believe me, I get it. I'm not your enemy. All I want to do is help you. Can you try and go a little easier on me?"

Jennifer sighed and looked down toward the ground. Lieutenant Michael thought she was either going to say something or start crying, but neither happened. Instead, she walked over to be beside him but she stayed an arm's breadth away from him. She continued to cross her arms across her chest.

Lieutenant Michael nodded and said, "Thank you for being so understanding, Jennifer."

As they walked down the street, side-by-side but at arm's length, Lieutenant Michael tried to keep their conversation going. He said, "So Jennifer, do you have anything you like to do in your free time?"

Jennifer shrugged her shoulders and said, "Not really."

Lieutenant Michael then said, "Do you like any TV shows? Valerie and Sarah like to watch Magical Girl Squad. Do you like that show too?"

Jennifer shook her head and said, "Magical Girl Squad is for little children."

Lieutenant Michael chuckled and said, "Yeah, well you won't get any argument from me on that. It was Mary's favorite show and she got Sarah hooked on it. Valerie was already a fan before she came to us." His smile faded away from his face as a twinge of pain gnawed at his heart again. Every time he thought about Mary, he felt this same pain in his heart. He always felt pain whenever one of his girls died, but this pain was different. It felt deeper then he remembered. He went silent.

After a few minutes of awkward silence, he focused his thoughts back on Jennifer and said, "Is there anything you want to know about me, Jennifer?"

Her face showed that she was thinking and then she said, "How old are you L.T.?"

A slight sense of relief came to his heart, he hoped that this was the beginning of Jennifer finally opening up to him. He said, "I'm twenty-five. I was born in what became the New Portland sector before it got destroyed. I lost both my parents when the Harvesters breeched the wall."

Instead of opening up, Jennifer went silent again. His relief started to turn to sorrow again.

After a few minutes of silence, Jennifer spoke up and said, "You lost both your parents?"

Lieutenant Michael nodded his head and said, "Yes, I did."

Jennifer, her arms still crossed over her chest and her face downward, said, "My parents lived in Los Angeles. They're dead now. Is that why you joined the Spirit Wielder Corp, because your parents got killed?"

Lieutenant Michael said, "That's part of the reason. I also joined the military because of my adopted brother Josh. He and I were inseparable so we decided to join the military together. He went into Military Intelligence. I wasn't smart enough for that so I joined the Spirit Wielder Corp."

When he said this, Jennifer started to laugh a little. From the sound of it, he thought that she was really laughing and not just faking it. He continued, saying, "Also, I wanted to get revenge on the Harvesters for killing my parents and I wanted to make sure that other people don't have to suffer a loss like I had."

Jennifer's momentary laugh was quickly erased. The humor on her face vanished and was replaced with a cold emotionless look. She looked down toward the ground and then gripped her right wrist again as hard as she could. She appeared to wince from pain.

Lieutenant Michael noticed the look of pain on her face and said, "Is your arm okay? You seem to be in pain."

Jennifer slowly released her right wrist and slightly shuddered, saying, "There's nothing wrong with my wrist, L.T."

Lieutenant Michael didn't believe her but said, "Okay, but if you ever have a problem, I want you to tell me so that I can help you fix it. Okay?"

Jennifer nodded her head and said, "Okay. I'm fine though."

Lieutenant Michael nodded his head and said, "Okay then. If there's anything that you feel you can't talk to me about, there's Doctor Lovecraft. She'd be happy to help you too. If you don't feel you can talk to an adult about it then I hope that you can trust Sarah or Valerie. They can help you get the help you need too."

Jennifer, still looking down toward the ground, said, "I'm fine. I don't need help from anybody. People always let me down."

Lieutenant Michael couldn't hide the disappointment on his face. He had hoped that she would be more open, but, in reality, she had closed herself off and covered it with hostility. He figured that this was her way of dealing with the grief that was no doubt inside her heart. He decided that he would have to endure it in the hope of cracking that hostile shell that seemed to surround her.

Lieutenant Michael contemplated whether he should try forcing her to open up or whether it would be better to let her close herself off. He scratched his head and wondered what he would want if he was in her position. *I'd probably want to be left alone*, he thought to himself. He decided that he wouldn't try to force her too much unless he had too.

Together they walked in silence. Jennifer didn't try to ask him any other questions and Lieutenant Michael didn't try to force her to talk. It felt very different to him. The other girls, especially Mary, wouldn't stop chattering his ear off. That was what he always expected from them. As he thought about Mary again, that same gnawing feeling tugged on his heart.

Finally, the Phoenix Guard Complex came into view. Now would be the time to see how Jennifer would interact with the other girls. He predicted that she would continue to close herself off to them as well. He just hoped that she wouldn't be as hostile towards them as she was to him.

Lieutenant Michael pointed at the building and said, "There's your new home, Jennifer. I bet Sarah and Valerie are getting anxious about meeting you. They were excited to hear about you." Jennifer didn't say anything but she did nod her head. That was something positive he supposed.

He opened the front door for her and then said, "I'll lead the way to your new home. We are Phoenix Guard Third Squad, so our door is marked with the number three. I guess I don't really need to explain all the floors since the Wielder Complexes are pretty standard no matter where you go. Out of curiosity, what squad number were you in at Leviathan?"

Jennifer said, "Second squad."

As they were about to go up the stairs, the voice of a man spoke out behind them. They turned around and Captain Faust walked quickly towards them. When he was close enough, he said, "Good morning, Lieutenant Snyder, and this must be Jennifer Gonzalez. Good morning to you Jennifer."

Captain Faust extended his hand to her. She stared at it and then reluctantly took it. It was the same hand that she had gripped the severed hand with. He shook her hand and smiled at her. He said, "I'm so sorry to hear about Leviathan Company. I hope that you can come to think of this place as your new home. You're really lucky to get to be with Lieutenant Snyder. He is one of my best Lieutenants so I'm sure that you'll get along just great."

Jennifer nodded her head and said, "Thank you, Captain."

Captain Faust let her hand go and said, "If there's anything you need, feel free to come see me. We'll do the best we can to help get you through this transition period."

Again Jennifer nodded and said, "I'm fine, Captain." A slight look of despair started to fall on her face. It was the sort of look that he had seen on Mary's face after she had gotten her first period. Jennifer quickly composed herself and began to squeeze her right wrist again. The look of despair on her face changed into a look of pain. She then released her grip on her wrist.

Captain Faust nodded his head and said, "Well, okay then, but my offer always stands so if you need anything at all, just let me or your Lieutenant know. I'll let you two get back to what you were doing." He shook Lieutenant Michael's hand and then walked back toward his office.

Lieutenant Michael turned back toward the door to the stairs and said, "Shall we keep going?"

Jennifer nodded and said, "Lead the way. I suppose we are on the fifth floor since we are Third squad."

Lieutenant Michael nodded and said, "That's right. I hope you like to climb stairs. We'll consider this climb today's exercise I suppose." He tried to chuckle but Jennifer just stared at him blankly, emotionlessly. He sighed and rubbed the top of his head. He then led the way up the stairs.

Lieutenant Michael and Jennifer stood in front of a door marked with the number three. Lieutenant Michael put his hand on the door knob. He turned his head toward Jennifer and smiled, saying, "Are you ready to meet the other girls." Jennifer, crossing her arms across her chest again, shrugged her shoulders. She didn't say anything.

Lieutenant Michael opened the door and stepped inside. Jennifer followed behind him. Sarah and Valerie were sitting at the dinner table. When the door opened they stopped talking and watched as Lieutenant Michael stepped inside. He took one look at them and smiled, saying, "Are you girls ready to meet Jennifer?"

Sarah stood up and said, "Of course."

Valerie also stood up and said, "Yeah, I'm ready."

Jennifer hid herself behind Lieutenant Michael. He stepped aside and shut the door behind them. Jennifer stood there with her arms crossed and her head subdued, looking somewhat towards the ground.

Sarah smiled at her and walked up to her. She put her hands behind her back and leaned towards her. Sarah said, "Hello, my name is Sarah."

Jennifer paused for a moment and appeared to be embarrassed. She said, "I ... I'm Jennifer ... not Jenny, not Jen ... Jennifer."

Sarah nodded her head and said, "Okay, Jennifer. I'm glad I can meet you. I hope that we can be good friends."

Jennifer began to grip her right wrist tightly again. Her face winced from what appeared to be pain. She said, "I'm not here to be anybody's friend. I don't need any friends."

Valerie, who was now standing beside Sarah, said, "You might not need friends now, but I think it's always good to have some friends. Friends are people you can trust and rely on. My name's Valerie. I was recruited two months ago so we're not that far apart."

Jennifer's small body began to slightly tremble. The look on her face changed from embarrassment to emotionless. She said, "I don't need to know anything about you to do my job."

Valerie, not knowing what to do, became sad and looked down toward the ground. She put her hands together and began flexing her fingers.

Sarah moved her hand to place it on Jennifer's shoulder but Jennifer smacked her hand away and coldly said, "Don't touch me!"

Sarah pulled her hand away and said, "Ouch, I'm sorry."

Lieutenant Michael stepped in and said, "Don't worry, girls. Jennifer just needs some time to adjust to her new home. Why don't we show Jennifer around?"

Jennifer spoke up, saying, "This place is the same as my old place. Just show me my room so I can lay down. I'm getting really tired."

Lieutenant Michael sighed and said, "Sure, that's fine. We can do that. Follow me." He walked around the corner and Jennifer followed him down the hall. Sarah and Valerie stood in the opening of the hallway looking sad and confused.

Lieutenant Michael stopped in front of Mary's old door and held his hand open, pointing at it. He said, "This is your new room. I got it all ready for you. Today, after lunch, we're going to the quartermaster and then we're going to do some shopping. Okay? So go ahead and lie down and we'll have lunch in a couple of hours. Do you have any questions?"

Jennifer put her hand on the door knob and stared at it. She said, "What are we going to have for lunch?"

Lieutenant Michael said, "Well, since you're new here, I thought I'd make one of your favorite foods. Is there anything you want to eat?"

Jennifer, still staring at her hand on the door knob, said, "Can I have a grilled cheese sandwich?"

Lieutenant Michael smiled and nodded, saying, "Sure, we can do that. We haven't had those in a long time. So go ahead and lie down. I'll come get you when it's time to eat if you are not out yet."

Jennifer nodded her head and said, "Thanks, L.T."

Lieutenant Michael gave her a thumbs up and said, "Sure, no problem."

Jennifer turned the handle of the door knob. She opened the door and quietly walked inside, shutting it behind herself.

Lieutenant Michael sighed and ran his hand through his hair. His face showed his disappointment in the situation. He turned to Sarah and Valerie who were still standing in the entryway to the hallway. He walked over to them and sighed as he put a hand on each of their shoulders. He said, "Let's go to the dinner table and talk about this."

Sarah and Valerie both nodded their heads and turned to the table. They both took a seat and Lieutenant Michael sat in between them. He clasped his hands together and leaned on the table top. He deeply sighed. He looked to Sarah and then to Valerie, saying, "Jennifer has suffered some serious emotional trauma. I think she is trying to put up a wall around herself so that she doesn't have to face her emotions."

Sarah nodded and said, "Yeah, I understand Lieutenant. It was hard enough to lose Mary. She lost her whole team. I wouldn't want to face that too."

Valerie said, "So she doesn't really hate us?"

Lieutenant Michael shook his head and said, "No, she doesn't hate us. She approved the transfer. Like I just said, she's trying to put a wall around herself. Just give her some time. Try not to force things with her. Let it happen naturally."

Sarah said, "I'll try to keep an eye on her, Lieutenant."

Lieutenant Michael smiled and rubbed the top of Sarah's head, saying, "Thanks, Sarah! Now, if she starts to get unreasonable go ahead and confront her, or you can just tell me and I'll take care of it."

Valerie smiled and said, "I'll try to make friends with her too, Lieutenant. I'm good at making friends."

Lieutenant Michael smiled at Valerie and rubbed the top of her head, saying, "Thanks, Valerie. But, don't try to push her too much. It might make her wall herself off more. Just be there for her and try to show her that she can trust us."

Valerie then asked, "Lieutenant, how come she called you L.T.?"

Lieutenant Michael chuckled and said, "L.T. is short for Lieutenant. Lieutenant has an 'L' and a 'T' in it so for short some people say L.T."

Valerie tilted her head and said, "Would it make you mad if I called you L.T.?"

Lieutenant Michael shrugged his shoulders and said, "Nope, you girls can call me whatever you want as long as you're nice about it."

Valerie thought for a moment and shook her head vigorously. She said, "I'm already used to calling you Lieutenant. I think I'll stick with that."

Sarah nodded her head and said, "Yeah, I think I prefer sticking with Lieutenant too. You'll always be my Lieutenant till the day I die, like Mary and Susan."

Valerie said, "Come on, let's not talk about dying right now, Sarah. It will make me sad again."

Sarah nodded and said, "Okay, Valerie. I'm sorry."

Valerie said, "When I thought about Jennifer, I thought she'd be more like Mary. But, she seems to be the opposite of Mary."

Sarah said, "Valerie, it's not a good idea to compare Jennifer to Mary. Everybody's different. It might make Jennifer sad if she thought she couldn't live up to Mary's role. Did we ever say you weren't like Susan?"

Valerie shook her head, saying, "No, I'm sorry. I didn't think of that. You're right. I promise I won't try to compare her to Mary or make her feel that she can't do it."

Lieutenant Michael spoke up, saying, "That's right, girls. We've got to help her feel at home and to help her find a way to break through the wall she's built around herself."

Jennifer sat on her new bed staring at the walls around her. She had kept the light off and the morning sun was still shining through the window shades.

The walls looked like her old walls but the room was void of all her things. There were none of her posters on the wall. The picture that she had taken with her old squad was no longer on her desk. It didn't exist anymore. They were nothing more than old memories that remained in her thoughts and her heart.

She took off her uniform jacket and placed it on the end of her bed. She stared at her right wrist. A number of scabbed over scars still remained on her wrist. She stared at them and remembered the pain that came from them. She felt the need to cry again. *I must not* cry, she thought to herself. Her body began to tremble from her emotions so she gripped her right wrist again. She gripped onto the scars that remained. The pain helped her to feel alive. It helped her to suppress the tears that wanted to come, the tears that she could not let come. *I don't deserve to let go of this pain*, she thought to herself again.

Jennifer rummaged through her jacket pocket and pulled out a small razor blade in a cardboard sheath that she had stolen from the hospital when the nurse wasn't looking. She pulled the small blade out of its sheath. She held the blade in her slightly trembling hand to her wrist. She slowly cut a shallow line across her wrist. A small trickle of blood seeped out of the line on her wrist. It was not deep enough to cause the blood to come flowing out, but it was deep enough to cause a little bit of blood to trickle. It was deep enough for her to feel the pain of it.

As she cut into her wrist she spoke softly saying, "Lieutenant, I'm sorry." She brought the razor back up and cut another line like the last one. Again, a small trickle of blood seeped out of the line. As she cut into her wrist the second time she said, "Julie, I'm sorry." After cutting herself the second time, she paused and closed her eyes. She felt the pain throbbing in her wrist. She felt the warm wetness of her blood. Emotions still remained so it still wasn't enough.

Jennifer brought the razor up to her wrist a third time and slowly cut across her wrist again. A small trickle of blood seeped out of the third cut line. As she cut herself the third time, she quietly said, "Annie, I'm so sorry I failed you." She lowered her arm and let it rest on the mattress of her new bed. She closed her eyes and felt the pain throbbing in her wrist. The tears that she felt coming went away. Her emotions were buried inside her again. Now it was enough.

Jennifer took the sheath of the razor and carefully put the razor blade back into it. She then stuck the razor into the drawer of her desk. She laid down on the mattress and let her right arm lay motionless and flat on her bed. She brought her left arm over her head and draped it over her eyes. She lay there and felt the pain throbbing in her right wrist. The pain in her wrist stopped her body from trembling. It stopped her emotions from coming. As she laid there, she slowly drifted off to sleep.

- 3 -

Sarah stood by the stove holding a spatula, waiting for the first grilled cheese sandwich. Valerie stood on her stepping stool next to Lieutenant Michael. She was buttering some bread as Lieutenant Michael was slicing some cheese.

Valerie turned her head to Sarah and said, "Try not to burn your hand again."

Sarah rolled her eyes and said, "Yeah, yeah, I know. I can be a klutz sometimes." She knocked herself on top of the head and stuck her tongue out.

Lieutenant Michael said, "Okay, girls. The cheese is all ready to go." He took some of the cheese and stuck it between two slices of buttered bread. He put the sandwich on the hot frying pan. Sarah watched it intently, waiting for it to be grilled to perfection. The apartment began to fill with the aroma of butter and toast with a hint of warm cheese.

As the three of them continued putting grilled cheese sandwiches together, Jennifer walked into the dining area. Lieutenant Michael noticed movement out of the corner of his eye and looked up. He saw Jennifer standing just beyond the exit of the hallway. He said to her, "Hello, Jennifer. Did the good smell of food wake you up?"

Jennifer shrugged her shoulders and said, "I could smell it from my room."

Lieutenant Michael smiled at her and said, "You want to help make lunch with us?"

Jennifer shook her head and said, "No. Is it okay if I just sit at the table?"

Lieutenant Michael nodded and said, "Sure, that's fine. Today's your first day so I'll go easy on you. But, I do expect everyone to help with the cleanup, okay?"

Jennifer nodded and said, "That's fine. I was expecting that." She pulled a chair out and sat down at the table. She rested her elbow on the table top and plopped her head onto her hand. There was a blank look of exhaustion on her face. Her lips frowned.

Lieutenant Michael changed the subject and said, "Were you able to get some sleep Jennifer?" He could still see the dark circles surrounding her eyes.

Jennifer shrugged her shoulders and said, "Yeah, I slept for a little bit. I've had trouble sleeping lately."

Lieutenant Michael nodded and said, "That's understandable. Hopefully you'll get settled down here and your body will start to relax and let you sleep better." He turned to Valerie, who was done buttering all the bread slices, saying, "Valerie, why don't you set the table now. We're almost done here."

Valerie smiled and nodded her head, saying, "Sure, Lieutenant!" She jumped off her stool and then scooted it over to where the cupboard with the dishes are. She climbed back on and pulled out four plates and four cups. She brought them to the table and began to set them in front of each chair.

When Valerie approached Jennifer's space, Jennifer would not move her elbow and arm off the table, so Valerie put her plate in front of her arm. She smiled at Jennifer. Jennifer smirked at her.

Valerie sat down in a chair across from Jennifer and said, "Did you watch Magical Girl Squad last night?"

Jennifer rolled her eyes and said, "Magical Girl Squad is for kids."

Valerie nodded her head and said, "Yeah, that's right. I'm a kid, so I watch Magical Girl Squad. You don't watch Magical Girl Squad?" Valerie's mouth dropped open and her eyes went wide with shock at the idea.

Jennifer sighed and said, "Only little kids watch Magical Girl Squad."

Valerie tilted her head to the side and looked confused. She said, "So … you're saying you don't watch Magical Girl Squad. You've never ever seen it?"

Jennifer shook her head as it rested on her hand, saying, "No, I've seen it. I think it is boring and meant for little kids."

Valerie's smile turned into a gloomy frown and she said, "I see. That's okay I guess. I like it though."

Sarah came over and wrapped an arm around Valerie's neck in a hug. She then sat down in the seat next to Jennifer, saying, "That's okay, Val. I like Magical Girl Squad too. We can at least watch it together."

Valerie perked back up and nodded her head toward Sarah. She said, "I can't wait to see what happens next Friday! They just got to make it inside of the fortress of the evil king! Then they can defeat him."

Lieutenant Michael came over with a plate full of grilled cheese sandwiches stacked on top of each other. He placed it in the middle of the table, saying, "Okay, everyone. Dig in!"

Valerie and Sarah began to shovel a few grilled cheese sandwiches onto their plates. Jennifer took one and placed it on her own plate. She stared at it in silence.

Valerie put her hands together and silently prayed over her food. When she was done praying, she turned to Lieutenant Michael and said, "Is Jennifer a goat?"

Lieutenant Michael looked at Valerie in confusion and said, "What? Did ... did you really just ask me if Jennifer is a goat?"

Valerie began to look worried and said, "You know ... a ... a goat ... like Tina."

Again, Lieutenant Michael stared at Valerie in confusion. He scratched his head as he thought about it, saying, "A goat like Tina?"

Sarah butted in and said, "I think she means goth, Lieutenant, not goat." Sarah began to laugh at Valerie.

Valerie blushed and looked downward in embarrassment, saying, "Oh yeah, I meant goth like Tina."

Lieutenant Michael chuckled and said, "Valerie, that was really cute." Valerie's shoulders slumped downward and her head lowered as she gave an embarrassed frown. He reached over to her and rubbed her on top of the head, saying, "Why don't you ask Jennifer if she's a 'goth'." He held up his hands and made quotation marks with his fingers as he said the word 'goth'.

Valerie turned back to Jennifer. She was still embarrassed and meekly said, "Jennifer, are you a goth?"

Jennifer shrugged her shoulders and said, "I don't even know what a goth is."

Sarah said, "A goth is someone who likes wearing black and likes dark things like skulls and bats. Tina, who's in Squad four, describes herself as being goth."

Jennifer shook her head and said, "No, I don't think I'm goth." She went back to staring at the grilled cheese sandwich.

Lieutenant Michael noticed her and said, "Is something wrong with your grilled cheese sandwich, Jennifer?"

Jennifer sighed and said, "No, I'm just wondering what real cheese tastes like."

Valerie said, "But ... but this is made out of real cheese, isn't it?"

Lieutenant Michael reluctantly agreed by slightly nodding his head. He sighed and said, "Yeah, real cheese was good. I miss it."

Both Valerie and Sarah looked a little shocked. Valerie gasped and said, "You mean this isn't real cheese?"

Lieutenant Michael shook his head and said, "No, I'm afraid it's not real cheese. Real cheese is made out of cow's milk. It's hard to get real milk. As far as

I know only a few places in the sector can get real milk. To get real milk you need to raise cows. In order to raise cows you need a lot of land. Thanks to the Harvester invasion, we don't have that much room to grow food or raise cows for milk. That milk you drink is a chemical invention made to simulate the taste of cow's milk. This cheese is made from oil and other chemicals to give it a flavor and texture like cheese, but, no matter what they do, it just doesn't taste the same. Oh, and most of that meat we eat once and a while, is actually made out of grains and compounds. It's very hard to raise animals for food here since we don't have the room. That's why everything is so expensive."

Valerie looked depressed and then said, "I wish I could try real food."

Sarah sighed and said, "Well, at least we don't know what we're missing. I wish the Harvesters would just go away."

Lieutenant Michael sat up straight and said, trying to cheer everyone up, "Don't worry, girls, this artificial food still tastes really good too. I just wish they could imitate real cheese better."

Jennifer picked up her grilled cheese sandwich and took a bite out of it. Everyone else went back to eating too. Lieutenant Michael reminisced in his mind about the creamy taste of the cheese he used to eat as a kid.

After lunch, they did the dishes together quickly. This time Valerie rinsed off the dishes that Sarah scrubbed and handed them to Jennifer to dry. After Jennifer dried them, she handed them to Lieutenant Michael to put away. It looked like things were beginning to get back on track to being somewhat normal.

Together, they left their apartment. Lieutenant Michael stopped for a moment in front of their door and appeared to be thinking. He seemed to sniff the air and looked towards Squad four's door. He stroked his chin with his thumb and index finger, saying, "While we're at it, why don't we introduce Jennifer to Squad four?"

Without waiting for the approval of the others, he walked over to Squad four's door and knocked on it. A moment later, the door opened, and an annoyed looking Giana stood there. She glared at Lieutenant Michael and said, "This better be important, I was in the middle of eating my dessert."

Lieutenant Michael rolled his eyes and said, "I'm sorry to infringe upon your dessert time, but I wanted to introduce you to our new girl, Jennifer."

Giana sighed and slumped forward, allowing her arms to hang dramatically. She backed away from the door and said, "Alright, come on in then.

I suppose I have time for that." Giana then turned and walked back toward the dining table where the rest of Squad four were sitting.

Lieutenant Michael, Sarah, Valerie, and Jennifer walked into the apartment to see Lieutenant Rachel, Giana, Tina, and Elsa sitting and enjoying what appeared to be a home baked chocolate cake. Sarah sniffed the air and then appeared to go into a trance like state. Her face morphed into an ultimate expression of nirvana. The word "chocolate" escaped from her lips.

Lieutenant Rachel said, "So girls, did you want some chocolate cake too?"

Sarah nodded and then looked to Lieutenant Michael with a hopeful smile. Lieutenant Michael said, "That's fine with me if you are willing to share it."

Lieutenant Rachel stood up and said, "Of course I'll share it if it's you."

Giana cried out and said, "No, don't share my chocolate cake. If you share, then I'll have to make do with less chocolate cake!"

Lieutenant Rachel swung her hand out and knocked Giana in the back of the head, saying, "Quit acting like a goof ball for Jennifer!"

Giana rubbed the back of her head and said, "Geez, Lieutenant! You didn't have to hit me that hard."

Lieutenant Rachel glanced at Lieutenant Michael with a mildly suggestive smile. She said, "Michael, do you want some of my cake too?"

Lieutenant Michael returned her smile and chuckled. He said, "Sure, if you are willing."

Lieutenant Rachel turned to Valerie and said, "I'm sure Valerie wants some too, right?"

Valerie nodded her head and said, "Of course I want chocolate cake! Lieutenant, how come you don't make us desserts like Lieutenant Rachel does for her squad?"

Lieutenant Michael looked away from her and shrugged his shoulders as if he was ignoring the question.

Lieutenant Rachel then turned to Jennifer and said, "Hello, Jennifer. My name is Rachel Harris. I'm the Lieutenant of Fourth squad. It's good to meet you. Would you like some cake too?"

Jennifer lowered her gaze to the ground and turned her head away. She crossed her arms across her chest, saying, "No, I'm not hungry anymore. I don't need your cake."

Lieutenant Rachel said, "Oh. Okay then. Let me know if you change your mind." She went into the kitchen to grab three small plates and forks. She returned to the table and began cutting up the chocolate cake.

Giana walked up to Jennifer and said, "My name is Giana." She pointed at her teammates, saying, "This is Tina and Elsa." Tina and Elsa waved at her.

Jennifer, still crossing her arms, shrugged her shoulders and said, "Hey."

Giana looked her up and down and then said, "It looks like we got another queen of darkness here."

Valerie joined by saying, "Yeah, I think she's a goth like Tina."

Sarah laughed and said, "Valerie thought that 'goth' was pronounced 'goat'."

Giana and Elsa began to laugh. Giana pointed to Valerie and said, "You idjit! Don't you know that a goat is an animal?"

Valerie balled her fists and stamped a foot. She glared at Sarah and said, "Why'd you have to go and tell them that?"

Tina got out of her chair, walked around the table and stood in front of Jennifer. She started to look Jennifer up and down. Jennifer started looking annoyed. She started to glare at Tina. Behind her glare, Tina could see the pain that hid behind her eyes. She could see the dark circles under them that showed her lack of sleep. Tina rested her right hand on her hip and said, "She's not goth, she's just emotionally depressed."

Valerie tilted her head in confusion. She brought a finger to her chin and said, "Isn't that the same thing?"

Tina sighed and rolled her eyes. She walked up to Valerie and put her hands on Valerie's shoulders. She said, "Valerie, a goth is someone who likes the macabre ..."

Valerie, still confused, said, "What is a macabre?"

Tina sighed again and said, "Geez ... The macabre are things that relate to darkness like ghosts, and skeletons, death, the dark arts. As I was saying, a goth is someone who is into the macabre. An emotionally depressed person is just sad. A goth would say 'everyone's life sucks because the world sucks.' An emotionally depressed person would say 'my life sucks so give me attention."

A light flicked on in Valerie's head and she said, "Oh, I get. Goths think that everything is bad, while an emotionally depressed person only thinks about themselves."

Tina patted Valerie on the head and said, "Yeah, that's close enough; I suppose."

Jennifer became angry and aggressively said, "So you think I only care about myself?"

Tina turned back toward Jennifer and looked her straight in the eyes. She said in her melancholy voice, "No, what I'm saying is that right now you are in so much pain that you can't see the pain that is on Lieutenant Michael's face. Nor can you see the pain that is on Sarah and Valerie's face. That is what I say."

Jennifer turned away from Tina and replied, "You don't know what you're talking about!"

Tina shrugged her shoulders and went back to her chair to finish her cake. She said, "Like I care what you do."

As Tina sat back down, Lieutenant Rachel handed everyone who wanted it a small plate with some cake on it. Sarah gratefully accepted it and began to savor every bite in exaggeration. Valerie, also thankful, dug into it as well. It did not take long for them to finish it.

Lieutenant Rachel said, "You know Michael, you have a habit of dropping by randomly whenever I make a dessert."

Lieutenant Michael raised his head up with a smile and pointed at himself with his thumb, saying, "Don't you know, Rachel? Detecting desserts is one of my seven senses."

Giana laughed and said, "What's your sixth sense then?"

Lieutenant Michael said, "Knowing when it's time to leave. And my sixth sense is telling me that it is time." He pointed at Jennifer who was standing next to the door with her back towards everybody. Her arms were still crossed across her chest.

Lieutenant Michael said, "Thanks for the cake, Lieutenant Rachel. As always, it was excellent. We're going to go to the quartermaster now and then we're picking up a few more things at another place. Guess we don't have too much time this afternoon."

Tina spoke in her melancholy tone, "The hands on the clock are like the reaper's scythe. It slowly falls upon the mortal threads to nothingness."

Elsa, who had been relatively quiet, said, "That was deep."

Giana pointed at Valerie and said, "Now Valerie, that was goat!" She placed her fingers over her lips and chuckled, she continued, "Oops, I mean goth." Elsa and Sarah laughed. Tina's lips began to form a slight smile. Laughter began to escape from her lips too. Valerie's shoulders slumped and she pouted her lips as if she were about to cry.

Lieutenant Michael pointed toward the open door and said, "Okay. Okay. Let's go girls. We've got quite the walk ahead of us today."

Sarah sighed and said, "How come they had to put our headquarters so far from the local Military base? It's going to take us about an hour to walk there."

Lieutenant Michael perked up and said, "Consider this your exercise for the day. We didn't do our morning exercises since I had to pick up Jennifer."

Jennifer turned around to face him and said, "You told me the walk from the hospital was going to be my exercise. Now you're making me exercise again?" She over exaggerated her voice.

Lieutenant Michael said, "It'll give us a good opportunity to get to know each other better. So buck up and let's get going." He then turned to Lieutenant Rachel and said, "Alright, I'll see you later."

Lieutenant Rachel waved goodbye as the four of them left. She sarcastically said, "Have fun on your hike girls!" There were several loud groans coming from Valerie and Sarah. They both drooped forward and let their arms hang dramatically toward the ground. Jennifer followed behind them with her arms still crossed over her chest again.

As they left, Lieutenant Rachel shut the door behind them. She sighed and rested her forehead on the door. She wished she could be closer to Michael.

Giana suddenly said, "That new girl's a bitch!"

Lieutenant Rachel swung her arm out and knocked Giana across the back of her head again, saying, "What'd I say about your language?"

Giana rolled her eyes and sarcastically said, "Only swear when you're out fighting in the field. But, Lieutenant, it's still true!"

Tina said, "That girl looks like she wants to die."

Elsa said, "At the very least you can see that she is very depressed. Giana, of course, is too dense to notice it."

Giana, rubbing the back of her head, said, "That's not true. I can see it but that's no excuse for her to act like a bi ... a female dog." Giana stopped herself and avoided getting knocked in the back of the head again.

Lieutenant Rachel sighed and said, "Come on Giana, just give her a break."

Lieutenant Michael walked down the street in his usual half pace that he kept when walking with the girls. It was easier for them to keep up with him this way. He was used to timing himself with Mary standing next to him. Now he was all alone. Sarah and Valerie linked arms like normal, following him from behind. Jennifer continued to keep her distance following behind Sarah and Valerie. He could hassle her again about it, but decided to just let it go. It wasn't like anybody could actually hurt her with her red Wielder abilities.

Sarah and Valerie continued to talk like they normally would. They continued like this for the first fifteen minutes of their walk. After that, Sarah turned her head toward Jennifer and said, "Why don't you come up with us, Jennifer. We'd love to talk to you too. We want to get to know you better."

Jennifer looked down towards the ground and said, "I think I'll pass."

Valerie, who had also turned her head to Jennifer, said, "Come on. Don't be like that. I think it would be more fun if we all got to know each other better."

Sarah said, "We could tell you all the secrets we know about Lieutenant Michael."

Lieutenant Michael, who was intently listening to their interactions with Jennifer, turned around and said, "What do you mean by secrets?"

Sarah turned back around to face him. She tilted her head and looked innocently at him while batting her eyes. She said, "Oh nothing."

Valerie copied Sarah with the innocent act and said, "Yeah, don't worry about it, Lieutenant. It's nothing."

Lieutenant Michael rolled his eyes and turned back around. He was at least happy that they were trying to befriend her.

Sarah and Valerie unlinked their arms and joined Jennifer on her left and right side. She was now surrounded. Jennifer crossed her arms over her chest again and looked down toward the ground."

Valerie said, "I like your hair style, Jennifer."

Jennifer mumbled, saying, "Thanks."

Valerie then said, "This butterfly clip is a gift from my dad, so I like to wear it as much as I can.

Jennifer shrugged her shoulders and kept her mouth shut.

Sarah tried to change the subject by saying, "We know you don't like Magical Girl Squad, but are there any TV shows that you do like?"

Jennifer mumbled again, saying, "I don't really like to watch TV anymore."

Sarah said, "Do you like to read anything?"

Jennifer said, "Yeah, I like to read."

Sarah smiled at her and said, "That's great! What do you like to read?"

Jennifer's mood began to perk up a little and she said, "I like to read fantasy type books. I have ... I mean I had the whole Lost Sword Saga. Of course they got all burnt up when Los Angeles got nuked by the World Government." Her countenance began to grow dim again.

Lieutenant Michael said, "Well, if you like it so much, why don't we drop by the bookstore after we stop by the quartermaster. I'm sure they'll have the Lost Sword Saga there. It is a popular youth novel series."

Jennifer looked up at him and said, "You mean it, L.T.?"

Lieutenant Michael turned around and said, "Of course! After all, we want to help you get back the stuff you lost in your last home."

Jennifer looked down to the ground. She began to grip her right wrist again and the look of pain returned to her face. Valerie noticed it and said, "Is there something wrong with your wrist? If it is injured I can probably heal it with my ability?"

Jennifer let go of her wrist and shook her head, saying, "No, there's nothing wrong with my wrist. It's nothing."

Sarah said, "Really? Because it sure looked like you were in pain now when you gripped your wrist."

Jennifer shook her head again and said, "Trust me, there's nothing wrong."

Sarah nodded and said, "Okay, I'll trust you. I was just worried that something was wrong. If you say it's fine I'll trust you since we're a team. I only hope that you can trust me too and if there's something wrong you'd tell me. Okay?"

"Jennifer nodded and tried to smile, saying, "I'm fine, so don't worry." The smile on her face was forced. It couldn't conceal the look of pain that was behind it.

Sarah nodded and said, "Okay." She let it go because she knew that Jennifer was trying to cope with her situation in her own way.

Lieutenant Michal pointed across the street and said, "Look, Jennifer. That's the bookstore. We'll go there after we get some new uniforms for Sarah." He then looked at his watch and said, "Wow, Sarah, you won't believe that it only took us a half an hour to get this far. This means that we cut our time down by fifteen minutes!"

Sarah said, "Well, I guess we're moving faster because Mary's not running to all the store windows and making us stop." Her smile went away and she began to look depressed again.

Lieutenant Michael regretted what he had just said. She was right. Mary was always running up to store windows and it would turn into an argument just trying to go somewhere. The pain of loss reappeared in his heart. The mask of happiness he wore fell off and his face showed his pain.

Jennifer stood there watching as both Lieutenant Michael and Sarah became depressed. Lieutenant Michael noticed Jennifer looking up at him. He focused his eyes on her and then put on his mask of happiness again. He smiled at her and then started to walk towards the base.

Jennifer said, "L.T."

Lieutenant Michael stopped and turned around again. He said, "Yes, Jennifer?"

Her head became subdued and she looked embarrassed. She brought her hands together and clasped them in front of her chest. She said, "I ... I'm sorry that Mary died."

Lieutenant Michael was surprised. It was the first time she had shown any empathy. He wanted to smile at her and rub her on top of the head but he had promised not to do anything like that so he kept his hand back. He said, "Thank you, Jennifer. We all loved Mary. We're all sorry about all the people you lost too. This was a horrible tragedy, but, despite that we all have hope that we can keep moving forward together."

Sarah said, "That's right, Jennifer. We look forward to being really good friends with you too."

Jennifer's hands began to shake. She began to alternate grasping her hands and sliding her hand over her fingers. Her eyes started to turn red as if she were about to cry. She grasped her right wrist again and seemed to grip it tighter than before. She stopped trembling and her eyes became clear again. She let her wrist go.

Sarah said, "If you need to cry, it's okay. I cried a lot. I might still cry later on so don't hold back."

Jennifer said with as much control she could muster in her voice, "Crying won't fix anything."

Valerie said, "Crying isn't about fixing things, it's about expressing yourself. Sometimes you just need to express yourself before you feel better."

Jennifer seemed to get annoyed. She said, "I don't need to express myself, I just need to kill some Harvesters."

Lieutenant Michael said, "I see, you're choosing the vengeance route. Well, that should work too. Come Thursday, I can promise you that we'll go out and kill some Harvesters. I'm going to ask the Captain to put us on hunting duty. You'll get to kill as many Harvesters as you want till you feel satisfied."

Jennifer smirked and said, "I won't be satisfied till every single one of them is dead!"

Lieutenant Michael nodded his head and said, "Yeah, me too." He turned back towards the base and began to walk again. Sarah, Valerie, and Jennifer followed together behind him. Jennifer was stuck in between Sarah and Valerie.

The quartermaster depot was near the entrance on the inside of the base. Above the front door was a plaque that read, "I AM QUARTERMASTER. I AM

PROUD." It was the ending of the quartermaster's creed. Lieutenant Michael opened the glass door and allowed the girls to enter first.

Inside the lobby it looked like a normal office waiting room. In the back there was a counter where another Lieutenant was sitting, reading over some papers. When the four of them entered into the lobby, the woman sitting at the counter looked up and greeted them. Lieutenant Michael greeted her back and walked up to the counter. She said, "My name is Lieutenant Summers. What can I do for you today Wielders?"

Lieutenant Michael said, "I am Michael Snyder of Phoenix Guard Company, Squad Three. Sarah Willard appears to have out grown her current uniform again."

Lieutenant Summers nodded and said, "I see. Sometimes they grow up so fast. Let me pull up your file." She turned to her computer and typed in Sarah's name and unit number. She read over the current sizes that were listed and said, "Okay, Sarah. Come with me and we'll start with the next size up."

Lieutenant Summers pointed to the chairs in the lobby and said, "Why don't you three have a seat and I'll take care of the rest."

Lieutenant Michael nodded and said, "Sure, no problem." He then went to a chair and sat down in it. Valerie sat down next to him. She looked up at him and smiled. She then began to swing her legs back and forth. Jennifer sat down next to Valerie and crossed her arms over her chest again.

Sarah followed Lieutenant Summers into the back changing room. The Lieutenant said, "Okay, Sarah. Go ahead and change out of your uniform and I'll get the next size for you." She left the room to go into the clothing storage area.

Sarah stood in the middle of the changing room. There was a large mirror on the back wall that allowed her to see her whole body in it. She began to unbutton her uniform jacket. She let it slide off of her arms and onto the floor. She then took off her blue tie and she dropped it onto the jacket. She unbuttoned the top two buttons on her dress and then lifted it up over her head and dropped it on the floor next to her jacket.

Sarah stood there in her underwear, socks, and combat boots. She turned to face the mirror. She tugged at the training bra that was feeling tight. She then ran her hands over her bust and wondered how much bigger they were going to get. As a soldier it would be inconvenient to have big breasts, but as a woman, she kind of hoped that they would grow more. There was also the danger that if she developed too fast, it would lead to a shortened life span. She then thought, *Why do I even need breasts? It's not like I'll ever have children.*

At that moment, she began to understand Mary a little bit more. The desire to obtain something that you would never be allowed to have. Mary had told her that she wanted to be a wife and mother. She would never reach that goal. She died. *I'll die before that too. I'll never know what it's like to fall in love with a boy and to have boys think I'm pretty,* she thought to herself.

When she first started to develop, she asked Lieutenant Rachel about it. She had told her that, "Yes, my breasts do get in the way of my military responsibilities, but there's not much I can do about it except to wrap them down when I need to."

Mary would often complain about Lieutenant Rachel's bust size. It wasn't so much a problem with Mary that Lieutenant Rachel had large breasts, it was the fact that her own size was very small. Sarah had already developed a little bit bigger than Mary was. She had teased her about it herself. She had only meant it as a joke though.

Lieutenant Summers entered the room carrying a new uniform. She handed the dress to Sarah and said, "Okay, Sarah. Try this on and tell me how well it fits."

Sarah took the new dress and slipped it over her body. She buttoned the top buttons like normal and then began to move her arms around to see how tight it was against her body. She said, "I think this is good. It feels slightly loose so I'll have a little room to grow but it is not so baggy that it will interfere in my work." She then took the jacket and buttoned it up. It too was a good fit.

Lieutenant Summers looked her over and said, "Well that was easy enough. I'll get you eight more uniforms to take home with you. Is there anything else that I can help you with?"

Sarah began to look embarrassed. She clasped her hands together and said, "My training bra is getting tight too. I'm a little embarrassed to ask my Lieutenant about it but I don't know what size to get. Do you think you can help me know what size to get?"

Lieutenant Summers smiled and nodded, saying, "Of course. I understand. It can be hard sometimes when you have a male Lieutenant. That's why they always have a female doctor as the medical officer. But, I'm happy to help too. Bra sizes are listed by the alphabet starting with double A and from there they go to A, B, C, and so forth. I can give you an exact measurement if you want, but just by looking at you I would think you are an A. Do you want me to measure you?"

Sarah nodded her head and said, "Sure. Thank you so much!"

Lieutenant Summers nodded and pulled a tape measure out of her pocket. She said, "Okay, to measure you, you're going to have to take off your dress again."

Sarah dropped her jacket onto the floor and then took off her dress. The Lieutenant wrapped the tape measure under her bust and said, "Exhale please." Sarah breathed out and held it out, while Lieutenant Summers measured her under bust. Then Lieutenant Summers measured her bust size and said, "Just like I thought. You are definitely an A cup."

Sarah nodded and said, "Thanks for helping me, Lieutenant Summers!"

Lieutenant Summers smiled and said, "Sure, no problem. Go ahead and get dressed again and then go back to your Lieutenant. I will get the other uniforms and bring them out to you."

Sarah nodded and began to dress herself again in her new uniform. As she dressed, Lieutenant Summers left the room to grab more uniforms. Sarah put the dress back over her head and let it slide down her body. She buttoned the top buttons and popped up her collar. She slipped the tie back over her head and tightened it. She then put her new jacket back on and buttoned it up. She looked at herself in the mirror and ran her hands down the blue stripes on her new uniform. She smiled at herself and nodded, saying, "Okay! I'm ready!"

Sarah left the changing room and walked over to her squad. She did a quick spin and then threw her arms open wide, saying, "Ta-dah! My new uniform! How does it look?"

Valerie clapped her hands and said, "It looks great!"

Lieutenant Michael gave her a thumbs up and said, "Yep, looks good."

Jennifer rolled her eyes and said, "It looks exactly the same as the old one."

Sarah dropped her arms to her sides and said, "I know that but I got to wear this stupid thing every day, so, at the very least, you can help me pretend that it looks good on me."

Jennifer shrugged her shoulders and said, "Whatever."

Soon Lieutenant Summers came out holding a large plastic bag full of new uniforms. She handed the bag to Sarah and said, "Here you go my dear." She then turned to Lieutenant Michael and said, "Don't forget to put the old uniforms in the uniform recycle container at your headquarters. I'll know if you don't."

Lieutenant Michael nodded and said, "Don't worry. I know what to do."

Lieutenant Michael held his hand out to Lieutenant Summers and they shook hands. He said, "Thanks, Lieutenant. We'll be heading out now."

Lieutenant Summers nodded and smiled. She patted Sarah on the back and said, "See you later, Sarah. Try not to grow too fast though!" Sarah waved goodbye as they left the quartermaster depot.

Sarah tossed the heavy bag over her shoulder and struggled to carry it. Lieutenant Michael noticed her and said, "Sarah, do you want me to carry that for you?"

Sarah looked at him and pouted her lips. She nodded and said, "Please do. It's heavy." Lieutenant Michael took it from her and swung the bag over his own shoulder. Sarah gave a huge sigh of relief and stretched out her arms. She said, "Thanks, Lieutenant. I don't think I could carry that all the way home."

Lieutenant Michael smiled at her and gave her a thumbs up, saying, "Don't worry. You can count on me."

Valerie said, "If something's heavy, we can always have Jennifer carry it. She's really strong."

Jennifer smirked at her and said, "I'm not your pack mule."

Sarah giggled and said, "She's not a goat either, Valerie."

Valerie slumped her shoulders and said, "Are you still laughing at that?"

Lieutenant Michael cut in and said, "That's enough of that. I don't mind carrying heavy stuff for you girls. I always try to be chivalrous."

Sarah began to think about what she had thought about earlier. She walked faster till she was standing beside Lieutenant Michael. She lowered her gaze and started to blush a little. She said, "Lieutenant, can I ask you a serious question?"

Lieutenant Michael turned his head toward her and looked a little concerned. He said, "Of course. You know you can always ask me anything. No matter what it is."

She paused for a moment and then said, "Lieutenant, do you think boys will think I'm pretty?"

Lieutenant Michael was not expecting a question like that. He stopped walking and looked up into the sky for a moment to collect his thoughts. He put his hand on top of her head and said, "So ... you're at that age where you start thinking about boys now are you?"

Sarah shook her head and said, "No, I don't really think about any boys. I was just wondering if you think boys would think I'm pretty."

Lieutenant Michael nodded and said, "Of course boys will think you are pretty. I think you're pretty."

Sarah blushed even more and said, "But I'll never get to go out with any boys, will I?"

Lieutenant Michael took his hand off of her head and ran his hand through his own hair. He said, "Well, probably not."

Sarah had stopped blushing and she looked down to the ground. She said, "I'll be dead before I'm old enough."

Lieutenant Michael's face began to look depressed. He sighed and said, "Well, I won't lie to you. You will probably be dead before you are old enough. Even then, there is the matter of having time."

Sarah looked up at him and grimly smiled. She said, "I'm sorry I made you look sad, Lieutenant. I was just thinking is all."

Lieutenant Michael started walking again. He said, "At the least, I hope that we can all have some fun together."

Valerie raised her hand and said, "I have lots of fun with you, Lieutenant!"

Lieutenant Michael turned his head to her and said, "I'm glad, Valerie. I have lots of fun with you too."

Sarah nodded and said, "I have lots of fun with you too, Lieutenant!"

The bookstore quickly came up since it was near the base. It was a small bookstore as there were not that many new books printed in paper now a days. Most books were read using electronic tablets. This bookstore sold both used and new books. As a plus, they also had a system set up where you can buy electronic books and download them directly to your reading tablet. Despite the ease of electronic books some people still preferred the old paper books.

Lieutenant Michael opened the door to the bookstore and allowed the girls to enter. He turned his head to Jennifer and said, "Okay, Jennifer. Let's find the Lost Sword Saga. That would be in fantasy I think. Do you want the electronic version or the printed version?"

Jennifer shrugged her shoulders and said, "If it's okay, I'd like the printed version."

Lieutenant Michael nodded his head and said, "Sure. I understand. I actually prefer the printed books too. I think it's easier."

Together they found the fantasy section and began to look for books that were titled: Lost Sword Saga. Jennifer said, "There are fifteen volumes, but I only had the first ten so far."

Lieutenant Michael said, "Well, if they have all fifteen, I'll just get them all for you as a welcoming gift." Jennifer didn't say anything but she looked like she was suppressing a smile on her face.

One by one, Lieutenant Michael began to pull Lost Sword Saga books off of the shelf and handed them to Jennifer. At the end, Jennifer held a large stack of books in her arms. Lieutenant Michael counted the books and the total came out to fifteen. He said, "It looks like we got all of them, Jennifer."

Jennifer suppressed her smile again but said, "Thanks, L.T., this means a lot to me."

Lieutenant Michael started to lift his hand to rub her on top of the head but then remembered what she had said. Instead he ran his hand over his own head and said, "Sure, no problem. I'm glad you're happy, Jennifer."

Lieutenant Michael turned to Valerie and Sarah, saying, "So, while we're here. Do you girls want any books too?"

Sarah shook her head.

Valerie thought for a moment and began to fidget. She said, "I wish I could buy a bible."

Lieutenant Michael nodded and said, "Unfortunately, the World Government doesn't allow the selling of religious texts. You can still download a free copy over the net though. Personally, I don't see what the problem is, but, whatever, I guess the government knows best. That's why they're in charge."

Valerie sighed and looked down cast. She said, "I know, Lieutenant. I have the free electronic version, but I miss the printed book that my dad had. I'm okay though, Lieutenant. I don't need any books today."

Altogether the books cost about two hundred dollars. Lieutenant Michael held the bag and said, "Do you want to carry your new books, Jennifer? Or, do you want me to carry them?"

Jennifer held out her hand and said, "It's okay, L.T. I don't mind carrying it by myself." She reached up and took the bag handle in her own hand.

Lieutenant Michael pointed towards the door and said, "Okay, we got uniforms and books. Now let's go to the clothing store to get the rest of what Sarah needs."

Unfortunately, the clothing store was in the opposite direction. They would have to walk all the way back up the street, past their headquarters, and then down to the clothing store. Lieutenant Michael scratched his chin and said, "Maybe we should have gone there first. Then we wouldn't have to carry all this heavy stuff."

Valerie said, "Too late to do anything about it now. Do you want to drop it off at home first?"

Lieutenant Michael shook his head and said, "No, then we'd have to go up and down all those stairs. It's not that far past home so I don't really mind."

Soon enough, they passed their home and came to the clothing store. Lieutenant Michael looked at the spot on the glass window front where Mary would press her hands and face on the glass when she wanted something. He thought he could see the print of her face and palms on the glass. He pushed the thought down inside of himself and opened the door for the girls, who walked in.

Sarah and Valerie were always excited to look through the clothing store, even if they were not planning on buying something. Jennifer's melancholy expression suggested that she didn't care at all.

Lieutenant Michael found his usual chair in the corner and sat down in it. He leaned back with his hands propped up behind his head. He relaxed his legs and let them stretch out where he sat. The girls would either finish quickly or take forever. Either way, he was going to enjoy sitting here while the girls did whatever they did when trying on clothes.

Sarah headed toward the underwear section for girls. Valerie followed behind her. Jennifer stood there in the aisle and again crossed her arms over her chest. She looked to Sarah and Valerie. She then looked to Lieutenant Michael. She was trying to decide who would be less annoying to go with. She looked to Lieutenant Michael again, who had just sat down and stretched out in a chair. She went to stand next to him.

Lieutenant Michael watched her walk over to him. She carried the bag of books with her. When she got close to him, he said, "Don't you want to help Sarah find some new clothes?"

She shook her head and said, "Not really."

Lieutenant Michael shrugged his shoulders and said, "Guess you're the loner type. I can appreciate that."

Jennifer sat down on the floor next to his chair. She reached into the bag and pulled out one of the books and began flipping through the pages. Lieutenant Michael watched her and began to think about if there was something else she needed. He began to inventory the things that he received for her the day before. Mainly, it was just uniform related. He then remembered that he did not remember seeing any pajamas among the stuff they brought for her. He said, "Jennifer, I was just thinking about stuff you might need and I don't remember seeing any pajamas."

Jennifer shrugged her shoulders and said, "That's okay, L.T., I don't mind sleeping in my underwear."

Lieutenant Michael shrugged his shoulders and said, "Well, don't you want something you can relax in during the evening? I don't know what you did before, but, around here, we tend to wear relaxing pajamas in the evening."

Jennifer stood up and said, "I suppose you're right. Guess I'll take a look at some pajamas while we're here."

Jennifer stood up and left her bag with Lieutenant Michael. He pointed in the direction where they were usually displayed. She walked over into that area and began looking for herself.

Sarah stood in the middle of the girl's underwear section. There were many different types of bras and she began to feel overwhelmed. Sarah brought her thumb up to her mouth and began to bite down on her thumbnail as she tried to think of what to do next.

Valerie saw the concern on her face and put a hand on her shoulder, saying, "Are you okay, Sarah?"

Sarah, almost coming to tears, said, "I don't know what bra I should get. I didn't know that there were so many kinds. I see wired bras, push-up bras, things I've never heard of before."

Valerie said, "What about the padded bra. That way if a Harvester hits you in the chest, you'll have extra padding to protect you."

Sarah's face became even more frustrated. Valerie said, "Why don't we ask the Lieutenant to help us then?"

Sarah shook her head frantically and said, "I'm too embarrassed to ask the Lieutenant about this."

Valerie tilted her head to the side and looked confused. She said, "Why are you embarrassed? I'm sure that the Lieutenant has had to do this before. At the least, he probably has some experience with this since he is a grown up."

Sarah again frantically shook her head.

Valerie rolled her eyes and said, "Why don't you talk to Lieutenant Rachel. She has really big breasts so I'm sure she knows a lot about bras."

Sarah looked down to the ground and sighed, saying, "But for me to talk to her, we'd have to go home first. That would be silly."

Valerie shook her head and said, "That's not true. We can have the Lieutenant call Lieutenant Rachel on his phone."

Hope began to fill Sarah's face. Her grim expression was replaced with a smile. She hugged Valerie and said, "Valerie, you're a genius! Will you help me with this too?"

Valerie said, "Of course. You want me to talk to the Lieutenant for you don't you?"

Sarah nodded her head in embarrassment. Valerie smiled and took Sarah by the arm. Together they walked over to Lieutenant Michael who was relaxing in his chair. He noticed them coming with empty hands. He saw the embarrassment on Sarah's face.

Valerie let go of Sarah's arm and stood next to Lieutenant Michael. She cupped her hand over her mouth and brought her face close to Lieutenant Michael's ear. She quietly said, "Sarah's too embarrassed to talk to you about bras."

Lieutenant Michael looked toward Sarah. She became even more subdued. Her lips began to tense a little. She brought her hands together in front of her skirt. She twisted her body slightly side to side as he watched her. He spoke quietly to Valerie, saying, "Really? She's embarrassed?"

Valerie quietly spoke back, saying, "Yeah. I told her you could call Lieutenant Rachel so she could speak to her about it."

Lieutenant Michael nodded and said, "Yeah, I can do that." He reached into his pocket and pulled out his cellphone. He scrolled though his number listing and clicked on Rachel. He brought the phone to his ear and waited.

After a moment, the phone picked up and Lieutenant Rachel spoke into his ear. He said, "Hi Rachel. Can you spare a moment to talk to Sarah for me?"

Lieutenant Rachel agreed so he handed the phone to Sarah who turned around and took a few steps away from them. With her back turned to them she began to speak, saying, "Hello Lieutenant Rachel."

Lieutenant Rachel responded and said, "How can I help you Sarah?"

Sarah lowered her voice and cupped her hand over her mouth and the phone. She said, "I don't know what kind of bra to get." She paused as Rachel replied to her. Sarah responded periodically, saying, "Yes" or "No". She then said, "Thank you" and hung up the phone and handed it back to Lieutenant Michael.

Lieutenant Michael said, "Did you get the answer you needed?"

Sarah, still embarrassed, nodded her head. She then left to go back to the underwear section. Valerie followed after her. Once there, Sarah began to look for some sports bras. She found some and tried them on to see how they fit. It seemed to fit her nicely so she went back to get some more.

In the meantime, Jennifer returned to Lieutenant Michael holding a white long pajama shirt with emerald green sleeves. He looked at it and said, "Did you find something you like?"

Jennifer nodded her head and said, "Yeah. I want this one."

Lieutenant Michael took it and said, "Okay. Looks good."

As he took Jennifer's new long pajama shirt, Sarah and Valerie returned. Sarah held onto a stack of bras in her arms as she clutched them against her chest. She still looked embarrassed. He held his hand open and said, "Go ahead and give them to me. I'll go buy these for you."

Sarah hesitated. Lieutenant Michael said, "I know you feel embarrassed, Sarah. I understand why you do. But you don't need to be so worried. This is just a normal part of life. You're not the first girl who I had to help with this you know. I would have thought that you had a little more trust in me."

Sarah handed him the bras she selected and said, "I'm sorry, Lieutenant. I just feel really embarrassed. I never had to do this before."

Lieutenant Michael took the bras into his hand and said, "Don't worry about it. Let's get going. It's almost time to make dinner in an hour or so." He walked up to the register and bought the items. He put the new bag into the bag filled with Sarah's new uniforms. Together, they left the store and headed back to their apartment.

- 4 -

After dinner, Lieutenant Michael, Sarah, Valerie, and Jennifer did the dishes together. Sarah scrubbed the dishes, while Valerie rinsed them. Jennifer wiped them dry and handed them to Lieutenant Michael to put away. Lieutenant Michael watched them work together well and hoped that they would be able to work as well together in the field too.

During dinner, Jennifer mostly just sat there quietly eating a bit here and there. Valerie and Sarah were always quite vocal together. They tried to get Jennifer to join in with them but she always put up a wall around herself. Especially when it looked like she might actually be enjoying herself a little. That was when she shut herself off the most. It was at that time when she would grip her wrist and show great pain in her face.

Lieutenant Michael thought back to when Valerie first came. Their first night, he suggested that the girls take a bath together so that they could have more time to get close to each other. He wondered if this tactic would work with Jennifer.

As he accepted a dish from Jennifer, he said, "Hey girls, why don't you take a bath together tonight after we're done here? That way you can have some alone time together without me getting in the way."

Jennifer quickly said, "I'll pass."

Valerie said, "Oh come on, it'll be fun. We take lots of baths together, all the time."

Sarah said, "Yeah, we got a really big bath tub so it's best used if we go at the same time. And the Lieutenant's right. There's lots of stuff we can talk about by ourselves in there. This way we can get to know each other better."

Jennifer's face showed her annoyance. She smirked at Sarah and Valerie, saying, "No thanks. I'll pass."

Lieutenant Michael's plan had backfired. Even if he could force her to do it, it would only make things worse. He said, "Don't worry about it everybody. You don't have to take a bath together. I just thought it'd be good for you girls to get to know each other tonight."

Sarah turned to Valerie and said, "You and I can still take a bath together tonight."

Valerie nodded and said, "Yeah, of course, but I was just hoping that Jennifer would come too. I just wanted to get to know her better."

Jennifer turned away from them and put the towel she was holding down on the countertop. She said, "Don't waste your time. There's no point in getting to know me." She then walked away without saying another word. The three of them stood there watching her go. None of them knew what to do. They heard a door open and then shut. Jennifer went into her room.

Valerie jumped off of her stepping stool and started walking towards the hallway. Lieutenant Michael reached out and grabbed her by the collar of her jacket. He said, "I think we should take this slowly. Let's not force her. She's been through something horrible and she needs time to think it out. That's why they give us a week off when we lose a teammate."

Valerie, still facing the hallway, started to cry. She said, "What does she mean that there's no point? That's ... that's just too sad."

Valerie stopped trying to move forward with Lieutenant Michael's hand grabbing on to her collar. Instead, she quickly turned and ran into Lieutenant Michael's chest. He wrapped his arms around her and held her tightly. She wept into his jacket. He said, "I know. I know, Valerie. Why don't you girls go take a bath now and I'll try to talk to her. Okay?"

Valerie stopped crying and nodded into his chest. He let her go and she turned away towards Sarah. Sarah held out her hand as she compassionately smiled at her. Valerie took her hand and together they walked towards the bathroom. They stopped in front of Jennifer's door.

Sarah knocked on the door and said, "Jennifer, we know you are hurting a lot. We just want you to know that we care about you no matter what."

Valerie added, saying, "Yeah, we care about you. Even if you don't think you are worth it." Jennifer said nothing in response to them through the door so they went into the bathroom to take a bath.

Jennifer laid on her bed in the darkness trembling. The wounds on her right wrist from earlier still stung. She gripped onto them tightly so that she could feel the pain from them. The pain helped to calm her trembling. She softly spoke to Sarah and Valerie, who had already walked away, saying, "I can't have friends because I get all my friends killed." She let go of her wrist and wrapped her arm across her eyes as she laid on her back.

After what seemed like only a few moments, Lieutenant Michael knocked on Jennifer's door and he said, "Jennifer, is it alright if I come in." There was no answer. Lieutenant Michael waited a moment and said, "If you don't respond to me Jennifer then I can use that as probable cause to justify entering without your permission to make sure you are okay."

Jennifer finally spoke, saying, "Come in."

Lieutenant Michael opened the door and turned on the light. Jennifer still laid on her bed with her arm resting over her eyes. It was only a few days ago that Mary laid on that same bed. He looked at the spot on the floor where he had sat, holding Mary, when she cried about getting her first period. Now he had placed another girl in this room, her room. A twinge of pain began to gnaw at his heart again.

Jennifer, still covering her eyes, said, "What is it, L.T.?"

Lieutenant Michael brushed his thoughts aside and focused on Jennifer. He walked over to her bed and sat down on the end of it. He waited for a moment, sighed, and then said, "I want you to talk to me, Jennifer. I don't care what you talk about, just talk."

Jennifer wrapped her other arm over her face too and said, "I don't got anything to talk about."

Lieutenant Michael said, "Yeah, you do. What you said to Valerie tells me that you need to talk to me. If you don't talk to me, I'll get Doctor Lovecraft to come here and talk to you about it. If you would rather talk to her, that's fine with me, but you are going to talk to someone."

Jennifer said, "I don't know what to talk about."

Lieutenant Michael said, "That's fair. Let me help you then. Why don't we talk about Lieutenant Sharon Thomas."

Jennifer said, "I don't want to talk about her."

Lieutenant Michael said, "Jennifer, I think you need to talk about your old teammates. I've read the file that Lieutenant Thomas wrote about you. Do you want to know what she said about you? She said 'Jennifer is a very nice girl who is easy to get along with. She is always smiling and looking to make friends.' That is what she thought about you."

Jennifer sat up and uncovered her eyes. She yelled, "You have no right to go through her things!"

Lieutenant Michael replied, "I am your Lieutenant now. I have every right to do something that pertains to your care. You've built up this wall around you that hides this Jennifer that Lieutenant Thomas wrote about. A girl who was nice to everybody and wants to be able to make friends with lots of people. Why don't you want to make friends with Sarah and Valerie?"

Jennifer sat there on her bed her face became blank from any expression. She looked down towards the floor. Lieutenant Michael said again, "Why don't you want to make friends with Sarah and Valerie too?"

Jennifer just sat there and continued to stare at the floor.

Lieutenant Michael said, "I know you need time to grieve for Lieutenant Thomas, Julie, and Annie. Sarah and Valerie also need time to grieve over Mary. I have hope that the three of you could help one another to get through this difficult time."

Jennifer, still looking down to the floor, finally spoke. She said, "I ... I was friends with them but being friends couldn't help them."

Lieutenant Michael nodded in understanding and said, "So you feel that because you were friends with Julie and Annie they died?"

Jennifer, without changing her expression, nodded her head. She continued to stare at the floor.

Lieutenant Michael said, "I don't believe that's true, Jennifer. This tragedy didn't happen because you were friends with them. It happened because we treated the Harvesters as if they wouldn't change their strategy. This has nothing to do with you being their friend. Now, I can't force you to be Sarah and Valerie's friend, but I hope you think about what I said. Sarah and Valerie are not going to die because they are your friends either. You can trust them. They are a good team."

Jennifer nodded her head and said meekly, "I'll try harder, L.T."

Lieutenant Michael stood up and said, "That's all I ask. It's okay to take it slow. Why don't you go take a shower now? Then you can get into your new pajamas and you three girls can sit down together and relax afterwards."

Jennifer nodded her head again and said, "Okay, L.T. I'll take a shower now."

Lieutenant Michael smiled at her and said, "Okay then. I'll leave you to it." He left her room and shut the door as he left. Jennifer slid over to the edge of the bed and waited a moment. She thought about how she acted toward Sarah and Valerie. In her own mind she didn't mean to act that way. She started to feel dirty inside herself. It just slipped out. She slid off of her bed and went to the bathroom.

Jennifer started to open the door to the bathroom. Sarah and Valerie immediately stopped talking and focused their attention on Jennifer who had just shut the door behind herself. Jennifer walked over to the bathtub. She began to fidget with her hands. She said, "I'm sorry I acted like that earlier. Please just give me some more time. I'll try harder, so please don't worry about me."

Sarah said, "I'm sorry if I'm pushing you too fast."

Valerie said, "Yeah, I'm sorry too."

Jennifer said, "I'm going to go take a shower now. After we're all done we can sit together and talk then. Okay?"

Sarah and Valerie perked up.

Sarah said, "Sounds good."

Valerie nodded her head and said, "Great!"

Jennifer walked over to her basket and began to take off her uniform. Valerie and Sarah watched her quietly. She made sure that she always kept her right wrist away from them so that they couldn't see it. That was the real reason why she didn't want to take a bath with them. She didn't want them to see the scars that represented her shame and pain over losing her teammates.

Jennifer walked over to one of the showers and turned on the water. When it was warm enough she walked in and let the water fall over her body. She felt so dirty all over her body. No matter how many times she washed herself, it didn't erase the dirtiness. The dirtiness was the shame she felt over what happened. It covered her whole body. No matter what anybody said, she knew deep in her heart that the reason everyone she loved was dead was because of her. She was the only one still alive and it was all her fault. No one would be able to convince her otherwise.

After their bath time, the girls got dressed in their pajamas and sat around the dinner table. Lieutenant Michael gave them some space by sitting in the recliner and watching the television.

The three of them sat awkwardly around the table. Jennifer sat there with the first volume of the Lost Sword Saga sitting in front of her on the table. Sarah and Valerie looked at each other. When their eyes met they both understood that they were waiting for the other to say something. Sarah, being the oldest decided to take the lead like Mary would have done. She said, "So ... Jennifer. I've never heard of the Lost Sword Saga. Would you mind telling me about it?"

Jennifer picked up the book and turned it over. She stared at the back and then flipped through the pages. She said, "It takes place in a fantasy world called Tiggdrasil. The people in this world live like it was the ancient days on earth. They live in small tribal villages. In the east, an empire begins to form under the rule of a bad man who wants to take over the whole world. To gain the ultimate power, he searches for an all-powerful magical sword that has been lost to time. The bad man uses magic to create these evil beasts that he uses to attack the towns and to search for the lost sword."

Valerie spoke up and said, "Wow, that sounds scary."

Sarah nodded her head and said, "Yeah, that sounds like an intense story."

Jennifer continued, saying, "There's more to it. In the west, a twelve year old boy is hunting near some caves. He sees a light shining in one of the caves and goes to see why. Inside he finds an old rusted sword sticking inside of a giant stone altar. The light is coming from the sword. When the boy gets close to it, the light stops. He grabs the sword by the handle and pulls on it. The sword slides out of the stone alter and magically changes into a sword that looks brand new. The boy found the lost sword. The whole series follows the boy as he hides from the evil ruler. He builds up an army and leads a rebellion. It gets really detailed."

Sarah said, "That sounds like an interesting story. I might like to borrow it sometime if you wouldn't mind."

Jennifer shrugged her shoulders and said, "Sure. I don't mind."

Lieutenant Michael, who was still watching television, called out and said, "Hey, girls! You all might want to see this."

Sarah, Valerie, and Jennifer rushed over to him as he sat in the recliner pointing at the television. There was an advertisement for a new show. Jennifer's eyes opened wide and her jaw dropped as she stood there in surprise as she watched. She said, "No way. Are they really making a Lost Sword Saga show?" Sure enough, at the end, they announced that it was the Lost Sword Saga.

Jennifer shrugged her shoulders and said, "I bet they'll ruin it. They always do."

Sarah said, "Well, at least they're making it. It's better than nothing."

Valerie said, "I want to watch it. It starts on Thursday night at eight. I'd love to watch it with you Jennifer. Then you can tell me when it screws up the story and you can tell me what it should be."

Jennifer looked downward and said, "I guess I can do that."

After the commercial was over, Lieutenant Michael shut off the television and said, "Time for bed, girls."

Sarah and Valerie said in unison, "Goodnight, Lieutenant." They both hugged Lieutenant Michael. Jennifer stood there and said, "Goodnight, L.T." The three of them walked toward their rooms.

They walked with Jennifer to her door. Sarah said, "Goodnight, Jennifer." She then turned to Valerie and gave her a hug, saying, "Goodnight, Valerie." Valerie hugged her back and also said, "Goodnight."

As Sarah walked away, Valerie reached out and embraced Jennifer in a hug. Jennifer's body went rigid and she said, "I thought I said I didn't want to be touched?"

Valerie let her go and said, "I know, but I love to hug people. And, when you stand there with that sad look on your face, I feel that you really want someone to hug you."

Jennifer crossed her arms in front of her chest and looked angry. She looked down to the ground and said, "Well, I don't, so don't do it again." Jennifer opened her door, stormed into her room and slammed the door shut behind herself."

Valerie looked to Sarah, who had turned around to watch the spectacle. Valerie sadly said, "Guess I did wrong again."

Sarah shrugged her shoulders and looked compassionately at Valerie. She said, "No, she does look like she needs a hug. But we can't help her if she don't want it." Sarah then opened her door and went into her room.

Valerie sighed and brushed her hair behind her ear. She went to her own room too.

As Sarah slept she began to dream. It was a new dream. She was alone in the apartment complex and was looking for Mary. As she looked for Mary she could hear the screeches of the Harvesters getting closer and closer. She could only find pieces of Mary scattered here and there. She tried to gather the pieces and put them together.

Eventually, she found Mary's head. It was hiding in Lieutenant Michael's room. She picked up the head and it came to life in her hands. Mary's disembodied head glared at her and said, "You did this to me."

Sarah dropped her head in shock. Mary's head rolled along the floor until it came to a stop. Mary's head said, "If you were stronger, this wouldn't have happened to me."

Sarah took a few steps backward and was getting ready to run. As she backed up she bumped into something cold and wet. She spun around to see the open mouth of a Harvester drooling. It screamed at her.

Sarah was startled awake. She lay there panting as she tried to figure out what was going on. "It was just another stupid nightmare," she said to herself.

She calmed her breathing down and wiped the sweat from her forehead. She threw back the covers and rolled out of bed. She made her way out of her room and went into Lieutenant Michael's room.

Instead of sneaking into the Lieutenant's bed like normal, she walked over to stand beside him. She placed her hands on his arm and began to shake him awake. She said, "Lieutenant, are you awake?"

Lieutenant Michael was forced awake and said, "Yeah, I'm awake. Is that you Sarah? Is something wrong?"

Sarah, standing there in the dark said, "I had a nightmare. Is it okay if I get in your bed?"

Lieutenant Michael was a little surprised. Usually, she'd just crawl in without even thinking about asking. He said, "Uh ... sure."

Sarah crawled onto his bed and slid under the blankets. He said, "Did you need to talk about your nightmare?"

Sarah hesitated for a moment and then said, "I had a new nightmare. The Harvesters were coming after me. I was looking for Mary but I could only find pieces of her. When I found her head, she told me that it was all my fault."

Lieutenant Michael could feel her body shaking on his mattress. He reached out and placed his hand on her arm. She slowly stopped trembling. He said, "This dream is just your mind trying to deal with some guilt that you feel. You feel that it is your fault, but I know that it's not."

Sarah started to cry, she said, "If ... if only I could have helped her. Maybe she'd be alive today."

Lieutenant Michael reached his arm over her and pulled her closer to him. He held her in his arm and said, "We can't say if that would of helped or not. We might all be dead if we tried that, like with Jennifer's squad."

Sarah began to stop crying. She said, "Sometimes I think it would have been better if I died with her."

Lieutenant Michael said, "No, Sarah, that's not good. Remember what Mary said? That as long as you're alive, she keeps living in your heart."

Sarah said, "Are you mad at me Lieutenant?"

Lieutenant Michael said, "Of course not, why would you think I'm mad at you?"

Sarah said, "Because I was too embarrassed to talk to you when we went clothes shopping for me."

Lieutenant Michael chuckled and said, "Oh that? No, that's not enough to make me mad. I understand that this can be an embarrassing subject for you. I was once your age and I had a mom who had to help me with embarrassing boy stuff too. So, I understand why you are embarrassed about it. I was too."

Sarah gave a sigh of relief and said, "I'm glad. I was worried about it all day. But I was nervous to ask you."

Lieutenant Michael said, "Don't worry, let's just put this behind us. I just hope that it will be easier for you next time something like this happens."

Sarah yawned and said, "Me too Lieutenant." She then drifted off to sleep.

When Lieutenant Michael was sure she was sound asleep, he let her go and rolled back over on his opposite side.

Lieutenant Michael shut his eyes and began to focus on going back to sleep. As he lay there, he heard the door open. He heard the shuffle of small feet trying to quietly approach his bed. The noise stopped and he felt a small body climb onto the edge of his bed. Lieutenant Michael quietly said, "Valerie, is that you?"

The figure on his bed stopped moving and quietly spoke, saying, "Yeah, it's me. I had a bad dream. Is it okay if I sleep in your bed?"

Lieutenant Michael said, "I guess so. Sarah is already there too. Do you want to tell me about it?"

Valerie finished crawling over to an empty spot on his bed and crawled underneath the covers next to Sarah. Valerie said, "My dream just represented my feelings that I'm never going to get stronger. I don't want to ever lose a friend again because I'm not strong enough."

Lieutenant Michael said, "I understand that feeling very well. When we go out into the field together, all I can do is stand there and watch you girls put yourselves into danger. I know that I'm never going to be as strong as you three are. Even you, Valerie, have more power and ability then I do. But, despite my lack of ability, I do what I can do."

Valerie said, "That's not true, Lieutenant. You do a lot. You help us to stay focused and organized. You can see things that we can't see or understand yet."

Lieutenant Michael said, "Thanks, Valerie. You do a lot too. You are our special healer. On top of that, you help give us hope for the future."

Valerie, confused, said, "How do I give people hope?"

Lieutenant Michael said, "Because you never give up. You help others to not give up because of that. Even when it is hard on you or dangerous. Like the time you ran out there first to save Mary. For that reason, I believe that you are going to be one of those really strong yellow Wielders. So try not to worry about whether you are going to get stronger or not. I already know that you will."

Valerie said, "I want to save Jennifer too. I want to be her friend. I think I made her angry again. I hugged her even though she told me not to."

Lieutenant Michael said, "Maybe. Then again, maybe not. I think that you should do what you think is right regardless of what others think. For all you know, it might just lead to something good. Of course, it can always make things worse. Since you never know what will happen, you might as well do what you think will best make you happy. That way it is easier to live with your choice."

Valerie yawned and said, "I understand now, Lieutenant. I'll try my best so I don't let you down."

Lieutenant Michael reached his hand out to her and rubbed the top of her head, saying, "Don't worry, Valerie. You could never let me down, no matter what."

Valerie yawned again and closed her eyes. She wrapped an arm over Sarah and felt the warmth from her sleeping body. She, too, quickly went back to sleep.

Again, Lieutenant Michael rolled over and faced the door. He began to think about Jennifer. He softly rolled out of bed so that he wouldn't wake Valerie or Sarah up again. He took a small flashlight that he kept next to his bed and went out of his room. He walked across the way and entered Jennifer's room.

The flashlight had a soft filter on it that made the light really dim. It was bright enough to see in a small room, but not so bright as to wake a person up; especially children. He shined the light to see Jennifer laying there staring back at him. She said, "Come to watch me sleep, L.T.?"

Lieutenant Michael said, "I'm sorry if I woke you. I was just worried about you and thought I'd check to make sure you were okay. Both Sarah and Valerie had nightmares and I was already up dealing with them. I thought I'd just see how you were doing while I was at it."

Jennifer said, "Don't worry, L.T. I was already awake. I've been having trouble sleeping since the Los Angeles battle. Every time I close my eyes to sleep, I just see images of what happened."

Lieutenant Michael said, "Talking about it might help, you know. Just like with a nightmare. Talking about it to someone can help your mind come up with a solution to making it stop."

Jennifer said, "I'm not ready to talk about it yet. Please give me more time."

Lieutenant Michael said, "Okay, Jennifer. I'll give you more time. Just don't forget that I care about you."

Jennifer said, "You hardly know me. How can you care about me?"

Lieutenant Michael said, "I want to get to know you better. That's enough for me to care about you."

Jennifer rolled over to face the wall away from Lieutenant Michael. She didn't respond to him. He turned off his light and said, "Goodnight, Jennifer. I'm there if you need me. Try to get some sleep." He walked out of her room and went back to bed.

After Lieutenant Michael left, Jennifer said to herself, "If you knew what I really was, you wouldn't care about me. If you knew what I did, you would hate me."

- 5 -

Over the next few days, Jennifer began to adapt to her new team a little bit better. She was mostly quiet still and kept to herself. She avoided saying things in a way that sounded like she was attacking them. It was an improvement from their first day together.

Lieutenant Michael could still see the dark circles that were under her eyes. She was still having trouble sleeping. He would check on her every night in the middle of the night and most of the time she was still awake. During emotional times, Jennifer would still suppress her sadness by faking that she lacked emotions. She continued to grip her wrist when she suppressed herself.

Sarah and Valerie continued to try to keep her involved in what they were doing, but Jennifer still resisted them. The walls that she had built up around herself were stronger than ever. When Jennifer got tired of talking to them, she would get her book and sit at the table to read. It was at that point that both Sarah and Valerie knew that they needed to stop and try again later.

On the Tuesday following Jennifer's arrival, Lieutenant Michael suggested that they make pizza again. Sarah and Valerie argued over the toppings. Valerie wanted to have mushrooms on the pizza, while Sarah wanted olives. Sarah, hoping to get Jennifer on her side, turned to her and said, "What do you want on the pizza?"

The dark circles that were under Jennifer's eyes were even darker than before. She must have had a really rough night. While Valerie and Sarah were having their friendly argument over pizza toppings, Jennifer stayed behind them and seemed even more melancholy then before. Jennifer shrugged her shoulders in response to Sarah's question and said, "I don't really care."

Valerie said, "Well if that's the case, why don't we just put both mushrooms and olives on the pizza."

Sarah appeared to be deep in thought as she stroked her chin. Lieutenant Michael intervened and said, "That's a good idea, Valerie. What do you think about that, Sarah?"

Sarah began to think out loud, saying, "I wonder if the mushrooms would drown out the flavor of the olives?"

Valerie said, "Geez, you are so obsessed with the flavor of food!"

Sarah retorted, "What do you think food is for? What's the point if I can't savor every flavor of it?"

Valerie, becoming frustrated said, "When you listen to music, there's not just one instrument. That would be boring. Instead you need a whole set of instruments to make the song reach its full potential! If we put both mushrooms and olives on the pizza, the flavors will combined to create a new song of flavors in our mouths!"

Sarah's face still showed signs of deep thought, she nodded as she stroked her chin. She said, "I see. I see. I suppose I can give it a try. I'm always up for experiencing new flavors."

Lieutenant Michael clapped his hands together once and said, "Excellent, then it's settled! We'll have a pizza with both olives and mushrooms." He turned to Jennifer and said, "If you want to add anything, Jennifer, now's the time."

Jennifer shook her head.

Lieutenant Michael sighed and said, "Okay then. Let's go to the store!" He pointed towards the door. Sarah went to grab the cloth shopping bag. Valerie began to spin in place in celebration of her successful negotiation. Jennifer crossed her arms and rolled her eyes at Valerie.

On their way to the store Valerie and Sarah walked on both sides of Jennifer again. Valerie said, "Sarah, do you remember the first time we had a pizza party?"

Sarah nodded and said, "Of course."

Valerie said, "I wanted mushrooms, you wanted olives, and Mary wanted pepperoni. I just thought it would be funny if Jennifer asked for pepperoni."

Sarah said, "I don't think that would have been funny."

Valerie focused her attention on Jennifer and said, "I know you are always sad, but you seem extra sad today. Is there something wrong about today? We're going to be having pizza so I thought that might cheer you up."

Jennifer's face drooped toward the ground. She shrugged her shoulders and said, "There's nothing special about today."

Valerie said, "Oh, okay." She dropped the issue and went back to conversing with Sarah about random things.

Inside the store, the four of them began to walk up and down the aisles of the store. Lieutenant Michael took the things off the shelf that they would need.

While Lieutenant Michael, Sarah and Valerie were focused on a few of the items, Jennifer noticed a small section that had party supplies. She left the others and walked toward the section. She picked up a small pack of birthday candles and held them in her hands. She stared at the pack intently.

Lieutenant Michael noticed that she had walked away. When he finished getting what he needed in that aisle, he walked over to her and said, "Do you like candles?"

Jennifer shook her head and put the birthday candle pack back on the rack. She turned away from it and waited for what he would probably say next.

Lieutenant Michael said, "Are you already thinking about your birthday? If I remember correctly, it's only in like two months right?"

Jennifer said, "Yeah, my birthday is in two months." Her face became expressionless again. She gripped her right wrist and her face winced in pain. Again, she seemed to be suppressing her emotions. Lieutenant Michael knew that there was no point in exploring it. She would just wall herself off more.

Lieutenant Michael, Sarah, and Valerie made the pizza together, while Jennifer sat at the table reading her book. Lieutenant Michael rolled out the dough, while Sarah grated the cheese. Sarah's hand slipped and she gasped in pain. Sarah looked at her knuckle and watched a trickle of blood come out of a fresh wound.

Lieutenant Michael said, "Sarah, did you just cut yourself on the grater?"

Sarah placed her knuckle in her mouth and sucked on the wound for a moment. She took her hand out of her mouth and watched more blood come out of the wound. She said, "Yeah, my hand slipped while I was grating the cheese."

Valerie jumped off of the stool and walked over to Sarah. Her eyes and hands began to glow yellow. She took Sarah's hand into her hands and said, "Don't worry. I'll fix it."

The yellow light radiating out of Valerie's hands began to spread over Sarah's hand. Sarah felt the warm glow of the light surround her hand. Valerie then let Sarah's hand go. She put a huge grin on her face and said, "All better!"

Sarah looked at the spot where the wound was on her knuckle. It was completely healed. Sarah looked back towards Valerie and matched her big grin with an even bigger smile. Sarah said, "Thanks, Valerie! I'm lucky to have you around. A klutz like me is always hurting myself stupidly." She then knocked herself on the head once and stuck out her tongue playfully towards Valerie. Valerie did a quick spin in place at Sarah's praise.

Lieutenant Michael shook his head and said, "I don't understand how you can do so well in the field and yet be such a klutz in the kitchen?"

Sarah looked towards the ground, flustered. She shrugged her shoulders and said, "I don't know. When I get in the kitchen, it's like my brain shuts off, and I do all these stupid things."

Valerie jumped back onto the stool and began to spread pizza sauce on the freshly rolled dough. When she was done, Sarah spread the grated cheese over the sauce. Lieutenant Michael then sprinkled mushrooms and olives on top and stuck it in the oven.

With their work done, Sarah and Valerie left the kitchen, and went to sit with Jennifer at the table. Jennifer continued to ignore them as she read her book.

Sarah stared at her for a while and then said, "How fast can you read that book?"

Jennifer shrugged her shoulders and said, "Depends how much time I get to read every day."

Valerie said, "What's the fastest time you've read that book in?"

Jennifer said, "A week, I think."

Valerie reacted in surprise. She said, "A week! That's really short. It would probably take a month for me to read that book."

Sarah said, "Well, you're not a very good reader, Valerie. You'd probably only spend half an hour reading before you pass out."

Valerie said, "Well, words are hard. I'd rather just watch it on T.V. anyway. Good thing they just finished making a show of it. In two days I'll get to see it and Jennifer will tell me how it's different from the book."

Jennifer sighed and flipped a page in her book.

Soon thereafter, the smell of baking pizza began to fill the room. Valerie began to bounce around in her seat and say, "Pizza! Pizza! It's almost ready!"

Valerie couldn't take it anymore and jumped out of her seat. She began to spin around in a circle and chant, "Pizza!" After a few moments of this she stopped and started to trip over herself from dizziness.

Lieutenant Michael said, "Geez, Valerie, if you have so much energy, why don't you set the table. It's almost ready."

Valerie jumped at the opportunity and said, "Leave it to me, Lieutenant!" She ran into the kitchen and began to get all the dishes that they would need. She quickly set the table and then went to sit in her seat again.

A timer went off and Lieutenant Michael pulled the pizza out of the oven. He placed the tray on the stove and turned off the oven. He pulled a round cutting board out of the cupboard and carefully slid the pizza onto it. He then cut the pizza into eight slices so that everybody could have two pieces.

Valerie began to rub her hands together greedily in anticipation. Lieutenant Michael brought the tray to the table and said, "Okay, girls! Dig in."

Valerie snatched two pieces of pizza and stashed them safely on her plate. She then pressed her hands together, closed her eyes, and bowed her head in silent prayer for a moment. She opened her eyes and noticed Jennifer staring right at her. Valerie smiled at her and picked up her first slice of pizza. She brought it to her mouth and then the entire front of the slice folded downward, dropping all the toppings of the pizza onto the skirt of her dress.

Valerie sat there in stunned horror. She stared at the now empty slice of pizza and then looked down to the skirt of her dress. A long red stain streaked down the front of her jacket. A pile of toppings sat in her lap.

Valerie cried out, "What?!" She put the slice back down on her plate and then picked up the pile of toppings out of her lap. She tried to spread them back on the crust, all while pretending to make crying noises, saying, "Not my special pizza!"

There were a couple of snorts and then laughter. Valerie looked to Sarah but it was not Sarah who was laughing. It was Jennifer. In shock, everyone turned in stunned silence to Jennifer.

Jennifer stopped laughing and quickly covered her mouth with both hands. She looked towards everybody staring at her. She looked surprised herself. She put her hands down and they all saw the embarrassment on her face.

Lieutenant Michael said, "It's okay, Jennifer. It was funny. It's okay to ..."

Jennifer pushed back her seat and jumped out of her chair. She then ran away from the table and into her room. *How could I let myself do that?* she thought to herself. Her own thoughts began to be flustered. She began to feel dirty all over her body again.

She walked over to her desk and opened the drawer. She pulled out the razor, unsheathed it, and stared at the blade. A knock came to the door. She heard Lieutenant Michael's voice through the door. Her mind was so scattered that she could not hear what he was saying. She would have to answer him to satisfy him so that he wouldn't pry deeper into her business. She called out to him, "Please, L.T., I need to be alone right now."

Lieutenant Michael said, "Okay, Jennifer, I'll let you be alone, but I also want you to know that you did nothing wrong there." She heard his footsteps walk away. He was gone.

She focused her attention back onto the blade of the razor. The shame she felt was deeper than she had ever felt before. She held the razor up to her wrist, but she couldn't find the will to cut herself like before. There were already at least a dozen cuts on her right wrist.

Jennifer re-sheathed the razor and stuck it into her jacket pocket. Her own voice in her head began to mock her, saying, "You were too much of a coward then, and you are still a coward now."

"I can do it!" she replied to herself.

The voice in her head said, "You mean like how you protected Annie? She's dead now because of you. They're all dead, while you get to go have fun and laugh it up with other people."

Jennifer brought her hands to her ears and said, "Shut up! Shut up! Shut up!" Her whole body began to feel dirty again. Her body trembled as she clasped her ears shut to try to drown out the voice in her head. She forced her emotions back down into the pit of her stomach before they became an overwhelming torrent. "I need to take a shower," she said to herself, "I have to wash this dirty feeling that's on me."

Jennifer rushed out of her room and into the bathroom. She stood there in front of the shower. She quickly stripped off her uniform and dropped it on the ground beside her. She turned on the water and let it warm up. When it was warm enough, she stepped into the shower and let the water run over her filthy body.

Jennifer began to rub her hands over herself but it was futile, and she knew it. No matter how many times she washed herself, she knew that she could never rinse the dirtiness that covered her.

The emotions that she had been suppressing inside of herself became a torrent again. Her eyes began to feel like they were burning. Tears wanted to come but she could not let them. She did not have the right to cry because she knew that it was all her fault. Despite her effort she felt a drop of water roll down her cheek. She couldn't tell if it was a tear that came out or if it was a random water drop that splashed on her face.

She stared at the jacket that was on the floor. It was the only way now to stop herself from crying. She stepped out of the shower and pulled the razor out that was in her jacket pocket. She unsheathed it again and let the sheath drop to the floor. She stepped back into the running water and stared at her right wrist again.

Jennifer brought the razor to an unscarred spot on her wrist and cut a shallow line into it. She couldn't feel the pain from it. Her whole wrist felt numb. She would have to cut deeper. She found another spot and let the razor sink in deeper as she cut a new line. It was too deep. Blood began to flow out of her wrist uncontrollably. She began to panic as an instinctive will to live took over. She lost control of her feet and slipped inside of the shower. Her head slammed against the hard tile and she went unconscious.

Lieutenant Michael went back to his seat and sat down. Sarah and Valerie looked depressed as they stared at their food. A long pizza stain colored the front of Valerie's uniform jacket.

Lieutenant Michael said, "I think Jennifer started letting her guard down, so she panicked, and ran away."

They then heard Jennifer's door open and shut. They assumed that she was coming back out to finish her dinner. Instead they heard another door open and shut.

Sarah said, "Guess she needs the bathroom."

A moment later they heard the water running through the pipes. The shower must be running. Valerie said, "Why is she taking a shower now? If anybody needs a shower now it's me."

Suddenly they heard a loud thud coming from the bathroom. All of them became startled as they looked towards the noise. Lieutenant Michael turned to Sarah and said, "Sarah, will you please go into the bathroom and see what that noise was."

Sarah nodded and slid her chair away from the table. She jogged down the hallway and to the bathroom door. She opened the door and called out, saying, "Jennifer, you okay?" There was no answer.

Sarah looked towards the shower and saw that it was still running but there was no one in it. She began to walk towards the showers and passed the bathtub. There was a red pool of blood on the floor. Sarah's eyes went wide as she examined the blood. She then saw Jennifer lying unconscious, on her back, on the floor. Her head had struck the edge of the walk in shower. Her arms were over her head on the floor.

Sarah, overcoming her shock, ran to the bathroom door and called out to Lieutenant Michael, saying, "Lieutenant! There's blood all over the floor!"

Lieutenant Michael jumped out of his seat, knocking the chair over on the floor. Valerie sat there in shock as she watched him run to the hallway. Valerie, realizing that Jennifer must be hurt if there was blood all over the floor, jumped out of her chair and ran to follow him.

Sarah stood in the hallway holding the door open. Her face looked white from shock. Lieutenant Michael stopped in front of her. She pointed towards the shower.

Lieutenant Michael, fearing water on the floor, carefully walked into the bathroom and towards Jennifer, who was still lying unconscious on the floor.

Valerie stood in the doorway with Sarah. She held her hands together, hoping that everything would be okay.

Lieutenant Michael stood over Jennifer's unconscious body. His military training prevented him from panicking. He carefully assessed the situation. He first reached into the shower letting the warm water soak into his jacket as he turned off the water. He looked at the blood on the floor and realized that it was too thin, which meant that it was blood mixed with water. He put two of his fingers on her neck to feel for a pulse. There was still a pulse.

Lieutenant Michael saw the wound on her right wrist. Blood slowly trickled out of it. He called to Valerie, who was still standing in the doorway. He said, "Valerie, come over here and heal her wrist and then try to heal her head."

Valerie nodded once and walked forward. She was scared of what she might see. As she walked around the bathtub she saw the blood on the floor and gasped.

Lieutenant Michael said, "Hurry, Valerie!"

Valerie said, "Sorry, Lieutenant." She moved quickly to his side. Valerie ignored her fear and dropped to her knees beside Jennifer. Her eyes began to glow with yellow light and then her hands radiated with the same yellow light. She placed her hands on Jennifer's wrist and the wound began to close up.

Lieutenant Michael then called to Sarah and said, "Sarah, please get me a bath towel."

Sarah nodded and went to the cabinet where the towels were kept. She brought it to Lieutenant Michael. He took it, unfolded it, and gently laid it over Jennifer's naked body.

Lieutenant Michael looked into the stand in shower and saw the small razor blade sitting on the shower stall floor. He picked it up and found the sheath lying on the floor. He stuck the razor blade back into the sheath and put it into his pants pocket. He then went back to kneeling beside Jennifer with Valerie.

With Jennifer's wrist now healed, Valerie focused her attention on Jennifer's head. There was a slight wound with a little blood but it was not that bad. Most of the blood had come from Jennifer's wrist.

After a moment of healing, Jennifer began to stir awake. She groaned in pain as she opened her eyes. For a moment she looked confused as she stared up toward the ceiling and blinked her eyes. She looked toward Lieutenant Michael who was staring down at her with concern on his face. She then looked towards Valerie, whose eyes were still glowing yellow. She then looked towards Sarah who was standing between them. Her face was pale and still in shock as she stared at her.

Jennifer looked back towards Lieutenant Michael and said, "What ... what happened?"

Lieutenant Michael said, "I was hoping you would answer that for me."

Jennifer looked back toward the ceiling and began to remember. She was cutting her wrist in the shower when she panicked, slipped, and hit her head. She began to realize that she was naked. She felt the towel that was over her body.

Jennifer began to blush. She looked towards the wall and said, "Did you ... did you see me naked?"

Lieutenant Michael, understanding that the question was directed towards him, said, "Unfortunately, you left me little choice, but I did put the towel over you."

Jennifer lifted her right arm and stared at the scars that were all over her wrist. She then drooped her right arm over her eyes.

Lieutenant Michael got off of his knees and sat down on his butt in the puddle of blood and water. He picked Jennifer up and helped her wrap the towel around her body. He then scooted her over to his lap and cradled her in his arms.

He somewhat expected her to protest, but she said nothing. She leaned her head into his chest and allowed him to embrace her. Her body was pale from the loss of blood. As he held her, his body began to tremble as his body began to react to the situation. He embraced her tighter. His voice was shaky as he began to speak, "I was so scared. Why would you try to kill yourself? Why didn't you try talking to me if you felt like killing yourself?"

Jennifer somberly said, "I'm sorry, L.T. I didn't mean to try to kill myself. It was an accident."

Lieutenant Michael, trying to control his emotions, said, "You mean you didn't mean to cut yourself?"

Jennifer said, "I didn't mean to cut myself so deep, but my shallow cuts weren't working anymore."

Lieutenant Michael took her right wrist and stared at all the scabbed over scars that were on her wrist. He said, "Now I know why you were constantly grabbing your wrist. You mean to tell me that you weren't trying to kill yourself, only cut yourself a little?"

Jennifer buried her face into his jacket and said, "Yeah. When I cut too deep, I panicked and I guess I slipped on the floor."

Lieutenant Michael let go of her wrist and wrapped his arms around her again. He said, "Why do you feel that you need to cut yourself like this? Why did you run away from us when we were having fun at the table?"

Jennifer kept her face buried in his jacket and didn't answer. Lieutenant Michael said, "Come on, Jennifer, I need you to talk to me about this. I won't know what's going on if you don't talk to me about it. Let me help."

Jennifer said into his jacket, "I cut myself because it helps me to get over my emotions. I need to punish myself, and when I do, I don't feel like crying anymore."

Lieutenant Michael said, "That's not a good reason to cut yourself, Jennifer."

Jennifer said, "I know, but I don't know what else to do."

Lieutenant Michael said, "If you feel sad, then you cry. Crying is normal and it helps us to feel better when it's over. What made you feel so sad earlier? Was it because you laughed?"

Jennifer said, "Today is Annie's birthday."

Lieutenant Michael said, "Annie was your teammate, right?"

Jennifer said, "Yeah, she was my teammate. We said that we were going to have a pizza party to celebrate it. Now ... now ..." she went silent. She brought her right hand up to his jacket and gripped the fabric in her palm. Her wet body began to tremble in his arms. For the first time since the tragedy Jennifer began to cry.

Lieutenant Michael began to rock her back and forth in his arms. He gently stroked her wet hair. He gently said, "We're sorry Jennifer. We didn't mean to be insensitive about your friend's birthday. We didn't know about it."

Jennifer, still crying, blurted out loudly, "I know! I know! It's my fault! It's always my fault! It's my fault that she's dead! It's my fault that they're all dead! I let them all die!" She continued to sob into his chest.

As Jennifer spoke, the memory of Mary's death returned to both Sarah and Valerie. Both of them remembered their own personal feelings. They both felt that it was their own fault too. Even the momentary thought that it would have been better to die with her.

Valerie put her hand on Jennifer's back and said, "When Mary died, I felt that it was my fault too. If I only had more power I could have saved her. But, Lieutenant Michael helped me to understand that it wasn't really my fault. It's not your fault either."

Jennifer didn't respond to her.

Sarah also put her hand on Jennifer's back and said, "Yeah. I felt the same way too. That it was my fault that Mary died. I was injured and I almost died, but Valerie kept me alive and Mary sacrificed her life to save me. I thought that if only I hadn't gotten injured then Mary might still be alive. Maybe that's true but I'll never know since I can't go back and redo it. But, I learned that it wasn't my fault. I know that it's really hard for you but we all know that it's not your fault, like it's not our fault that Mary died."

Lieutenant Michael said, "Yeah, Jennifer. I know that all you can feel right now is shame and regret, and that's okay, but, we all know that you are not the reason they died. They died because we all underestimated the Harvesters. When you understand that, then you will know that it wasn't your fault."

Jennifer didn't respond to any of them but she slowly stopped crying. When she had stopped, Lieutenant Michael said, "I'm going to have to report this, Jennifer. I think I should ask them to take you off duty for now. I think you should just focus on getting better."

Jennifer quickly wrapped her arms around his neck and began to beg him, "Please! Please let me keep fighting! I think that if I go back to fighting, it will help me. This is all I have left! Please don't let them take it away from me!"

Lieutenant Michael sighed and said, "Okay. But, if I help you, you are going to have to agree to my conditions. First, you are not allowed to be alone till I think you are better. This means that you are going to have to sleep with either Sarah or Valerie, or both. I don't care who, but, you are not allowed to be alone. This also means going to the bathroom and taking baths, dressing yourself ... I mean everything. Second, you need to spend time every night talking to me about how you are feeling. If you feel like cutting yourself again, talk to me first. It's okay to feel that way but it's not okay to do it. Talking about your feelings will help you to deal with it. Do you agree to those two conditions?"

Jennifer said, "Yeah, I agree."

Lieutenant Michael said, "Okay then. Can you walk?"

Jennifer nodded and said, "Yeah, I can walk."

Lieutenant Michael said, "Okay, then I want you to go with Sarah and get dressed. You can wear your pajamas if you want."

Sarah extended her hand to Jennifer and said, "Okay, Lieutenant." Jennifer took her hand and allowed Sarah to help her up. She grasped onto the wet towel that was around her body. Sarah led her out of the bathroom and to Jennifer's own room.

Lieutenant Michael then stood up and examined his uniform. It was wet and his pants were stained pink from Jennifer's blood mixed with water. He stared at Valerie, whose skirt was also stained pink from Jennifer's blood mixed with water. He said, "I hate to do this to you Valerie, but would you mind cleaning this up?"

Valerie nodded and looked toward the mess on the ground. She said, "Lieutenant, why would someone want to hurt themselves?"

Lieutenant Michael put his hand on her shoulder and said, "Sometimes when people get really depressed, they do things that they don't really mean to do. Sometimes it involves hurting themselves. Sometimes it involves hurting others. When you are depressed the only thing you can think about is yourself. Everybody deals with it differently. Jennifer tried to deal with it by hurting herself. She couldn't see any other way out of it."

Valerie said, "I'm glad I have you, Lieutenant. You helped me not to be so depressed. I hope that you can help Jennifer too, like you helped me."

Lieutenant Michael said, "Don't worry, Valerie. I'm going to do everything I can to help her. But, ultimately, the choice is hers. I'm going to go change my uniform and then I'm going to talk to Doctor Lovecraft. After you clean up here, you can change into your pajamas too, and join Sarah and Jennifer."

Valerie nodded her head in silence. She lowered her gaze to the puddle of blood and water. Lieutenant Michael rubbed the top of her head and said, "Thanks." He walked out of the bathroom leaving Valerie behind.

Valerie went into a cabinet and pulled out a fresh towel. Fortunately, the blood was mixed with lots of water so it would be easier to clean it up. She got onto her knees again and began to soak up the puddle of blood and water. The white bath towel was stained pink.

Sarah led Jennifer into her own room. Sarah was still pale and solemn from the shock of the incident. The vision of Jennifer lying in a puddle of her own blood kept replaying itself in her mind.

Jennifer, still wearing the wet towel, sat on her bed. Her body was pale from the loss of blood. Her eyes were red from crying. Her face was downcast as she sat on her bed staring at the floor.

Sarah shut the door behind herself and said, "Let's get you dressed."

Jennifer stood up and allowed the wet towel to fall to her feet. She then went into her drawers and pulled out a pair of underwear. She put it on and then sat back down on the bed. Sarah found her new pajamas and helped her to put it on.

Sarah stared at Jennifer's right wrist as she helped her put on the white long pajama shirt with emerald green sleeves. Sarah took her wrist in her hand and looked at it even closer. Jennifer allowed her to do it, but she turned her face away from her. Sarah said, "I'm sorry I didn't notice this before. I should have been paying closer attention to you."

Jennifer said, "No, I was trying to hide it. It's my fault. Don't worry about it."

Sarah let her wrist go and said, "Is this why you wouldn't take a bath with us?"

Jennifer, still looking away, said, "Yeah."

Sarah sat down beside her on the bed. She put her arms around her and said, "I'm sorry that you feel so much pain. You really scared me there. I don't ever want to see you like that again. Please, I'll be sure to take better notice of you, so please depend on me. You can also depend on Lieutenant Michael. He is a really good Lieutenant."

Jennifer said, "I'm sorry."

There was a knock on the door and then Valerie said, "It's Valerie, I'm coming in." The door opened and Valerie entered. She was wearing her white and pink pajamas. She walked over to the bed and sat down on the other side of Jennifer.

Valerie said, "Lieutenant Michael is going to talk to Doctor Lovecraft now. If you want to change into your pajamas, Sarah, I'll be with Jennifer now."

Sarah nodded her head and said, "Okay. I'll be right back then."

Sarah left and Jennifer and Valerie sat there next to each other silently. After a moment, Jennifer said, "Do you think they are going to kick me out of the Spirit Wielders?"

Valerie shook her head and said, "Lieutenant Michael said that he'd do everything he could to help you. I think he's going to do everything he can to let you stay because the Lieutenant wants to help you."

Valerie brought her hand up to Jennifer's face and brushed her wet hair back. She said, "Let's brush your hair before it dries like that."

Jennifer nodded.

Valerie stood up and took Jennifer's hand. She pulled her up and led her to the bathroom. Jennifer did not fight her at all but allowed Valerie to lead her. Valerie brought her to the sink and mirror that had belonged to Mary. She opened the top drawer and pulled out a brush. She began to run it through Jennifer's wet hair.

Lieutenant Michael went into his room and took off his clothing. He then walked over to his desk and picked up the intercom phone. He dialed a number and Doctor Lovecraft picked up. He said, "Hello Doctor Lovecraft. This is Lieutenant Snyder. I need to speak with you urgently in your office. Can you meet me now?"

Doctor Lovecraft said, "Yeah, I'll be right there."

Lieutenant Michael said, "Thanks! I'm going to ask Captain Faust to come too. See you soon."

Lieutenant Michael then dialed another number and asked the Captain to meet him at Doctor Lovecraft's office. He then got dressed and went to the meeting he himself had arranged.

At the meeting, Lieutenant Michael rehearsed to both of them everything that had happened. Sadness fell upon both of them as they listened to him about Jennifer.

When he was done, Captain Faust said, "That's horrible. I've seen major depression before but I've never had a girl in my unit who cut herself like this before."

Doctor Lovecraft said, "Doctor Paulos talked to me earlier. He had suggested that Jennifer be taken off of combat duty, but the higher-ups decided to put her back out in the field because they are worried about the loss of Leviathan Company. We could use this to push the issue."

Lieutenant Michael said, "I'll agree that that is probably a good idea but she begged me to help her to stay in the field. She says that if we take this away from her she will have nothing left. I'm no expert in child psychology, but right now she probably needs stability. She's already familiar with me and the other girls. If we pull her out and take her away from us, it might cause more harm than good. For all we know, maybe what she really needs is to go out and fight the Harvesters. Helping her get some vengeance might help her to overcome her depression. And think about the other side. What will the World Government do? They'll shut her in a room until she self-destructs. I don't think that is very helpful."

Doctor Lovecraft sighed and said, "You've got a point. I'll agree to this on one condition, Lieutenant. I want daily reports, and I mean daily reports, on her condition. I'll want to see her every week starting tonight too."

Lieutenant Michael nodded his head and said, "That's fine with me. I put two conditions on her myself. She's never to be alone until I say it's okay and she's to talk to me every day about her feelings. What do you say Captain?"

Captain Faust stroked his chin as he leaned back in a chair. He sighed and said, "Yeah, I'd rather not lose her too. If we can help her without removing her, that is probably what's best. I'm leaving the decision up to you Lieutenant. Of course, Doctor Lovecraft can overrule you, but if you are in agreement then I am fine with it."

Lieutenant Michael nodded his head and smiled. He said, "One more thing, Captain. I'd like to take my unit out on a hunting party tomorrow. I know it's a day early but I want to get Jennifer out in the field as soon as possible."

Captain Faust looked to Doctor Lovecraft and said, "I'll allow it if Doctor Lovecraft allows it. Let her see Jennifer first and then she'll let you know."

Lieutenant Michael nodded his head and said, "Okay. I'm ready to go up now if you are Doctor."

Doctor Lovecraft nodded and said, "Yeah, I'm ready."

Together, they left her office and walked up to the apartment. When they entered, Sarah, Valerie, and Jennifer were sitting on the couch watching television. Lieutenant Michael called out to Jennifer, saying, "Jennifer, would you please come to the table."

Jennifer got out of her seat and cautiously walked to the table. Sarah turned off the television and both Sarah and Valerie turned around on the couch to watch what would happen. Jennifer sat with Doctor Lovecraft and Lieutenant Michael.

Doctor Lovecraft looked at the scars on Jennifer's arm and asked her questions about it. They talked about her desire to stay in the field. After her questions, Doctor Lovecraft then examined her body a little bit and then she excused Jennifer to go sit back with her teammates.

Lieutenant Michael and Doctor Lovecraft stepped outside the door. He said, "So, Doctor. What do you think? Can I let her go out tomorrow?"

Doctor Lovecraft said, "Yeah, I'll allow it. But make sure that you keep a close watch on her. If something like this happens again, I will force the issue and have her removed. For now, I think you might be right that it would be better to keep her here since she is already familiar with you all. We'll believe her for now that it was an accident and that she wasn't really trying to kill herself. If she does show signs that she is wanting to kill herself, then I really will have to pull her off duty."

Lieutenant Michael nodded and said, "Thanks, Doctor Lovecraft. I understand. I'll be sure to report to you tomorrow."

Lieutenant Michael went back inside and walked up to the girls. Jennifer sat in the middle of Sarah and Valerie. She held onto each one of their hands as they sat together. He said, "Good news, Jennifer. They have agreed to let you stay here on the condition that I report to the Doctor everyday about your status and you also have to meet with the Doctor once a week."

Jennifer tried to smile, but it was hindered by her depression. She said, "Thanks, L.T. for helping me to stay."

Lieutenant Michael said, "I also asked to let us go out on a hunting party tomorrow. So when you girls wake up tomorrow, we'll be going outside the wall."

Sarah said, "While you were gone, we decided that we would all sleep together in Jennifer's bed."

Lieutenant Michael said, "Great! It's like having a slumber party. Oh, guess I forgot about the dishes."

Valerie said, "Do you want us to help?"

Lieutenant Michael said, "No, you girls just relax. You had a pretty hectic day. I'll take care of the dishes tonight. You three just relax and watch some more television together. Tomorrow though, I expect a lot out of you three."

Valerie and Sarah in unison said, "Aye, Lieutenant!"

- 6 -

The next morning, Lieutenant Michael made sure to wake up earlier than normal. He quickly changed out of his tan shirt and olive green pajama pants, and put on his white uniform with the black stripes. Today they would be going back into the field. This time they would be hunting instead of defending.

Hunting parties were so much easier, in his opinion, since you had much more freedom to act. You didn't have to worry about defending anybody, except your own team.

He quietly stepped out of his room and walked across the way to Jennifer's room. As quietly as he could, he turned the knob to the door and opened it just enough so he could poke his head into the room.

He took a quick look around the room and focused his attention on the bed. He saw Jennifer lying in the middle between Valerie and Sarah. Both Valerie and Sarah had an arm draped over Jennifer as if they had been hugging her. He hoped that maybe this was a start of a new tradition. A new tradition where they actually sleep in their own beds and leave his own bed alone. One can dream.

Despite the drama that had happened last night, it seemed to be the thing that Jennifer needed to help break down the walls she had built around herself. For the first time, he was finally seeing her softer side. He smiled at the thought and shut the door quietly.

The night before, he had told himself that he would make pancakes for the girls' breakfast. He went into the kitchen, pulled out the mixing bowl, and began making the pancake batter. As he worked, a memory of Mary returned to him. In the past, he was making pancakes. Mary was standing next to him. They were making it together.

It had been so hectic with the problems surrounding Jennifer that he had not had so much time to think about Mary. He supposed that it was a good thing, but thinking about her now made him feel guilty. A twinge of guilt gnawed at his stomach again. Pancakes was the last thing that Mary made for a meal. She had insisted on making it herself. Now they were going back into the field. He was making the pancakes. There was always a possibility that one of them might not come home. He quickly tried to suppress that thought.

As he worked, he heard an alarm clock going off. Soon the girls would be joining him. He hoped that they were able to bond even more last night. As soldiers, it is very important for them to form bonds. That friendship allowed them to fight even harder. It is easier to fight for your friends then it is to fight for yourself. By yourself, you are more likely to fall into despair and give up ... like Jennifer. Only time would tell if Jennifer could make it through her despair. He believed she would.

The alarm clock went off at six-thirty like normal. Sarah, who was laying on the front edge of Jennifer's bed, waved her arm around till she found the alarm clock. She turned it off and tried to sit up.

Valerie and Jennifer began to stir. It would be harder to get up because, despite going to bed on time, they stayed up late to talk. For the first time since Jennifer came, she began to feel that they were a team.

Valerie sat up. She stretched her arms and yawned deeply. She shook her head and said, "Good morning every one!"

Jennifer sat up and rubbed her eyes. She looked at Valerie and then at Sarah. She stared blankly and said, "Good morning" in her melancholy tone. She still had black circles under her eyes, but they actually looked better than the days before.

Sarah said, "How are you doing, Jennifer?"

Jennifer said, "I still feel like crap ... but ... but I guess I feel a little bit better."

Valerie reached over and hugged Jennifer. Jennifer didn't push her away. Valerie said, "I'm so glad that we were able to start being friends."

Sarah began to sniff the air. She stepped out of bed and sniffed the air again. She said, "I ... I smell pancakes!" Her body started to move on its own accord. She started to run for the door.

Valerie yelled out, saying, "Hold on Sarah, aren't you forgetting something?"

Sarah stopped dead in her tracks. Her arms and feet froze in the position of a runner in mid run. Valerie said, "One of us has to stay with Jennifer."

Sarah dropped her hands and lowered her foot. She sighed and said, "That's right, the smell of food almost made me forget. Valerie, you help her get changed and I'll get dressed, then I'll come back and you can get dressed." Valerie nodded her head in agreement. Sarah walked toward the door and left.

Jennifer slid out of bed and said, "Don't worry. I can dress myself, you just sit there and watch."

Valerie scooted to the edge of the bed and said, "Okay, but if you need help just let me know."

As Jennifer changed out of her pajamas, she said, "Do you think you can actually protect your friends in the field?"

Valerie looked down to the ground and thought for a moment. She said, "I believe I can. If I don't believe I can then I will probably fail. I'd rather believe that I can, and do everything I can, than think I can't so I give up."

Jennifer said, "I thought I could protect my friends too, but I couldn't."

Valerie said, "But I'm sure you tried really hard."

Jennifer said, "I wish I tried harder."

Valerie slid off the bed and walked up to Jennifer. She got really close to her face and put her hands on Jennifer's shoulders. Valerie said, "I'm going to do everything I can to protect you today. So do everything you can to protect me too."

Jennifer stared back at Valerie. Her eyes became watery. She wiped the moisture out of her eyes and said, "Please don't put your trust in me. I'll only let you down like I let my team down. It's too much for me to carry."

Valerie dropped her hands and then reached around Jennifer's body. She rested her head on Jennifer's shoulder and embraced her, saying, "Don't worry. Lieutenant Michael won't let you fail. Trust him. You'll see." Jennifer didn't say anything. Valerie let Jennifer go.

The door opened and Sarah came in wearing her white uniform with the blue stripes. Sarah gave Valerie a thumbs up, so Valerie left and Sarah took her place.

After Jennifer got dressed, they went into the bathroom. Sarah started brushing her own hair. Jennifer stood in front of her own mirror and stared at her own reflection. She saw the ugliness inside of herself.

The voice in her head began to speak to her again, saying, "You're just going to get them all killed again. They trust you and you are going to betray them."

Jennifer continued to stare at herself in the mirror. She wanted to argue with the voice, but she couldn't argue with it because it was right. She was going to betray them like she betrayed all her friends. She stared at the hand that had held Lieutenant Sharon's hand.

Her thoughts were distracted when Sarah started brushing her hair. Sarah pulled her hair back behind her head and pulled a black hair band out of the drawer. Sarah said, "This hair band belonged to my best friend Mary. Now it's yours. I hope that you will be one of my best friends too."

Sarah finished putting the band in Jennifer's hair. She then stroked her hair and said, "You have really thick and wavy hair." Jennifer didn't say anything in response to what Sarah said, except for, "Thank you."

Valerie then walked into the bathroom and began to brush her hair too. She was about to put the butterfly clip in her hair but then remembered what both Sarah and Mary had warned her about. She put the butterfly clip back in the drawer. Instead she pulled out a cheap hair clip and pulled the hair over and back behind her right ear.

When they were all done, Valerie took hold of Jennifer and Sarah. She put a hand on each of their shoulders and said, "Today's our first mission as a new team. I promise to do my best to protect you."

Sarah smiled at her and put her own hand on Valerie's shoulder as well as on Jennifer's shoulder. She said, "Yeah, we're going to protect each other and come back home today. All of us."

Jennifer looked down to the ground and said, "I don't know if I can, but I'll try."

Sarah smiled at her and gently shook her shoulder, saying, "That's enough. Just do your best! We will all do our best today, and we'll help each other."

With that, they let each other go and went to the dining room where Lieutenant Michael was setting the table.

Valerie raised her hands high above her head and shouted, "Yes! Pancakes!" She spun in a circle as she made her way to her chair.

Sarah sat down in her chair and said, "Valerie, try not to drop your food in your lap this time." She laughed at her own joke.

Valerie pulled her chair out and pretended to pout, saying, "My pizza!" She then turned her head towards Lieutenant Michael, who was putting the last of the pancakes on a platter, and said while pouting, "Since I spilled my pizza, I think we should have another pizza."

Lieutenant Michael laughed and said, "Why, you'd probably spill that one too."

Sarah laughed again.

Jennifer made her way to her seat. She pulled it out and sat down. She gazed down at her plate. Her face still showed signs of her deep depression. This was actually an improvement. She was finally allowing her emotions to come out. The wall she had built up around her was starting to crumble down. Lieutenant Michael knew it would not be easy, but anything was an improvement.

Lieutenant Michael put the platter of pancakes on the table. Like vultures, Sarah and Valerie began to grab at pancakes, tossing them onto their own plates. Jennifer waited for them to finish. When they were done, Jennifer picked up a few of her own.

Valerie put her hands together, bowed her head, and said a silent prayer. Lieutenant Michael waited for her to finish. When she opened her eyes, he said, "After breakfast, we'll do the dishes together, and then we'll go out on a hunting party."

Jennifer stared at her food and avoided looking him in the eyes. She was probably embarrassed about what happened last night. He turned to Jennifer and said, "Jennifer, this will be the first time we get to see your abilities. We'll be counting on you."

Jennifer shrugged her shoulders and put a piece of pancake in her mouth.

Valerie excitedly said, "I'm ready, Lieutenant!"

Lieutenant Michael reached over and rubbed her on top of the head, saying, "I'm counting on you, Valerie."

Sarah, not wanting to be left out, said, "I'm ready too, Lieutenant." She tilted her head towards him.

Lieutenant Michael took the hint, reached out to her, and rubbed the top of her head as well. He said, "I'm counting on you too, Sarah." She smiled and blushed a little. She lowered her face and went back to eating her pancakes.

Lieutenant Michael turned his attention to Jennifer. She continued to keep her gaze lowered as she ate her own pancakes. He said, "Jennifer, are you ready to go back to combat?"

Without saying anything she nodded her head. She still looked so depressed. He wished he could comfort her. Hopefully today's sortie would help her to feel better.

After the dishes were done, the three girls lined up by the table. Lieutenant Michael gave each one of them their com unit, which they promptly stuck in their ears. They did a radio check to make sure that their com units were all working properly. They appeared to be just fine.

Lieutenant Michael handed Sarah her belt with the two scabbards. She checked the two metal sticks that hung in their scabbards. Next, he handed her a backpack that had water and rations in it. He said, "We probably won't be back for hours, so we'll have to eat some rations when we get hungry." Sarah saluted him and said, "Aye, Lieutenant!"

Lieutenant Michael handed Valerie her cattle prod gun and holster. She slung it over her back and checked the magazines in the pockets to make sure that they were fully loaded. He also handed her a small backpack that had rations and water in it. Valerie smiled and said, "Thanks, Lieutenant!"

Lieutenant Michael handed Jennifer her own backpack, saying, "Here's your rations for today. Don't eat them all at once."

Jennifer said, "Don't worry. Who'd want to eat cardboard all at once?"

He chuckled and said, "They're not that bad." He pointed toward the door and said, "Let's go! Our first hunting party awaits!"

Sarah and Valerie threw their hands up and shouted, "Let's squash some bugs!" Jennifer, without passion half-heartedly raised her right fist into the air and said dispassionately, "Yeah." When she raised her arm, the sleeve lowered and revealed the scars that still remained on her wrist. She realized what she had done and lowered her arm. She looked embarrassed again and covered her right wrist with her left hand. Lieutenant Michael noticed her. He didn't want her to feel even more embarrassed so he decided to ignore it.

Since they were on a mission, the girls formed a straight line behind Lieutenant Michael, and followed him out the door, down the hallway, and onto the street. Instead of flying there by helicopter, they would simply climb over the wall, and start hunting the Harvesters.

Together, they stood at the base of the inside of the wall. The small rungs ascended up to the top. Lieutenant Michael climbed up first, followed by Sarah, Jennifer, and Valerie. Together they stood at the top of the wall. No matter how many times you see it, it was always a shocking sight. The difference between the inside of the wall and outside of the wall were night and day. The inside of the wall was a safe haven to humanity. The outside of the wall was nothing but death and destruction.

Lieutenant Michael said, "Alright, girls, activate your powers."

The girls in unison, said, "Aye, Lieutenant," except for Jennifer who said, "Aye, L.T." Their eyes began to glow with their colors. Sarah's eyes radiated with a light blue light. Valerie's eyes radiated with a sharp yellow light. Jennifer's eyes radiated with a bright red light.

Lieutenant Michael said, "Okay, girls. This is our first mission together. It's going to be a little harder at first because we're not used to working together. So let's take it slow. Remember to follow my directions. Look out for each other. Keep a sharp look out for Harvesters."

The girls in unison, said, "Aye, Lieutenant" again, except for Jennifer, who again said, "Aye, L.T."

Lieutenant Michael said, "I want Sarah to go down first, then Jennifer, then Valerie, and finally I'll go down last."

The girls nodded their heads and said in unison again, "Aye, Lieutenant," except for Jennifer, who again said, "Aye, L.T."

Lieutenant Michael motioned for them to go down, so Sarah led the way. After she climbed over the edge, Jennifer followed behind her. Valerie then went down, followed by Lieutenant Michael.

All together, they stood on the burnt remains of vegetation. Next to where they stood, there was an old road that had once led out of the area. The road had become broken up and lots of plants had grown through it. A few burnt out cars laid in the road, their frames filled with holes from shrapnel. Further down the road were abandoned houses. Trees had grown up around them, causing some of the houses to be pushed aside. There was a silent breeze that flowed through the region.

Lieutenant Michael pointed down the road and quietly said, "Okay, girls, let's go down this way. I want Sarah on point and Jennifer on rearguard." Sarah nodded her head and started walking in front. Jennifer fell back and walked behind Lieutenant Michael.

They tried to be as quiet as they could. The only sounds they made were the shuffling of their feet over the broken asphalt and the occasional comment through the com unit. The houses blocked their view of the surrounding area. The trees towered over the houses further obscuring their view.

They walked for about an hour without seeing anything except for a few rats that were scurrying over the remains of what was once human civilization. A few birds flew through the trees and chirped their songs. The animals did not have that much fear of humans. They were not used to being around people so they did not know to be afraid of them.

Sarah stopped in her tracks and pointed at a collapsed building. Inside the collapsed framework there were four baby Harvesters. If there were babies here that meant that there would most certainly be larger ones nearby.

Sarah held her hand up and said, "Don't worry, Lieutenant. I've got these ones." She stretched out her hand toward the baby Harvesters. Her hand radiated with blue light and a beam of blue light flowed out of her hand. She picked off the babies one by one. The last baby Harvester let out a shriek of terror before it died. Its shriek was answered by a distant screech. There was no doubt that this area would soon become full of Harvesters.

A pack of six junior sized Harvesters of various ages stumbled into the area. Jennifer's hands and feet quickly lit up with red light. She leapt forward and slammed into the closest Harvester. She quickly caught it by the mandibles, flipped it over onto its back, and stomped onto its head several times. Its head was crushed under her foot and yellow goo spilled out of the opening.

As Jennifer leapt toward the closest harvester, Valerie quickly pulled out her cattle prod gun off of her back. She pointed it to the ground and pulled the lever that allowed the first round to enter into the chamber. The first round clicked into place.

Sarah stood in front of Lieutenant Michael and Valerie. She held her hands out again and started shooting her spear of light at the approaching Harvesters.

Jennifer punched the next Harvester in the head. It shrieked at her and trembled. A second Harvester attempted to charge at her from behind, but Sarah shot it dead in its tracks. It skidded to a halt a few feet behind Jennifer. Jennifer grabbed the mandibles of the Harvester she was already fighting and started kicking it in the mouth. Clear slime drooled out of its mouth as it shrieked in pain at her.

As Jennifer fought it, memories of the Los Angeles battle flooded back into her memories. She tried to ignore them. The voice in her head said, "You're going to get them all killed, then you're going to run away. Just like last time." Jennifer gave the Harvester one last kick. Its head split open and yellow goo began to pour out. It rolled over on to its side and died.

"It's all your fault that they died. You let them all die!" The voice mocked her again in her head. The memories continued to flood into her thoughts.

"Don't worry, I'll protect you ..." that is what she had said to her team. "Take my hand Lieutenant ..." she had taken her hand. All that was left of her was a bloody stump of a hand. The rest had been torn off by a fully-grown Harvester.

Jennifer leapt toward the fifth junior Harvester, crashing into it. The force of the blow caused the Harvester to roll over onto its side. It rocked itself and then got back up. It trembled and screamed at Jennifer. It charged at her. Jennifer caught it by the mandibles and began to kick its head until the shell cracked and yellow goo spilled over the ground.

The voice in her head said, "You don't deserve to live after what you've done." Jennifer said to the voice, "I know ... I don't deserve to be the one to live."

Sarah killed the last junior Harvester with her spear of light ability. It rolled over and yellow goo flowed out of its side. She turned to Valerie and gave her a thumbs up. Valerie smiled and gave her a thumbs up back.

Lieutenant Michael smiled and said, "You girls did a really good job working together there. I'm impressed for your first time. Even you, Jennifer, did very well."

Jennifer spoke into her com unit softly, saying, "Thanks." His words meant nothing to her. The memories of her friends, who were all dead, flooded into her mind. They looked so disappointed in her.

The voice in her head said, "If they knew what you did, they would never trust you."

Jennifer said to the voice in her head, "I know. I should have died with my friends."

Out of nowhere, there was a large crash to the left of Jennifer. They all turned to see a fully-grown Harvester crashing through the rotted side of an abandoned house. It stared at Jennifer and shrieked with its horrible voice. The Harvester drooled as it shook its giant mandibles at Jennifer.

Time seemed to slow down in Lieutenant Michael's mind. He saw the Harvester charge at Jennifer. He saw Jennifer's expression change to a peaceful clarity. Or, was it acceptance? What had she accepted? Jennifer smiled as the Harvester charged at her. The red lights that emanated from her hands turned off. She dropped her hands to her sides and stared vacantly into the nothingness. He realized what she was thinking. She was going to let herself get killed.

Without thinking, Lieutenant Michael bolted toward her. It was a race to see who would get to her first. The Harvester was quicker, but he was more determined. He ran as fast as he could and then ran a little faster. In only a moment, the Harvester would snatch up Jennifer in its mandibles and snap her in half.

Without thought to his own safety, he leapt toward Jennifer. If he was a millisecond too slow, he would also be swept up in the Harvester's mandibles. He opened his arms and grabbed Jennifer in them. The force of the blow knocked Jennifer out of the way of the Harvester.

Together, they crashed onto the ground and rolled over each other a couple of times before finally coming to a stop. The charging Harvester ran past them at full speed and crashed into the side of another abandoned building.

Both Sarah and Valerie stood there in shock as they tried to process what was happening. Lieutenant Michael had taken off so fast that they were still trying to make sense of what was happening.

Lieutenant Michael shouted, "Sarah! Shield!"

Sarah and Valerie ran next to Lieutenant Michael and Jennifer. Sarah brought her blue-glowing hands together next to her heart and slowly separated them. A small blue sphere of light came out of her chest and expanded over them, forming a shield that guarded all of them together.

Jennifer laid on her back in the dirt, gasping for air. The force of Lieutenant Michael's tackle knocked the wind out of her. She quickly regained her breath. Her arms were spread out on the ground. Lieutenant Michael laid protectively on top of her.

After Sarah's shield extended over them, he lifted himself off of her body. He grabbed her arms, pinning them down. He pinned her legs together with his knees. He shouted, "What the hell were you thinking, Jennifer? Were you really just going to let that thing kill you?"

The fully-grown Harvester pulled itself out of the rubble. It turned to see all four of them under Sarah's shield. It screeched and charged at the shield. The Harvester crashed into it causing a shower of sparks to spray in all directions.

Lieutenant Michael turned his head to Sarah, saying, "Can you hold it back for a little bit, Sarah?"

Sarah nodded as she continued to hold the shield up, saying, "Yeah, there's only one, so I'll be good for a long time Lieutenant."

Lieutenant Michael looked down at Jennifer's face. Jennifer looked disappointingly into his eyes. Tears started to stream out of her eyes and ran down the sides of her temples, into the dirt. She started crying again, she said, "Why? Why won't you just let me die? I … I can't take this pain anymore. I don't deserve to live! Please just let me die!"

Lieutenant Michael became frustrated. He lifted her arms and upper body up off the ground and slammed them back down on the ground. He grunted in frustration. He shouted, "Damn it, Jennifer! I'm not just going to stand there and watch you do something stupid to yourself. Second, I need you to help me keep Sarah and Valerie alive. I am not going to damn well allow you to get them killed with you!"

Jennifer, still crying, said, "If you knew what I really did, you'd think I should die too!"

Lieutenant Michael shook his head and shouted, "Fine! Tell me what the hell you did and then let me be the judge of it. Just don't assume I'd think something without asking me. Why do you think you deserve to die?"

Jennifer turned her head to avoid looking at him. Lieutenant Michael grabbed her by the chin and forced her face to look back at him. He said, "No, Jennifer, I'm not going to allow you to run away from this. You are going to tell me why you deserve to die!" He let go of her face and placed his hand on her arm again.

Jennifer started to sob uncontrollably, she said, "Because … because … I was the one who said I'd protect them. If … if I hadn't convinced them that I could do it, then they would all be alive now." She turned her face to avoid looking at him again. She continued to cry as she laid there in the dirt.

Lieutenant Michael closed his eyes and took a deep breath. He exhaled and softly said, "Jennifer, there is not a single Spirit Wielder girl who, once they get used to fighting, thinks that they can't handle every situation. Every single one of them promises their teammates that they are going to protect them. The truth is that we can't protect every single person that we want to protect. Sometimes we lose. Sometimes we're not strong enough."

Valerie started to cry. Lieutenant Michael turned his head to see what she was doing. She had dropped to her knees and covered her face with her hands. As she cried, she said, "I promised that I'd protect everybody! I thought I was strong enough! I wasn't! All I could do was stop Sarah from dying, and because of that Mary died. I ... I thought I could protect her too! But, even though Mary died, I know ... I know that she wanted me to live. I know your friends would want you to live too!"

Sarah stood there trembling, her arms continued to stay outstretched as she held up the barrier that was keeping them alive. The Harvester circled around them like a cat stalking its prey. It occasionally struck the barrier, causing a shower of sparks to fly in all directions.

Lieutenant Michael was sure that it was taking all of Sarah's willpower to not drop to the ground like Valerie had done. Tears dripped from her eyes as she thought of Mary again. She said, "I thought I was strong enough too, but I wasn't. I was almost killed, and Mary sacrificed herself to save me. She's dead and I'm alive. I got to keep living or else her death was meaningless!"

Valerie dropped her hands from her face and wrapped her arms around Sarah's right leg.

Jennifer said, "But ... but ... when we tried to make it out together, when we got overwhelmed. I didn't stop them from getting killed. Instead, I ran away. I should have stayed and fought even harder. If I'm with you, I'll just get you all killed too, like before!"

Lieutenant Michael shook his head and said, "I don't think you just ran away. Do you remember that you were holding onto your Lieutenant's hand when I first met you on the helicopter?"

The memory began to return to Jennifer. She stood on the top of a fully-grown Harvester's head. She looked back to Annie and Julie. They were surrounded but they were safe underneath Annie's barrier. Lieutenant Sharon on the other hand, had been snatched up in a Harvesters mandibles. She decided to save Lieutenant Sharon first. A second Harvester came and began to tug on Lieutenant Sharon's legs. Lieutenant Sharon screamed from the pain.

Jennifer grabbed her hands and began to pull. As she pulled, she looked back to see Annie and Julie. A pack of eight to ten fully-grown Harvesters had descended upon the barrier now. She heard Annie's voice in her ear, "I … I can't hold much longer!"

Jennifer said, "I'll be there in a moment. Don't worry. I'll save you!" She began to stomp on the head of the Harvester that had her Lieutenant in its mandibles. The other Harvesters continued to slam against Annie's barrier causing huge showers of sparks. The barrier began to crack and then it shattered. Annie and Julie were shouting into the ear piece.

Annie said, "Jennifer, where …" she was quickly cut off. The Harvesters descended upon the now helpless Annie and Julie. They were quickly devoured in only a few moments. Jennifer heard their death screams in her ear piece and then it went silent as their voices were cut off.

Jennifer cried as she continued to tug on Lieutenant Sharon's hand. Lieutenant Sharon looked up at her with pain in her face. Blood flowed out of her mouth. She opened her mouth and said, "Run, Jennifer." As she spoke, more blood spilled down her once white uniform. She passed out and was probably dead.

Jennifer shook her head and said, "No, I got to save you!" She pulled using all the strength she could use as a red Wielder. With the force of her strength, Lieutenant Sharon's hand separated from her wrist. Jennifer was knocked back from the sudden loss of tension. She fell to the ground. A Harvester kicked her. She rolled from the force of the blow. When she stopped, she looked back to where Annie and Julie had been. All that remained of them was a blood stain on the ground with tattered pieces of uniform and a few uneaten body parts. Lieutenant Sharon was devoured right in front of her. Lieutenant Sharon's head was snapped off of her body and it landed in front of Jennifer's face. Her now lifeless gaze was frozen in place. Jennifer stared at it in horror. The screech of a Harvester woke her up from her trance. She jumped to her feet and ran. She ran and jumped as far as she could using all her power. She still gripped Lieutenant Sharon's hand in her own hand as she ran.

Jennifer continued to cry as she remembered all of it. Through her sobbing, she told the story to Lieutenant Michael, who was still holding her down.

Lieutenant Michael softly said, "See, you didn't just run away. You saw that Annie and Julie were safe for the moment so you tried to help Lieutenant Sharon who was in danger. You were overrun and Annie's power got depleted.

You made the right choice. You thought that you would have more time. Then, when it was pointless to stay you retreated. Even Lieutenant Sharon told you to run. She wanted you to live. Every Lieutenant wants their teammates to live. If I was going to die, I'd tell you all to run away too."

Jennifer looked back towards his face. Her cheeks were stained with mud from the dirt mixed with her tears. She said, "But ... still, it hurts so much. I miss them so much! I don't know if I can live like that."

Lieutenant Michael smiled compassionately at her. He brushed her mud-stained cheek with his right hand and then placed his hand over her heart. He said, "There once was an ancient general who said after a really costly battle, 'What you leave behind is not what is written on stone, but in the hearts of men.' Do you know what that means, Jennifer?"

Jennifer shook her head and said, "No."

Lieutenant Michael said, "It means that the only thing that matters are the memories we have of our friends that have died. Nothing that we put in a memorial can equal the memories that we have. Your friends: Lieutenant Sharon, Annie, and Julie, their memories exist in your heart alone. Mary told me that as long as I'm alive, a part of her will keep living on in my heart. Your friends live in your heart too. As long as you are alive, they'll keep living inside of you. If you die, then they die with you because there is no one else here that can keep them in their heart. I keep on living through the pain so that Mary can keep living inside of me. Will you try to keep living so that they can keep living inside of you too?"

Jennifer started to cry again, she nodded her head and said, "Yes, Lieutenant. I'll keep living so that I can keep their memories in my heart. Please help me to keep living!"

Lieutenant Michael nodded and said, "That's what I've been trying to do already. Are you ready to fight this last Harvester, Jennifer?"

Jennifer nodded. Lieutenant Michael let go of her other arm and scooted back so that he was no longer on top of her. She stood up and brushed the dirt off of the back of her dress. She put her hands up in a fighting stance and reactivated her powers. Her hands and feet glowed with their bright red light.

The Harvester continued to circle around the barrier like a tiger in a cage. Jennifer stared at the alien and said, "I'm going to kill you, and keep living for my friends!" She braced her feet and said, "Okay, Sarah, drop the shield."

Sarah looked for confirmation from Lieutenant Michael. He nodded his head.

As the shield disappeared, Jennifer leapt forward. She yelled a war cry and grabbed onto the Harvesters mandibles. The Harvester screeched at her. Drool spat into her face. She yelled, "When I stabilize it, Sarah, you give it a blow with your sticks."

Sarah pulled her two metal sticks out of their scabbards and held them up. She used her power to cover them with her blue light. She said, "I'm ready!"

The Harvester pushed against Jennifer. Her feet started to slowly scrape backward along the ground. Sarah ran up alongside it and started to hack at one of its legs.

Behind her there was a large crash. Sarah turned her head and saw another fully grown Harvester that had crashed through the remains of an old abandoned house. It was charging straight at her. Out of reflex, Sarah crossed her two sticks together and held them in defense. The Harvester mandibles crashed into the blue light of the sticks, causing a shower of sparks to spray into its face. The Harvester jerked to the side as the sparks surprised it, which prevented Sarah from being thrown across the area. Sarah dropped her two sticks and erected a barrier around herself. The Harvester charged at her again and crashed into the barrier, causing even more sparks to fly.

Lieutenant Michael said out loud, "This isn't good. He pulled out his own cattle prod gun and pointed it toward the Harvester that Jennifer was pushing against. She was in the way so he was hesitant to shoot at it in case he hit her.

Behind Lieutenant Michael and Valerie, there was a third shriek. A mid-sized Harvester appeared behind them. Lieutenant Michael and Valerie spun around with their cattle prod guns raised. Both of them began to shoot it in the face.

Valerie's first magazine clicked empty. She let it drop and grabbed the second one on her belt. She slammed it into the empty slot and pulled the ammo loader back. She raised the cattle prod gun again and fired into its face alongside Lieutenant Michael. Again the magazine clicked empty. She let it drop and grabbed the third magazine off of her belt. She slammed it into the empty magazine slot and pulled the ammo loader back. Again, they both fired into the Harvester's face. Again, their magazines clicked empty.

The Harvester's face was nothing but an open hole now. Yellow goo poured out of the open wound and the now dead Harvester rolled over onto its side.

Lieutenant Michael looked at Valerie and said, "I got one magazine left. How about you?"

Valerie allowed the empty magazine to drop to the ground. She pulled out the fourth magazine and slammed it into the empty magazine slot. She pulled the ammo loader back and said, "Yeah, me too."

Lieutenant Michael said, "You help Jennifer. I'll help Sarah. Be careful."

Valerie nodded and said, "Aye, Lieutenant! You too!"

Valerie ran over to Jennifer's side. She shoved her cattle prod gun onto the side of its head and fired at point blank range. The Harvester screamed as a small hole was blown into its head. The magazine clicked empty. The Harvester was still alive.

In frustration Valerie turned the gun around and grasped onto the barrel. She began to hit it over the head, shouting, "Why won't you just die!"

Jennifer, who was still grasping onto its mandibles, yelled at her, saying, "Get back, Valerie! You're just pissing it off!"

Valerie shouted back, saying, "No! I'm not going to lose another friend to these bugs!" She continued to beat the Harvester over the head. A few moments later, there was a crack and the butt of her gun broke off.

Valerie shouted in frustration and threw the broken gun onto the ground. Jennifer continued to be slowly pushed backward as her feet dragged along the ground. Valerie grabbed onto the mandibles of the Harvester alongside Jennifer. She braced her feet on the ground and pushed against the Harvester with all of her strength.

Jennifer shouted, "You don't have my power, Valerie! You're just going to get hurt! Get away from here!"

Valerie yelled, "Die, damn you! Die! Die! Die! I want you to just die!" Valerie's eyes suddenly began to grow brighter than ever before. Her hands began to glow with yellow light even though she didn't put any power into them. Instead of power flowing out of her body, she began to feel a power she never felt before flowing into her body.

The Harvester began to screech and tremble. Valerie's hands glowed brighter than ever. The Harvester stopped pushing against Jennifer. It seemed to grow weaker and weaker. It finally stopped moving and collapsed under its own weight. It was dead.

Valerie, confused, looked at her hands and said, "What's happening?"

Jennifer let go of the dead Harvester and looked just as surprised. She said, "I ... I think you stole all its energy?"

Lieutenant Michael's voice came into their ears, saying, "If it's dead, help Sarah, and me while you're at it!"

Jennifer snapped out of her confusion and looked toward Sarah and Lieutenant Michael. The Harvester and Lieutenant Michael were running around in a circle around Sarah. More accurately, the Harvester was chasing Lieutenant Michael, while he placed Sarah's barrier in between himself and the Harvester.

Jennifer leapt toward the Harvester and grabbed onto its mandibles, trying to stabilize it. Valerie, her hands still glowing brightly, grabbed onto the Harvester alongside Jennifer. She expected the same thing to happen but nothing was happening.

Valerie said, "It's not working!"

Jennifer said, "Try focusing on killing it in your mind."

Valerie said, "Okay."

Jennifer was right. With the last Harvester she sincerely wanted it to die. She began to focus on wanting this Harvester to die. She thought about it harder and harder. She felt power began to flow into her body again. The Harvester stopped pushing forward. It screeched at them and started to tremble. It then collapsed under the weight of its dead body.

Valerie stepped back from the dead Harvester. Her hands were glowing even brighter than before. She started panting heavily. Sweat dripped down her forehead and the sides of her face. The power that had flowed inside her felt like a burning fire. Her hands grew hotter and hotter. She dropped to her knees and cried out, "My hands are burning!" She became afraid and started to cry.

Sarah and Jennifer, who were now standing next to her, dropped to their knees too, and held onto her arms to hold her up. Lieutenant Michael, still panting, ran over to her and said, "You've absorbed too much power. You have to release it or it will kill you."

Valerie cried out, "How do I release it?"

Lieutenant Michael said, "The same way you do when you heal somebody."

Sarah grabbed one of Valerie's hands and said, "Release it into me! I'll help you get rid of it, Valerie."

Jennifer grabbed Valerie's other hand and said, "Yeah, give some to me too. We'll help you hold it together."

Valerie closed her eyes and focused on healing Sarah and Jennifer even though they didn't need it. The power that Valerie had absorbed started to leave her body and flowed equally into Sarah and Jennifer.

Yellow light flowed from Valerie's hand and covered Sarah and Jennifer's arms. The yellow light was warm and soothing to their tired muscles. They felt a new power overtake them. They felt like they could fight even more.

The pain in Valerie's body left her. She stopped pouring energy into them. The Light that had covered them returned inside Valerie. Slowly her breathing returned to normal. She opened her eyes. Lieutenant Michael sat kneeling in front of her. Jennifer and Sarah continued to hold onto her trembling hands.

Lieutenant Michael could not hide the excitement that he felt. He grabbed onto Valerie's arms and said, "Valerie, do you know what this means! You can steal energy now! You can use your power to fight too!"

Valerie, who was still a little confused, said, "All ... all I wanted was for the Harvester to die. I wished it with all my heart and then I just felt power flowing into me. I never felt anything like it before. It was scary."

Lieutenant Michael stood up. Jennifer and Sarah then stood up. They pulled Valerie up off the ground and helped her to her feet.

Sarah said, "Valerie, that was super cool what you just did!"

Jennifer said, "Yeah, that was so amazing Valerie!"

Valerie blushed and looked down toward the ground. She said, "I ... I just wanted to protect you."

Lieutenant Michael ran his hand through his sweaty hair and said, "Yeah. I thought we were all going to die for a moment there. I'd have to say Valerie, that we're all alive thanks to you. I think you deserve a pizza party."

Valerie looked straight up at him with a huge smile on her face. She threw her fists up in celebration and jumped up and down, saying, "Yes! I love pizza!"

Lieutenant Michael waved his hand and said, "Calm down, we got to make it home first. Normally, they'd expect us to be out here a few more hours but I think we did enough to head on home now."

The four of them headed back the way they came. On the way back, they ran into several more groups of Harvesters. Valerie, using her new power helped too. When the power started getting hot she released it into one of her teammates. By the time they made it back over the wall, they had slaughtered a total of thirty-one Harvesters: two fully-grown ones, eleven mid-sized ones, fourteen junior-sized ones, and four baby ones. They spent about four hours in the field.

The three girls climbed down the ladder on the side of the wall and stood together side by side at the bottom. Lieutenant Michael stood in front of them. He smiled at them and said, "You three did very well today. Better than I ever thought we could do. I'm very proud of you."

Lieutenant Michael rubbed the top of Sarah's head. She looked up and smiled back at him. Jennifer stood in between Sarah and Valerie. Lieutenant Michael remembered her yelling at him that she didn't want to be touched so he skipped over her and rubbed Valerie on the top of her head. Valerie looked up and smiled back at him.

Jennifer looked disappointed. He started to turn away from them but Jennifer reached out and grabbed his hand. He stopped moving and looked back at her questioningly. She put his hand on top of her head and held it there. She looked up at him with a slight pout and wanting in her eyes. She said, "I ... I don't mind, Lieutenant, if you want rub my head too."

Lieutenant Michael smiled at her and rubbed the top of her head. She let his hand go and smiled back at him. He said, "So Jennifer ... you going to call me Lieutenant now?"

Jennifer nodded her head and said, "Yeah, after all, you're my Lieutenant now." She started to blush. She brought her hands together and twirled her thumbs. She looked down to the ground and said, "I ... I ... I ..." she stopped speaking and blushed even more. She said, "I think you're a really good Lieutenant so please take care of me."

He smiled at her again and rubbed her head, saying, "Thanks, Jennifer. I'm really glad that you're on my team. Don't worry I'll take care of you. I promise." He took his hand off of her head and turned around. Together, the four of them walked back to their apartment.

- 7 -

As Squad three entered into their hallway, the door to Squad four opened. Lieutenant Rachel and Giana exited their apartment. Giana's face was gloomy, her shoulders drooped forward and her arms hung toward the ground. She looked like she had been crying. Lieutenant Rachel did not look happy either.

They noticed Squad three at the end of the hallway. Giana looked toward the ground to avoid making eye contact with anybody. She wiped her eyes with her hands. They started walking toward the end of the hallway. Lieutenant Michael and his team started walking toward them.

Giana rolled her head and said out loud, "Geez, why'd they have to come back now?"

Lieutenant Michael, confused, said, "Sorry, we just got back from a successful hunt. What's wrong?"

Giana looked toward the ground again and mumbled something.

Lieutenant Michael said, "Huh? What was that?"

Giana rolled her head and said a little bit louder, "I ... I got my first period. There, you happy now that I said it?"

Lieutenant Michael's eyes went wide and instinctively he looked toward Lieutenant Rachel. She nodded her head. He looked back toward Giana and put his hand on top of her head, saying, "I understand. I'm sorry, Gianna. Just a couple of weeks ago Mary got hers."

Giana said, "Yeah, I knew it was coming. I'm getting old after all. Mary and I always did stuff together ... so ... so ... I." She started to cry a little. Lieutenant Rachel wrapped her arm around Giana's shoulders and pulled her close to her chest. She rested her head on Giana's head. Giana quickly composed herself and said, "I'm okay." She tried to put a smile on her face.

Lieutenant Rachel let Giana go. Sarah and Valerie went up to her and hugged her together. Jennifer stood there next to Lieutenant Michael. She took hold of the fabric on his sleeve.

Jennifer said, "I'm sorry, Giana. I'm also sorry that we fought earlier. I was not acting like myself."

Giana stepped toward her, squared her arms on her hips, and bent forward. She stared at her deeply and said, "Don't worry about it, shrimp. You look much better then you did the last time that I saw you."

Jennifer said, "Yeah, Lieutenant Michael helped me."

Giana laughed and said, "No, I meant that you look much better covered in dirt and Harvester goo. It seems to fit your personality more."

Jennifer let go of Lieutenant Michael's sleeve and crossed her arms across her chest. She rolled her eyes and said, "Pff ... you are ..."

Lieutenant Michael waved his hand in between them and said, "Come on girls, this is not the time to fight."

Lieutenant Rachel nodded her head and said, "Yeah, we got to go see Doctor Lovecraft and you four need to take a shower."

Giana plugged her nose and said, "Yeah, Jennifer smells like Harvester guts."

Lieutenant Michael put his hand on Giana's shoulder and gently squeezed it. He looked at her compassionately and said, "If you need anything from us, let me know. We'll help where we can."

Giana became glum again and lowered her head. She said, "Thanks. I guess we'll see you later."

Giana and Lieutenant Rachel walked off towards the end of the hallway where the exit was. Lieutenant Michael stood there and watched them leave. As they exited through the doorway, Lieutenant Rachel looked back towards

Lieutenant Michael. The look of exhaustion filled her face. She attempted to smile at him but it looked more like a frown. His face filled with a look of understanding towards her.

Jennifer, still crossing her arms, said, "I don't really stink do I. I only got a little bit of the Harvester goo on me."

Lieutenant Michael jokingly sniffed the air and said, "Well, only a little bit."

Jennifer sighed and said, "Fine! I guess I'll have to take a bath."

Valerie said, "Yeah, let's all take a bath!"

Sarah nodded her head and said, "Yeah. This will be our first time too!"

Jennifer nodded her head and said, "Yeah, I think I'm ready to take a bath with you."

Lieutenant Michael opened the door to the apartment and said, "It's settled then. You girls will take a bath. I'll take a shower and then get dinner started. But, before that, we need to talk about something very important."

They went into the apartment. Lieutenant Michael pointed them to the dinner table. They all sat around it waiting for Lieutenant Michael to speak. Lieutenant Michael leaned forward and said, "We had a really good day today, but there is one problem. Jennifer tried to get herself killed today."

Jennifer looked down toward the table, embarrassed.

Lieutenant Michael continued, saying, "Doctor Lovecraft said that if Jennifer tries to kill herself she is going to be removed from the Spirit Wielders. They let the last incident slide because we felt that it really was an accident."

Sarah and Valerie looked down toward the table. Valerie said, "But ... but, I don't want Jennifer to leave. We finally became friends!"

Sarah said, "Yeah, I don't want to lose Jennifer either."

Jennifer continued to look down toward the table. She said, "I know I did something I shouldn't have done. If they are going to remove me for it, then I guess I have no choice."

Lieutenant Michael held his hand up towards her and said, "Wait one moment. They don't know what really happens out there unless we tell them. If we all agree to it, then we just won't mention that part. Okay?"

Sarah nodded her head and said, "I can keep it a secret, if it means Jennifer gets to stay."

Valerie nodded her head too and said, "Yeah. I won't tell anybody either."

Lieutenant Michael looked towards Jennifer and said, "The choice is yours, Jennifer. This will be the perfect opportunity to leave if you want. I can tell them what you did and they'll remove you. Then, you won't have to worry about fighting anymore. Or, we can keep this a secret and you get to stay with us. Which path do you want to take?"

Jennifer looked up into his face and said, "Lieutenant, please help me to stay. I don't want to leave this team anymore. I want to keep fighting Harvesters for my friends."

Lieutenant Michael nodded his head and said, "Okay, Jennifer. But, if you really want to stay, I can't have a repeat of you doing anything like that again. This is your third chance with me. I'm not going to give you another. The old deal we had still stands. I want you to still talk to me every day about your feelings. You will still have to stay with your team twenty-four seven until I say so. You will still have to talk to Doctor Lovecraft every week. Okay?"

Jennifer nodded her head and said, "Okay, I understand."

Lieutenant Michael pretended to seal his lips with a zipper and said, "Alright, you girls worked hard today so go on and take a bath now. I'll take a quick shower and then start making dinner."

Sarah and Valerie stood up from their seats. They walked up to Jennifer, who was still sitting. She looked up at Sarah and then turned her head to look up at Valerie. She smiled at them and slowly pushed her seat back. She stood up and the three of them slowly started walking towards the hallway.

Before they entered the hallway, Jennifer suddenly stopped. She turned around and looked towards Lieutenant Michael, who was still sitting in his seat. Valerie and Sarah stopped walking and turned around to see what Jennifer was going to do.

Jennifer ran up to Lieutenant Michael and threw her arms around his shoulders as he sat there. Lieutenant Michael raised his arms and returned her embrace. She quickly let him go, so he let her go too. She stepped back from him. Her cheeks were blushing red. She looked down toward the ground to hide her embarrassment. She said, "I know that you risked your life to save me today. I ... I was just hugging you to thank you for saving me. It's not like I really wanted to hug you."

Lieutenant Michael nodded his head and said, "Okay, I get it. Don't worry. I saved you because I think you're worth saving."

Jennifer spun around and ran in between Valerie and Sarah into the hallway. Sarah and Valerie glimpsed at each other. They smiled and chuckled. Lieutenant Michael shrugged his shoulders and pushed his chair back. With a tired sigh he stood up and stretched. Valerie and Sarah went into the hallway and entered the bathroom.

Jennifer was already standing beside the tub. She had turned the water on and was staring at the water rising in the bathtub. Sarah unbuttoned her jacket and tossed it into her laundry basket. She lifted her dress over her head and tossed it on top of her jacket.

Valerie followed suite. She unbuttoned her dress jacket and tossed it into her laundry basket. She slipped out of her dress and kicked it into the laundry basket. She stretched her arms and legs, saying, "Ah! That's much better! We sure worked hard today."

Sarah nodded her head as she slipped out of her underwear, saying, "Yeah. That was really dangerous though. We're really lucky. We're even luckier that you were able to develop that ability."

Jennifer began to get undressed. She said, "Yeah, I never met a Yellow Wielder that could pull the life out of Harvesters before. I mean, I heard about it, but I've never seen that before."

Valerie walked up to Jennifer with a smile. She took one of Jennifer's hands into her own hands and placed it over her own heart, saying, "I ... I was just so afraid that I was going to lose you. I thought as hard as I could about killing it and then it happened."

Jennifer placed her other hand over Valerie's hands and said, "I'm glad you are my friend too. Thanks for helping to save me."

Valerie nodded and let her hands go. She felt the water and then slipped into the tub with a sigh of relief. She said, "It was really scary when my hands started to feel like they were on fire. I thought that power was going to kill me."

Sarah slipped into the tub and sat down across from Valerie. She said, "It can kill you. That's why your hands were burning because you took too much energy into your body at once. You should only use that power if you really have too. If you take too much energy into your body, it will self-destruct."

Jennifer finished getting undressed and got into the bathtub. She turned off the water. She sat down in the spot between Valerie and Sarah. Valerie and Sarah stared at the scars on her right wrist.

Valerie said, "Yeah, I get it. I'll only use my new power if I really need too. It's just ... it's just ... I wish I could have had it when we fought in Los Angeles. Then I probably could have saved Mary."

Valerie quickly turned to Jennifer and held up her hands, saying, "I'm sorry, Jennifer. I don't mean that I don't want you to be here too, it's just ..."

Jennifer waved her hand in protest and said, "Don't be sorry. I know what you mean. If I could be with my old team, I'd ... but, I do like being with you too."

Sarah leaned back against the bathtub wall and relaxed even more, saying, "Don't worry. Missing your old friends who've died in the war is normal. It doesn't take away from your new friends that are still alive. Trust me. I'm older so I've dealt with this before."

Valerie and Jennifer both somberly nodded in agreement.

Valerie said, "Well, if anything you are definitely right that you are older."

Jennifer laughed.

Sarah smirked at Valerie and lightly splashed water in her face.

Lieutenant Michael got out of the shower and dried himself off. He thought about the report that he would have to write. It's not like he was going to lie on the report. He was just going to omit a small detail that didn't really matter in the long run. Of course, there was always the possibility that Jennifer could have a relapse. It could be dangerous if she did. But, he wanted to believe in her. She seemed genuinely better now. Not all better, but the walls that she had built around herself had finally come crashing down. He was finally seeing the real Jennifer, the Jennifer that he read about in the reports.

Lieutenant Michael got dressed into a new uniform and went into the kitchen. He looked around the cupboard to see what he should make. There was lots of spaghetti still in the cupboard. He decided that it was time to make more pasta. He pulled a pot out of a cabinet and filled it with water. He placed it on the stove and waited for it to start boiling.

After dinner, the girls got into their pajamas as Lieutenant Michael began to write his after action report at the dinner table. It was Sarah's turn to be with Jennifer as she got dressed in her room.

Valerie ran into the living room wearing her white and pink pajama top and bottom. She tossed herself onto the couch. Soon it would be time to watch the re-run of Magical Girl Squad. Valerie reached for the remote, but it was not in its usual spot. She sighed out loud and started to look for it. She looked on both sides of the couch, but it was not there. She overturned one of the cushions and found it jammed underneath. "Thank goodness!" she said to herself.

Valerie clicked on the television and set it to the right channel. As she put the remote back into its proper place, Sarah came out in her blue and white long pajama shirt. She sat down next to Valerie and said, "Did I miss the beginning?"

Valerie shook her head and said, "Nope! Still just commercials."

Jennifer came out of the hallway behind Sarah, wearing her long white pajama shirt with the emerald green sleeves. Much to their surprise, she was not carrying her favorite book. Jennifer shyly walked up to Valerie and Sarah. She stood there, her right arm crossed over her chest and her hand gripping onto her left arm. She said, "Can I watch Magical Girl Squad with you?"

Valerie and Sarah looked surprised.

Valerie said, "I thought you said that you hated Magical Girl Squad?"

Jennifer said, "No, I was … lying. I … I was afraid to watch it without my friends. I felt bad that I got to watch it and my friends won't ever get to see it again."

Sarah scooted herself over with a smile. She patted the now open spot with her hand and said, "Of course! Sit down right here."

Jennifer nodded, saying, "Thanks." She sat down between Valerie and Sarah.

Valerie wrapped an arm around Jennifer's arm and said, "I always believed you liked Magical Girl Squad. There is no girl our age that doesn't like it."

Sarah wrapped her own arm around Jennifer's other arm and said, "Let's make a new promise to each other: No more lying to each other. Okay?"

Jennifer nodded her head and said, "Yeah, I'm sorry I lied. I just … I …"

Sarah stopped her and said, "Don't worry about it. We understand that you were having a really hard time. From now on, we'll help each other and be honest with each other."

Jennifer nodded her head. Valerie smiled at her and nodded her head too. The introduction music for Magical Girl Squad began to play. The three of them stopped talking and focused on the television.

TEARS OF DARKNESS

CHAPTER 05

THE WALLS OF JERICHO

- 1 -

Over the next few weeks, Jennifer continued to improve. She talked to Lieutenant Michael every evening and allowed either Sarah or Valerie to remain with her always.   She talked to Doctor Lovecraft every week without any arguments. It was decided that Jennifer was going to be okay, so Lieutenant Michael and Doctor Lovecraft relaxed the restrictions placed on her. She no longer had to be with someone twenty-four seven and she no longer had to have daily and weekly meetings.

Valerie, Sarah, and Jennifer continued to grow closer together. They continued to work together well during hunting parties. On Wednesdays and Fridays they watched Magical Girl Squad together. On Thursdays they watched the Lost Sword Saga. As promised, Jennifer provided ample commentary on the differences between the show and the book.

By the end of two months being together, it was Jennifer's tenth birthday. It happened to fall on the same day as Unity Day, which was July twenty-first. Lieutenant Michael held a pool side party and Squad four came too.

Lieutenant Michael sat on the edge of the pool, allowing his legs to hang in the water. Lieutenant Rachel sat next to him. She wore her olive green bikini; the familiar scar visible on her stomach.

Tina laid on her back pretending to be dead again as she floated across the top of the water. Lieutenant Michael watched her as she floated by. It astonished him why she was always focused on death so much. Her body randomly floated toward where Lieutenants Michael and Rachel were sitting.

As Tina drifted by, Lieutenant Michael said, "Tina, why do you like death so much?"

Without hesitation, Tina replied in her melancholy tone, "Death is the sweetest of fruits and it can only be eaten once."

Lieutenant Rachel shook her head and pushed Tina in the other direction with her foot. She said, "I wish you wouldn't say stuff like that, Tina. It's so depressing. Being alive is not that bad."

Tina, still pretending to be dead on the water, said, "But Lieutenant, it's true. Living in this messed up world is really bad. I'm just glad I get to die sooner than everyone else. My whole life is devoted to killing and dying."

Jennifer spoke up saying, "That's a harsh way of putting it. There are lots of good things we can experience in this life."

Giana stopped swimming and stood up, she turned to Jennifer and pointed at her. She said, "That's funny! Queen of Darkness number two telling the Queen of Darkness number one not to be so depressing."

Jennifer turned to Giana and slapped her palms against the water, shouting, "I'm not a Queen of Darkness, stupid!"

Giana shouted back, "Those cuts on your wrist say otherwise!"

Jennifer became subdued. She brought her right wrist up to her chest and covered it with her other hand. Her lip began to quiver and she looked like she was going to cry.

Valerie came to her defense and said, "Stop teasing Jennifer, it's her birthday!"

Jennifer said, "It's okay, Valerie. Giana is just trying to pick a fight again. I don't feel like fighting today so I'll just let it go. I'm more mature than her anyway."

Elsa said, "That was pretty low, Giana. You know that's a sensitive issue."

Giana squared her hands on her hips and said, "Pff ... I thought Jennifer got thicker skin than that."

Tina floated by, saying, "Giana, you never know when to quit."

Giana rolled her eyes and pushed Tina in the opposite direction. Giana said, "I do what I want to do when I want to do it!"

Lieutenant Rachel waved toward Giana and said, "Giana, come here."

Giana turned toward Lieutenant Rachel and tilted her head. She blinked her eyes and said, "Why?"

Lieutenant Rachel smiled deceptively and said nonchalantly, "So I can whack you upside the head."

Giana gasped and put her hands on top of her head. She started to back up and said, "No, why do you got to hit me all the time?"

Lieutenant Rachel tilted her head and said in the same tone, "Because it's the only thing that seems to work on you."

Giana began to swim in the opposite direction. Lieutenant Rachel slid into the water and started wading toward her.

As she started walking away, Lieutenant Michael stuck out his legs out and wrapped them around the sides of her waist. She stopped wading forward and turned around. She looked at him, waiting for him to speak. Her heart began to beat a little faster.

Lieutenant Michael dropped his legs and slipped into the pool. He took a step forward and stopped right in front of her. He took her by the forearm and pulled her closer to himself. She felt his strength hidden behind his firm grasp. She looked up at him. Her eyes began to glaze over and her heart began to beat even faster. She thought to herself, *Is ... is he going to kiss me?* She let her lips open a little and started to blush in embarrassment.

Lieutenant Michael said, "So, Rachel ... do you want to watch the Unity Day speech together at my place?"

Lieutenant Rachel said, "You can ... wait ... what?"

Lieutenant Michael repeated himself, saying, "Do you want to watch the Unity Day speech together at my place?"

Lieutenant Rachel sighed in disappointment, but said, "Oh yeah, the Unity Day speech. Sure. I thought that was the plan already."

Giana stopped swimming away and looked toward them. She sighed in relief and shook her fist in victory. She said quietly to herself, "Saved by manly interference."

Lieutenant Michael let Rachel go and said, "All right, girls. It's almost time for the Unity Day speech so let's go on up and get ready."

After drying off, they all left the pool together and went back to their apartments to change.

Lieutenant Rachel shut the door behind herself. She leaned against the door and held her hand against her chest. She still felt a little restless about the way Michael had grabbed her arm and pulled her close to himself. He had never done that before.

Giana noticed it and said, "So ... you thought he was going to kiss you, eh? When I saw it I almost choked on the water. But, as usually, it was nothing."

Lieutenant Rachel stood up straight and said, "No, I wasn't expecting that. Don't think I've forgotten about smacking you upside the head!"

Giana's face dropped in shock and she quickly turned, running into her room before Lieutenant Rachel could move toward her.

After they got dressed, both squads gathered in Squad three's apartment. They all were wearing their white uniforms with their colored stripes. Lieutenant Michael sat down next to Lieutenant Rachel on the stairs that led down to the sitting area in the living room. Giana and Sarah sat in the recliner chairs, while Elsa, Tina, Valerie, and Jennifer squeezed together on the couch.

In Denver Sector, the world's capitol, there was a stage constructed underneath the great wall that surrounded the sector. On the stage was a podium. Behind it were rows of chairs where officials of the World Government sat. There was a band playing the World's Anthem in the back ground.

The stage was set in the World Heritage Park that was dedicated to the struggles of humanity in the two alien invasions. A monument was erected to the fallen with the words engraved along the bottom, "Our hope has not faded, we shall persevere."

An older women with short gray hair, stood up from her seat and approached the podium. Over the television there could be heard the cheers and applause of a large crowd. The camera panned to show that the whole area had become crowded with people. A voice came over a loud speaker, saying, "I present to you the second President of the World Government, Madam Regina Fantoccio!"

The music began to fade and the jubilation of the crowd died down. The woman at the podium raised a hand and waved to the crowd of people. She lowered her hand and said, "On this day, twenty years ago, we violently learned that we are not alone in the universe. It was because of this knowledge that we were able to cast off the old traditions of the world that held us back and to put together a New World Order to stand against all those who seek to destroy humanity. It was thirteen years ago that the Harvesters fell from the sky. If not for our unity, we could not have survived that vicious assault. It is thanks to these walls that shelter us now so that we can continue to live in peace and safety. The Harvesters thought to wipe us out! But, we are still here today!"

There were more cheers from the crowd. A wave of applause came from the huge crowd in front of her. The people behind her clapped their hands with the same level of enthusiasm.

After a moment, the uproar died down. She continued her speech, saying, "Yes, we are still here. We will not be outcasts on our own world. This is our world! They are the invaders and we will reclaim it from them. Every centimeter that we have lost will be reclaimed! Our scientist have been working night and day. We are at this moment preparing to unleash new weapons in our war against these merciless invaders!"

Suddenly there was a loud screech from the speakers and the microphone cut off. The people of the crowd looked around in confusion. After a moment the speakers then crackled back on. President Fantoccio tried to speak again but the sound of her voice did not come through the speakers. Several people got up and began to check the wires on the podium.

Suddenly, an odd clapping noise began to come out of the speakers. It was loud yet slow, but increased in speed. It sounded like two leather-gloved hands were clapping over the loud speakers. People looked left and right to try to see what was going on.

The clapping was soon replaced by the sound of a man laughing psychotically. After a few moments of laughter, he stopped. The sound of a man clearing his throat came, followed by a voice that rang through the loud speakers, saying, "Pardon the interruption citizens of the world. Excuse me, Madam Puppet, but this shall not take long. I have hacked into your sound system to deliver this very important message to the world. If you would all turn your attention to the top of the wall, I shall introduce myself."

Valerie turned her face towards Lieutenant Michael and said, "Lieutenant, what's going on?"

Lieutenant Michael shook his head and said, "I've got no idea."

The television camera panned upward and a man appeared on the top of the wall. The man wore an eighteenth century style navy blue frock coat with red lining. He wore a white waist coat with a white silk cravat. He wore white breeches that tucked into knee length black leather boots. He wore a black tricorn hat. On his face was a mask. The mask was divided into two colors: on the left side it was black and on the right side it was white. The mask projected a wide sinister smile that alternated its color on each side of the mask. On the right side it was black and on the left side it was white. Around the right eye hole there was the shape of a black sun and to the side of the left eye hole there was a white crescent moon.

The man took off his hat, placed it over his heart, and bowed deeply before the crowd. He then lifted himself up and replaced the hat onto his head. He shouted, saying, "Ladies and Gentlemen! I bring glad tidings to you, O citizens of this brave new world!"

The man threw his arms wide open. He said, "I am Justice! The justice of a vengeful God! I have come to bring justice upon this corrupt government. The government that you see is nothing more than a puppet show, and our beloved President is the chief marionette. If only you people knew who really pulled her strings. All that you hear is a lie! All that you see is a lie! All that they do is a lie!"

World Police started to scramble as the man revealed himself to the crowd. Riffles pointed at the man and fired. The bullets that were fired seemed to deflect away from him mysteriously.

The man continued, saying, "The World Government has constructed these walls as a form of population control! You think you are safe behind these walls! From time to time these walls fall when your population reaches their limits. These walls are nothing more than chains to bind you till they are ready to slaughter you! But, fear not! I have come to break your chains! Behold, O Jericho! When the walls fell!"

Suddenly there was a bright flash and a loud boom from the base of the wall. Shatters of cement sprayed in all directions. A cloud of dust began to surround the area. People began to scream and scatter in all directions. One after another more explosions could be heard setting off a chain sequence that seemed to surround the entire city.

Sarah said, "Did ... did the wall just explode?"

Lieutenant Michael sat there in shock, he shook himself at Sarah's voice and said, "It looks like someone planted bombs along the base of the wall."

Lieutenant Rachel said, "But that's crazy! Did that psycho just blow himself up?"

Valerie said, "Are we going to deploy?"

Lieutenant Michael said, "I doubt it, they'll all be dead by the time we get there."

The television camera was left on but abandoned. It had gotten knocked over by the force of the explosion. But, it was angled in such a way as to show the wall. As the dust began to settle, the area of the wall became visible. Instead of being able to see the wall, there was nothing but shattered remains of concrete blocks and open air. Screeches of Harvesters could be heard in the distance. Then, the camera went black.

Lieutenant Michael jumped up and exclaimed, "One sec!" He ran towards his room, flung open the door, and grabbed the laptop sitting on his desk. He ran back into the living room and sat down next to Lieutenant Rachel again. He said, "I can try to use my Military access code to get more information."

He opened the laptop and anxiously waited for it to turn on. After what felt like a long time, it finally booted up. He opened the World Government Access page. Under the news feed there was a notice that read, "Please stand by."

He manually inputted a back door code into the login request and accessed the emergency military website. He said, "I was able to access it."

The girls got out of their seats and huddled around him waiting to see what it would say. Lieutenant Michael watched as real-time updates began to appear in the news feed. He read them out loud as they appeared: "Denver capitol attacked in major terrorist event. Denver Sector outer wall demolished. Key governing members in process of evacuation. All units ordered on stand-by. Prepare for potential activation. Harvester units advancing on all fronts. All personal assigned to Denver capitol to withdraw as able. Denver capitol projected losses: twenty million."

Lieutenant Michael shut the laptop and closed his eyes. He felt a sudden rage at all the people who were going to die. His body began to shiver at the thought of it. Twenty million people were suddenly made defenseless by the sudden loss of the wall.

Sarah's voice finally reached him. She had been talking to him but he could not hear her words. She repeated herself, "Lieutenant, are you okay?"

Lieutenant Michael opened his eyes and turned his head toward Sarah. He stared at her blankly. Her eyes were starting to get watery as tears began to appear. He said, "I'm ... I'm okay, Sarah."

Jennifer shut off her emotions and sat there as memories of the Los Angeles massacre returned to her mind. She held onto her right wrist and rubbed her left hand thumb in a circle over the scars that remained on her right wrist. Lieutenant Michael saw the look of despair on her face and recognized it. He reached out to her and put his hand on her shoulder and said, "Try not to worry. We'll get through this together like we always do."

Jennifer slowly nodded her head and brought herself back to the present. She nodded again and said, "Yeah, I know. We're not involved in it this time."

Valerie's lips pouted and her eyes were wide open. She said, "There's no way we can save those people, is there?"

Lieutenant Michael said, "No, the wall is completely destroyed. It's not a breach. The entire wall is destroyed. It would take us like four or five hours to get there and the Harvesters are already swarming into the sector." Valerie covered her face with her hands and started to cry. Sarah reached out to Valerie and pulled her into an embrace.

Tina, in her melancholy tone, said, "See, our lives here are nothing but death and killing. That's what I was trying to say earlier."

Elsa leaned over on Lieutenant Rachel's shoulder and said, "Why would people want to blow up the wall? The wall is the only thing keeping us safe."

Lieutenant Rachel said, "We've been cooped up behind these walls for around thirteen years now. I guess some people are getting cabin fever."

Elsa said, "What's cabin fever?"

Lieutenant Rachel said, "That's when a person has been stuck inside for too long and it makes them go crazy. I guess these terrorist felt that blowing up the capital of the World Government would send a message to the rest of humanity."

A chime sounded over the loud speaker and Captain Faust's voice spoke, saying, "All Lieutenants, please report to my office immediately."

Lieutenant Michael stood up and said, "Well, that's our cue." He held out his hand to Lieutenant Rachel and she accepted it, allowing him to help pull her up from where she sat. Lieutenant Michael held up his hand and said, "You girls, wait here. We'll be back as soon as we're done." Together, Lieutenants Michael and Rachel quickly left the apartment.

Giana plopped back down in the recliner and sighed loudly. She covered her face with her hands and said, "I'm so sick of this crap! I'm starting to look forward to my body's structural collapse soon."

Elsa threw her hands down and started to cry, she shouted, "Don't say that Giana! That's ... that's ..." She then took off running down the hallway and entered the bathroom, slamming the door behind herself. She ran into a toilet stall and sat on the toilet. She locked the stall door and cried.

Giana rolled her eyes and sighed again. She lifted herself out of the chair and said, "Geez, not again. I'll be right back."

Giana walked down the hallway and entered the bathroom. As she opened the door, she could hear Elsa crying. Giana stepped inside and said, "Geez, are you still crying about this?" There was no reply.

Giana saw the locked stall door and walked up to it. She knocked on it three times and said, "Elsa, won't you open the door so we can talk?" Still there was no answer.

Giana said, "Look, I'm sorry I said something insensitive. I wasn't trying to upset you. You're my friend and I love you. You know that."

The sound of crying stopped. The lock on the stall clicked. Giana pushed the door open and found Elsa sitting on the toilet. Her knees were straight up and her feet sat on the edge of the toilet seat cover. Her arms were wrapped around her legs and her face was buried in her knees.

Giana bent forward and hugged Elsa's huddled frame. She said, "Come on, Elsa. It's going to be okay."

Elsa said, "I'm sorry I overreacted. I guess I'm already worked up because of Denver."

Giana patted her head and said, "Don't worry about it. Why don't you come back and join everybody. They are worrying about it too, so we can go back and help each other deal with what happened today." Elsa nodded her head and stood up. Giana took her hand and pulled her close to her body. She embraced her for a moment and then led her back to the living room where everyone was waiting for them.

Lieutenants Michael and Rachel entered into Captain Faust's office. They saluted and then sat down next to each other in the chairs by the Captain's desk. The Captain was still on the red emergency telephone that sat on his desk. Despite the modern convenience of the new communication systems, the military still used direct line phone systems. Probably because of its reliability during emergency situations.

One by one, the other Lieutenants filed in and sat in the remaining chairs. The Captain said, "Thank you, sir. Good bye, sir." He hung up the old style telephone and sat up straight in his chair. He shook his head and said, "We never expected a terrorist group to ever attack the walls. I guess we just assumed that nobody would do that because it's the only thing stopping the Harvesters from wiping us all out."

Lieutenant Lloyd of First squad said, "Did the terrorist group give any reason for why they did it? Do we know who they are?"

Captain Faust shook his head and said, "That's a no for both questions. We can only suppose that they are an anti-government group. The man who spoke at the speech is most likely dead from his own explosion. That means they are suicidal. Those are the most dangerous types. From his own words I'd say that the group believes in bringing punishment to the World Government for some supposed crime. They also claim that the walls are a form of population control. Where they get these insane ideas from, I don't know. But, I guess that humans have been cooped up behind these walls for too long. I suppose that some people are starting to go insane being stuck behind them."

Lieutenant Lloyd asked, "Did we get any orders from the brass?"

Captain Faust nodded his head and said, "Yeah. In addition to our other duties, we're also going to have to check the walls every day. Since we got five squads, we'll have two squads check the inner side of the wall. Two squads will check the outside perimeter of the wall. One squad will check along the top of the wall. The squad that checks the top may divide itself into two teams so that they can each do half of the wall. The two inner and outer squads will start at the same place and go in opposite directions till they meet back up with their counterparts. You will start right now: First squad and Second squad check the inner portion of the wall. Third squad will check the top of the wall. Fourth and Fifth squad will check along the outside perimeter of the wall. We'll do it this way till I come up with a better plan."

Lieutenant Lloyd looked a little apprehensive, so did the other Lieutenants. He said, "Sir, it will probably take us four to six hours to check the wall in this fashion."

Captain Faust nodded his head and said, "I know. We'll come up with something better in a day or two. For now, get your teams out there and start checking the wall. If you see anything suspicious, radio us and let us know the location immediately. We're also placing the citizens on Martial lockdown for today till the wall has been checked. Take your time, but speed is of the essence. Just do a thorough job, that's all I ask. Dismissed."

The Lieutenants stood up and saluted before they left. Outside the Captain's office Lieutenant Lloyd said, "Let's all meet at junction thirty-three since it's the nearest point on the wall from here. We'll divide up from there." The other Lieutenants agreed and quickly returned to their waiting teams in their apartments.

Lieutenants Michael and Rachel walked into his apartment together. Lieutenant Rachel called out saying, "Okay, Squad four, let's get ready for combat duty."

Giana said, "Are we deploying to Denver?"

Lieutenant Rachel shook her head and said, "No, we're going to check along the wall for explosive devices. Our squad is checking the outside part of the wall."

Giana jumped up and tilted her head questioningly. She shrugged her shoulders and said, "How the hell am I supposed to recognize an explosive device. We don't use that kind of stuff."

Lieutenant Rachel replied, "We're just looking for something that doesn't seem to belong. Besides, would you rather wait and do nothing while terrorists blow up our wall?"

Giana sighed and said, "No. I'll check. But this is going to take hours if we have to fight off Harvesters while we're trying to check."

Lieutenant Rachel said, "I know, so we better get started now. Get your gear."

Giana, Elsa, and Tina walked toward the door and left for their own apartment. Lieutenant Rachel turned to follow them. Michael reached out and grabbed her arm again. She stopped and turned her head towards him. He said, "Be safe."

Lieutenant Rachel nodded and gave him a thumbs up, saying, "Don't worry, we got this."

He let her go and she continued out of his apartment with her squad. She opened the door to their own apartment and said to herself out loud, "Did I really just give him a thumbs up?"

Giana giggled and said, "Yes. Yes you did. Wow, Lieutenant Michael is starting to get a little bolder. That's the second time he's grabbed you like that, both times today! I bet your heart is racing."

Lieutenant Rachel shook her head and said, "Just go get ready for combat."

As Squad four left, Sarah, Jennifer, and Valerie stood up. Sarah said, "Are we going outside the wall too?"

Lieutenant Michael shook his head and said, "No, we got the top of the wall. But, I still want you to bring your combat gear. Since it is just us on top of the wall, we're going to divide ourselves into two groups. I will take Valerie with me and you, Sarah, will go with Jennifer in the opposite direction. If you see anything that looks like it doesn't belong there call me over the radio and give me the coordinates so I can contact H.Q."

Lieutenant Michael then opened the cabinet that contained their combat gear. He pulled out the box that held their com units. He handed each one to the girl it belonged to. They put it in their ear and switched it on. Lieutenant Michael then put his own in his ear and switched it on, causing it to crackle to life. He said, "Radio check."

Sarah said, "Blue on."

Jennifer said, "Red on."

Valerie said, "Yellow on."

They all heard each other in their own ears.

Lieutenant Michael handed Sarah her belt with the scabbards. She wrapped it around her waist and then checked the two metal sticks in the scabbards.

Lieutenant Michael handed Valerie her shoulder holster. She strapped it on her back. She checked the magazine pouches to make sure they were full.

Lieutenant Michael asked, "You girls ready?"

Together the girls raised their fist high in the air and said together, "Let's go!"

They walked out of the apartment together. As they left, Squad four also came out of their apartment too. As they walked down the stairs together, Giana said, "Geez, how come Squad three gets it easy? I got to go out and fight Harvesters while checking for bombs!"

Jennifer said, "Don't worry! I'll wave to you from on top of the wall so you don't feel so alone."

Giana replied, "Pff ... I'll give you my own special wave with my special finger!"

Valerie said, "I hope this doesn't take too long. It's Friday so I don't want to miss Magical Girl Squad."

Sarah said, "Don't worry, Val. It's only fourteen hundred hours and Magical Girl Squad starts at twenty hundred hours. It should take us only four hours to go through our section of the wall."

Tina said, "If we run into a pack of harvesters it will take us much longer than four hours to do our section."

Jennifer gave her two thumbs up with a huge grin on her face. She said, "Do your best!" Tina rolled her eyes in response.

As they stepped outside the Phoenix Guard Complex, the streets were empty. All the citizens were under Martial lockdown in their own homes. Any person that was found outside their homes could be arrested, or, even worse, shot dead in the street. They could already see that Squads one and two were ahead of them. They walked down the street behind them toward junction thirty-three of the wall.

- 2 -

When all the teams gathered at the base of the wall at junction thirty-three, they departed for their assignments. Squad four climbed up the wall first, followed by Squad five. Squad three then followed them up and stood at the top while watching the other two squads climb down the outer wall.

Jennifer stood over the top of the ladder and watched as Giana climbed down the wall. As Giana climbed down, Jennifer said, "I feel much better knowing that you're down there checking for bombs."

Giana looked upwards and said, "I can see the zoo animal prints on your underwear!"

Girls from multiple squads started to chuckle. Jennifer stepped backwards and pushed the hem of her dress closer to her body. She started to blush and avoided looking at the others.

Valerie said, "There's nothing wrong with that. I got underwear with cute little butterflies on them. I also got underwear with bunnies on them in my drawer. They're really cute!"

Jennifer looked over the edge again and shouted to Giana, who was now on the ground, "You're just jealous that you can't wear cute things anymore!"

Giana cupped her hands around her mouth and shouted, "I'm still cute! But I can also wear underwear with sexy lace on them!"

Jennifer blushed again and turned around to try to hide it.

Lieutenant Michael shook his head and spoke to Jennifer, saying, "All right Jennifer. That's enough horsing around. We've got work to do."

Lieutenant Michael turned to Sarah and said, "Sarah, you're taking Jennifer and heading in that direction. Valerie and I will go in this direction. And we'll meet somewhere in the middle on the other side. Just walk there and keep your eyes open. If you see anything suspicious, don't forget to radio me."

Sarah saluted Lieutenant Michael and said, "Aye, Lieutenant!" She then took Jennifer by the hand and the two of them began walking in the direction that Lieutenant Michael had pointed at.

Valerie then grinned at Lieutenant Michael and saluted in her childish manner, saying, "I'm ready, Lieutenant!"

Lieutenant Michael nodded his head and said, "Yep, let's get going now so we can get back in time for Magical Girl Squad."

Valerie raised her fist high in the air and said, "Yeah! Let's go!"

Together, they walked down the path on top of the wall in the opposite direction that Sarah and Jennifer went in. Valerie walked and occasionally skipped beside him. He thought it was not a good idea to have children look for bombs. Not only for safety reasons, but also because he wasn't sure that they could focus on the task and identify explosive devices. The wall could also suddenly explode while they stood on top of it if there really were bombs planted here. It made him a little nervous.

Though Valerie was always alert to her surroundings during missions, she often had the problem that she would sing when she was board. After being quiet for some time on top of the wall, Valerie started singing the Magical Girl Squad theme song. It was apparently one of her favorite songs:

> When evil covers the land,
> It's time for girls to take a stand!
> Deep inside you a power is sleeping.
> Magical power to illuminate the world!
> Fight the darkness that surrounds you.
> When girls combine nothing can stop you.
> With your friends by your side,
> You transcend above the darkness below.
> With a shot of love your powers flow,
> You've tasted the fruit that fell from the tree.
> Rise up and fight the foe, it is your destiny!
> The Path of the Future calls you!
> You are Magical Girls!
> Your destiny is calling you!

Lieutenant Michael had never really listened to the song before, but Valerie had memorized it and he began to think about it since there was not much else to do as they looked for bombs. He said, "You know, Valerie, those lyrics seem pretty deep. Have you ever thought about what they mean?"

Valerie stopped singing and thought for a moment. She tilted her head and brought her right index finger to her lips. She said, "Well, it sounds like they are saying that girls have all the power so they should work together as friends to fight evil."

Lieutenant Michael nodded and said, "Yeah, I get that part. It just seems to me that they made this show to help Spirit Wielders get ready for service."

Valerie nodded her head and said, "I never told anybody this but I started watching Magical Girl Squad because of my powers. It made me feel that I had these powers for a reason. Even though I was really sad to leave my parents, I also felt like I was one of the Magical Girls. I was joining the Spirit Wielders to become a Magical Girl. Does that sound weird, Lieutenant?"

Lieutenant Michael shook his head and said, "No, that's not weird at all. When you think about it, we might as well call you girls 'magical', because there's no other explanation for your powers. You become Spirit Wielders to fight the evil Harvesters that are trying to destroy humanity."

Sarah and Jennifer continued to walk along the top of the wall. They had been at it for two hours already and they had not noticed anything that looked suspicious. Of course they had no idea what bombs really looked like so they weren't sure if they would be able to recognize it. At the least, they didn't notice anything that looked like it shouldn't be there.

Jennifer walked over to the side of the wall and looked over it. To her surprise Squad four was just a little ways behind them below the wall.

Jennifer shouted at them, saying, "Hey there! Do your best!" She raised her hands and waved at them in an exaggerated way.

Elsa and Tina waved back at her. Giana raised her hand high and then stuck out her middle finger. Lieutenant Rachel reached over and slapped Giana across the back of the head.

Jennifer chuckled and turned to Sarah. She said, "Giana just flipped me off and Lieutenant Rachel smacked her on top of the head again."

Sarah chuckled too and said, "Yeah, that's funny. But, try to stay focused on what we're supposed to do."

Jennifer shrugged her shoulders and said, "Yeah, yeah, but this is so boring. We've already been out here for two hours."

Sarah replied, "Yeah, I know. But, we got to do it so we can make sure this sector is safe. We don't want a repeat of what happened in Los Angeles."

Jennifer stopped walking and looked downward. She wrapped her arms across her chest and held herself tight.

Sarah stopped walking and turned around to face her. She said, "Are you okay, Jennifer?"

Jennifer dropped her arms and nodded, saying, "Yeah, I'm okay. I was just remembering what happened in Los Angeles."

Sarah stepped towards her and put her hand on her shoulder, saying, "I'm sorry I brought it up, but we need to stay focused on what we're doing. We don't want to miss anything and let that psycho blow up another wall."

Jennifer nodded and said, "Yeah, I know. But it's still boring."

Together they continued to walk down the path on top of the wall trying to find anything that looked suspicious.

Jennifer said, "Did you have another nightmare last night?"

Sarah nodded her head and said, "Yeah, how did you know?"

Jennifer said, "You weren't in your bed when I went into your room in the morning. So, I thought that you had a really bad dream and went to sleep in the Lieutenant's room."

Sarah said, "Yeah, you are right. I had a nightmare."

Jennifer said, "I'd be too embarrassed to sleep in the Lieutenant's room."

Sarah said, "Yeah, I understand that. But, it helps me to feel safer. When you have a nightmare you crawl into either my own or Valerie's bed. That helps you feel safer too. If you went looking for me then you must have had a bad dream too."

Jennifer nodded her head and said, "Yeah, I had that same dream again. I see my friends dying in Los Angeles. It's happening less often though. I guess I'm getting over it now."

Sarah said, "I don't think any of us get over it fully. I think we all just adapt to it."

Jennifer looked toward the landscape over the wall and said, "I wish we didn't have to."

Valerie pointed in the distance and excitedly said, "Look, Lieutenant! It's Sarah and Jennifer!" Valerie raised her hand high and waved toward them. Sarah and Jennifer waved back.

Lieutenant Michael wiped the sweat on his forehead from the July sun and said, "Thank goodness, we're finally done. I hope they come up with a better plan. This takes up too much time."

Valerie took off running towards Sarah and Jennifer. She ran up to them and began jumping up and down excitedly, saying, "We made it. We'll get to watch the new episode of Magical Girl Squad on time!"

Sarah put her hand on top of Valerie's head and said, "Have you already forgot about the potential for bombs being on the wall?"

Valerie calmed down a little. She started to twist her body side to side and said, "No ... I didn't forget. But, if there was a problem, I'm sure we'd have heard about it already. We didn't find any bombs. Did you?"

Jennifer shook her head and said, "No, we didn't see anything that we thought was a bomb. It seemed pretty normal."

Sarah said, "Yeah, but we don't know too much about bombs so I hope that we didn't accidently miss one."

Lieutenant Michael walked up behind Valerie and said, "Gee, thanks Val for leaving me to check the last section by myself."

Valerie turned around and held her hands together in front of her dress. She looked downward and started to pout her lips. She said, "I'm sorry, Lieutenant. I just got excited when I saw Sarah and Jennifer."

Lieutenant Michael put his hand on top of her head and said, "Don't worry. I was just teasing you. I know this mission was pretty boring for you girls. But, at least we got to make sure that the wall was safe. If anything happens to this wall … well, I don't think I need to remind you of what will happen."

Jennifer looked downward as she remembered the chaos that unfolded in Los Angeles. Lieutenant Michael noticed her change in attitude and put his hand on top of her head. He said, "Good job, Jennifer."

Jennifer shrugged her shoulders and said, "I didn't really do anything." Despite her somewhat gloomy attitude, her mood seemed to perk up at his complement.

Lieutenant Michael put his hand on top of Sarah's head and said, "You did a good job too, Sarah. Thanks for keeping Jennifer focused."

Sarah looked up at him and smiled, saying, "Thanks, Lieutenant. It was really hard keeping her focused."

Jennifer pouted and said, "I stayed focus … most of the time."

Lieutenant Michael pushed the button on his earpiece that allowed him to communicate with the other Lieutenants. He said, "Squad three has completed their assigned area."

Lieutenant Lloyd of First squad replied, "Roger. First Squad near completion.

Lieutenant Adams of Second Squad said, "Second squad is near completion too."

Lieutenant Ackley, the new Lieutenant of Fifth Squad said, "Fifth squad is near completion but we've run into a pack of Harvesters so we'll be delayed."

Lieutenant Lloyd asked, "Do you need assistance?"

Lieutenant Ackley replied, "I don't think so. It's very light resistance."

After a moment the radio clicked on and Lieutenant Rachel's voice came into the com unit. She sounded out of breath as she spoke, "This is Squad four. We've run into heavy resistance. Since Squad three is complete, we could use your assistance."

Lieutenant Michael pushed the button on his com unit and said, "Copy that Squad four. Squad three is moving to assist. What is your nearest junction?"

Lieutenant Rachel replied, "We're at junction one hundred and eight."

Lieutenant Michael said, "Copy that, we're nearby so we'll be there soon."

Lieutenant Ackley said, "Squad five is heading that way too."

Lieutenant Rachel replied, "Thanks! A pack of fully-grown Harvesters has appeared so we could use all the help that we can get."

Lieutenant Michael said, "Come on, girls! Let's jog down to junction one hundred and eight. We've got to help Squad four!"

Sarah, Jennifer, and Valerie raised their fists high in the air and shouted together, "Let's go squash some bugs!"

Together they ran down the path. Junction one hundred and eight was only one junction away. It would take them about ten minutes to get there. As they ran, Valerie said, "I hope we'll be back in time for Magical Girl Squad."

Jennifer said, "I hate to be the one to break it to you, but there's a possibility that they won't show it tonight. The disaster in Denver might cause the television schedule to be pushed back for news."

Valerie almost tripped over herself. She wailed, "What!? Say it's not true!"

Lieutenant Michael said, "Sorry, Valerie. Jennifer might be right. There might be nothing but news on tonight. We won't know till we get back."

Valerie pretended to cry and whimpered, "Why'd they have to mess with my Magical Girl Squad!"

Sarah said, "Don't worry, Valerie. If it's canceled tonight, they'll show it on either Saturday or Wednesday like normal."

Valerie said, "I know, but I wanted to see it tonight."

Lieutenant Michael interrupted them and said, "Look, girls. There's the ladder for junction one O' eight. Activate your powers and get ready to fight. I want Jennifer to go down first, then Sarah and Valerie. I'll follow Valerie. Be careful and watch out for each other."

Jennifer said, "Don't worry, Lieutenant. I'm going to make sure Giana owes me one."

Jennifer's eyes began to glow with their red light. Her fists and feet also radiated with the same red light. She grabbed onto the handle of the ladder and swung herself over. She hurriedly descended toward the ground.

Sarah's eyes and hands also began to glow with blue light. She followed Jennifer down the ladder.

Valerie activated her own power and her eyes began to glow with their yellow light. As she was about to descend, Lieutenant Michael said, "Remember, Valerie. Don't use your power unless you have too. Okay?"

Valerie saluted him and said, "Aye, Lieutenant!" She then quickly descended down the ladder. Lieutenant Michael followed behind her.

On the ground below, Lieutenant Michael assessed the situation. Lieutenant Rachel and Elsa were huddled around Tina's legs. Tina had erected a barrier and was protecting them. She had made the barrier smaller so that it would be harder to break. A group of four fully-grown Harvesters were smashing themselves against the barrier. Showers of sparks flew in all directions as the Harvesters crashed into the shield barrier.

Giana was jumping among another group of four fully-grown Harvesters. Instead of fighting them she was employing a strategy of distracting them. It was a smart strategy considering it was very unlikely that she could fight them on her own, especially now that she was in greater danger of self-destructing due to age. The Harvesters, both confused and annoyed ran around in circles as they tried to corner Giana, who simply would jump out of the way.

Lieutenant Michael pointed toward Giana and said, "Jennifer, go help Giana. If you can, work together to try to smash them when they're moving around. Don't try to hold them down; there's too many of them."

Jennifer nodded her head and said, "Aye, Lieutenant!" She then started leaping toward Giana.

Lieutenant Michael said, "Okay, Sarah. From here, use your spear of light ability to assist Jennifer and Giana."

Sarah nodded her head and said, "Okay, Lieutenant!" She brought her hands together and pointed her palms toward a Harvester. The blue light of her hands joined into one and grew brighter. A blue beam of light began to pour out of the place where her hands met. She shot out the beam of light over and over again agitating one of the Harvesters.

Valerie pulled the cattle prod gun out of the holster on her back and pulled the ammo feed lever back, allowing a bullet to be fed into the propulsion chamber. Lieutenant Michael looked at her in confusion.

Valerie noticed the look on his face. She looked up at him, smiled, and said, "Don't worry, Lieutenant. I'm not going to run out there. I'm just getting prepared in case they charge us."

Lieutenant Michael accepted this explanation and nodded his head. He returned his attention to Jennifer, who had just reached Giana's position.

Giana stood on the back of one of the Harvesters waiting for Jennifer to arrive. Jennifer leapt onto the back of the Harvester and landed in front of Giana. Giana stood there with her arms crossed, her right foot tapped on the Harvesters steel-hard shell. She scowled at Jennifer and said, "Geez ... what took you so long?!"

Jennifer said, "Don't worry, mam. I'm here to help you. I know old people like you get tired easily. If you want, you can take a little nap and I'll make it all better."

Giana squared her arms on her hips and said, "I'm only thirteen! I'm not a mam yet!" Giana pointed at the Harvesters head and said, "Stop goofing around and help me crack this nut!"

Jennifer gave her a thumbs up and said, "I'm on it!"

Together, Giana and Jennifer carefully walked up to the head. They took each other's arms in their hands for support and began to stomp on the head using their full power. Each time their feet smashed on top of its head, a shower of sparks sprayed upward. After several hits, the head split open and Harvester goo sprayed in the air, showering both Giana and Jennifer's legs and dresses with yellow goo. The Harvester shrieked a death cry and then collapsed under the weight of its dead body.

Giana shouted, "Damn it! Now I'm going to stink."

Jennifer chuckled and said, "You smelled bad already. I think it's an improvement over your old woman smell."

Giana rolled her eyes and said, "Come on! Let's grab the next one." Together, they dropped to the ground. Another Harvester charged at them. They leapt into the air and allowed the Harvester to slip underneath them. They leapt at another Harvester and landed on its back.

Giana landed perfectly on its back. Jennifer landed a little too far on the curving edge. She started to wobble and spin her arms as she tried to avoid falling over backwards onto the ground. Giana quickly reached out and grabbed her by the jacket and pulled her towards herself. As she dragged Jennifer next to herself she said, "Geez, how long do I got to keep helping all these noobs?"

Jennifer shyly chuckled and looked embarrassed. She said, "Thanks, Giana."

Together, they walked over to the head again and smashed on it till the head cracked open. More yellow Harvester goo spilled out onto the ground. The Harvester shrieked more death cries and collapsed under its dead weight.

With the second Harvester dead, the other Harvesters began to get even more agitated. The Harvester that Sarah was shooting at began to buck up and down. It spun in a circle trying to figure out what was going on. It stopped and stared right at Sarah. Its body quivered and it shrieked loudly at her. Drool spilled from its mouth as its mandibles clicked open and shut. It then charged at her.

Sarah immediately brought her hands together in front of her chest. A blue sphere of energy came out of her chest. Sarah threw her arms apart and the sphere of energy expanded, forming a protective bubble around herself, Valerie, and Lieutenant Michael. The Harvester rammed into the shield and sparks flew from the impact.

The Harvester backed up and seemed to be dazed. It had charged at her with all its might. Sarah dropped her shield and pulled her two metal sticks out of the scabbards on her belt. The blue light of her hands extended around them.

Sarah dashed forward and shoved the two sticks into the open mouth of the Harvester. She then pulled them out and backed up. She held the two sticks up in a defensive posture.

The Harvester screamed. Yellow Harvester goo began to pour out of its mouth. Valerie ran up besides Sarah. She pointed the cattle prod at the Harvester and fired half of the bullets in her clip. The face of the Harvester collapsed. Even more Harvester goo spilled onto the ground. The Harvester leaned forward and collapsed under the weight of its dead body.

Sarah and Valerie looked at each other and smiled. They both nodded their head once and gave each other a high five.

As Giana and Jennifer finished off the fourth Harvester, Squad five finally showed up. The four Harvesters that were attacking Tina's barrier finally stopped and began to shriek and focus their attention on the new comers.

Lieutenant Ackley began to issue orders and Veronica, the red Wielder of Squad five, leapt toward Giana and Jennifer. Together, the three of them began to assault the next Harvester.

Lieutenant Ackley ran up to Lieutenant Michael with the rest of her squad. May, the blue Wielder of Fifth Squad, stood next to Sarah and the two of them began to assault another Harvester. The Harvester's shell broke and it rolled over dead.

In a short time, the rest of the Harvesters were killed and the area was clear again. Tina let her barrier drop. Lieutenant Rachel and Elsa stood up. Lieutenant Rachel put her hand on Tina's shoulder and said, "Good job, holding out against all those attacks."

Tina nodded her head with a slight smile. She spoke in her melancholy tone, saying, "I didn't have much of a choice."

Lieutenant Michael ran up to Lieutenant Rachel and said, "You okay, Rachel?"

Lieutenant Rachael dusted the dirt off of her uniform pants and said, "Yeah, we're fine. Thanks for coming to our aid."

Lieutenant Michael nodded his head with a smile. He ran his hand through his hair and said, "Of course. I'll always come to help you."

Giana, who stood a little ways off behind Lieutenant Michael, wrapped her arms around herself and made kissy faces in the air. Lieutenant Rachel tilted her head and glared at Giana. Lieutenant Michael turned around and saw Giana standing there acting innocent. She held her hands together in front of the skirt of her dress. Her body twisted from side to side. She tilted her head and smiled at him, while batting her eyes. Lieutenant Michael shook his head and turned back around to face Lieutenant Rachel.

Lieutenant Michael turned to Lieutenant Ackley and said, "Did your squad check the section up to this point? Or do we need to finish checking it now?"

Lieutenant Ackley shook her head and said, "Don't worry, we checked the wall on our way here so we're good up to this point now."

Lieutenant Michael sighed in relief and said, "Great! Now we can get the hell out of here. Come on girls. Time to go back up the wall!" There were cheers from the girls and all the teams headed for the nearest ladder.

Lieutenant Rachel walked over to Lieutenant Ackley and said, "Thanks for coming to help too!"

Lieutenant Ackley said, "Of course. We're a team!"

One by one everyone climbed up the ladder and then down on the other side. There was already a military transport truck waiting for them. Squads one and two stood in front of it as they waited for the others to arrive.

When Squads three, four and five came, Lieutenant Lloyd waved his hand and said, "Alright. Everybody in the truck. You get a free ride home tonight."

They all climbed into the back of the truck and sat on the benches alongside the walls of the cargo hold. Lieutenant Michael looked at his watch and said, "It's already nineteen hundred hours. Looks like you'll make it in time to watch Magical Girl Squad, Valerie."

There were multiply cheers from girls as some of them showed their excitement. Lieutenant Michael continued, "Assuming of course it's not canceled tonight."

Valerie showed an exaggerated look of pain on her face as she was reminded of the possibility that it might not be on.

The ride back to headquarters was uneventful. The Lieutenants sent their girls upstairs as the five of them went to meet with Captain Faust. Again, they sat around his desk according to the number of their squad. Captain Faust said, "The good news is that all the top government officials were able to escape out of Denver. They have gathered in New York Sector, and, New York will be the new capital for the time being." There were sighs of relief from the Lieutenants.

Captain Faust continued, saying, "We've decided that it is inefficient to have you check the whole wall every day. Military personal will check the inside and top of the wall every day. Your teams will check the outside of the wall every day. If we do it this way, then it should only take an hour out of your time. Of course, defensive missions are your top priority. We'll just have to risk it if your teams need to deploy and you haven't checked the wall yet."

Lieutenant Lloyd asked, "Have they identified the people responsible yet?"

Captain Faust shook his head and said, "No, they still don't know who did this. No one is bragging either. I've seen reports from other sectors coming in and so far there have been no other bombs discovered. For the time being, we are lessening the state of emergency, but we are going to stay in alert standby so be ready to deploy in a moment's notice."

Sarah, Jennifer and Valerie walked into their own apartment. Sarah yawned and stretched, saying, "I'm tired and hungry."

Valerie nodded her head and said, "Yeah, me too. We missed dinner time thanks to those crazy people."

Jennifer pointed to her legs and said, "And I'm covered in Harvester goo. I want to take a quick shower. Do you girls want to jump in the bath with me?"

Valerie nodded her head and said, "Sure! That sounds like fun."

Sarah shrugged her shoulders and said, "I guess. Hopefully when we get out, the Lieutenant will have made dinner."

Valerie said, "We only got half an hour before Magical Girl Squad starts. So let's get started."

Sarah said, "Do you really think it's going to be on tonight?"

Valerie clasped her hands together and raised them to her chest as if in prayer. She looked upward and said, "I have to live by hope, otherwise, I'll end up like Tina."

Together they went into the bathroom. Sarah turned on the water to the bath tub. She began to take off her uniform and threw it into her basket. Valerie quickly stripped her uniform and threw it in her own basket. She took off her underwear and held them up, saying, "Look Jennifer, see, I got butterflies on my underwear. So it's okay if you got zoo animals on yours."

Jennifer started to blush and looked embarrassed. She brushed the yellow Harvester stains on her dress and then lifted the dress over her head, throwing it into her basket. As she stood there in her underwear, Sarah pointed at her and chuckled, saying, "Look! Zoo animals! That's just so cute!"

Jennifer rolled her eyes and said, "Yeah, yeah, get it out of your system." She took off her underwear and tossed it into her basket.

Sarah felt the water to the bath and stepped in. She hung her body over the side, hanging her arms over the rim as she stared at Jennifer and Valerie.

Valerie joined Sarah in the bath. She sat across from Sarah. Jennifer pulled the band out of her hair, put it on the counter of her sink, and walked over to one of the showers. She turned on the water and waited for it to warm up. It was the same stall that she had used when she cut her wrist too deeply.

Sarah watched her stand at the stall. Her memories from that time came back to her. She saw the blood all over the floor. She saw Jennifer lying unconscious on the floor. Sarah tried to shake the thought out of her mind.

Jennifer stepped into the water stream as it poured out of the faucet. She rinsed her legs that were splattered with Harvester goo. She turned the water off and joined Sarah and Valerie in the bathtub.

After the meeting, Lieutenant Michael stepped into the apartment and heard the water to the bath running. He said to himself, "Guess I'll make dinner while they're taking a bath." He started to search in the food cabinets and pulled out two cans of soup. He said, "It's late so I'll make something easy."

After the soup was hot he put it into four bowls and put the bowls on the table. He knew that, if Magical Girl Squad was on, they'd want to eat it in the sitting room. But, if it wasn't, they would stay at the table. He heard doors opening and closing. They'd be out soon.

Valerie came out first wearing her white and pink pajama top and bottom set. She ran out of the hallway and looked at the clock on the wall. She said, "Oh good! I still have one minute." She ran past the table and jumped onto the couch. She turned on the television and turned it to the channel that Magical Girl Squad would be on. She knelt on the couch, clasping her hands together as if she was praying.

Lieutenant Michael walked over to her and said, "Your dinner is ready, why don't you come take it. I'll let you eat it while you're watching TV."

Valerie, still focused on the television screen, said, "I'll get it in a moment, Lieutenant."

Jennifer came out next wearing her long pajama shirt that was white with emerald green sleeves. She went to the table and picked up a bowl of soup from the table. She sat down on the couch next to Valerie.

Sarah soon followed Jennifer. She wore her blue and white long pajama shirt. She went to the table and took a bowl of soup and also sat down on the other side of Valerie, who still looked like she was praying.

Suddenly the screen flashed with brilliant colors and the Magical Girl Squad theme song began to play. Valerie bounced up and down in her seat and threw her arms up, shouting, "Thank you, God! I still get to see it tonight!"

Sarah and Jennifer tilted their bowls to stop the soup from spilling out as Valerie bounced around on the couch.

Valerie jumped up and bolted for the table. She calmly picked up the soup and carefully brought it over to the couch where she was sitting before. As she walked by Lieutenant Michael, she said, "You shouldn't scare me like that, Lieutenant. I thought they might not actually show it tonight."

Lieutenant Michael shrugged his shoulders and said, "I wasn't trying to scare you. It was possible that they might not have shown it."

Valerie raised her hand from the couch and shushed him, saying, "Not while my show is playing."

Lieutenant Michael rolled his eyes and shrugged his shoulders. He sat down at the table by himself and ate his soup."

After the show ended, Lieutenant Michael grabbed the black case from the cabinet and pulled out the injector for their weekly shots. He pulled out a small vial and put it into the injector. He then took Sarah's arm, pressed the needle against her skin, and pressed the trigger. There was a small click and Sarah winced from the momentary pain. She then said, "Good night" to everyone and went into her room.

Lieutenant Michael pulled out the empty vial and inserted a new one. He brought the injector to Jennifer's arm and pulled the trigger. Again, there was a small click and Jennifer, who was slightly more resistant to the pain blinked her eye and said, "Thanks, Lieutenant. Good night!" She then got up from the couch and went into her room.

Again, he removed the empty vial and inserted a new one. Valerie held out her arm and closed her eyes. Every time he gave her the shot she kept her eyes closed. He pressed the point against her skin and pulled the trigger. There was a small click and Valerie winced from the pain. She opened her eyes and rubbed the spot on her arm. She jumped up from the couch. Smiled at him and said, "Good night, Lieutenant!" She left and went into her room.

Lieutenant Michael put the injector back into the case and closed it. He put it back into the cabinet and sighed. He was still wearing his dirty uniform. He went into his room, took off his clothing and got into the shower before going to bed.

- 3 -

Valerie stood in between Sarah and Lieutenant Michael in the ruins of an old city. Jennifer stood in front of them looking outward. They stood in the middle of what used to be an intersection of a major street. Dead and ruined cars littered the streets. In addition to the dead cars, the ruins of old sky scrapers surrounded them. Many old windows were cracked or smashed entirely. The outside shell of the buildings were rotting off of their structure's frames. The sound of large claws stampeding over the cracked pavement echoed throughout the ruins. Shrieks of Harvesters soon joined the echoes.

Valerie said, "Don't worry, we can do it if we work together!"

Sarah nodded her head and said, "Yeah, if we work together, we can overcome anything!"

Jennifer nodded with a smile and held out her hand. Sarah put her hand on top of Jennifer's hand. Valerie put her hand on top of Sarah's hand.

Suddenly there was a whizzing sound and Valerie and Jennifer turned around. In the distance a large Archer-class Harvester shot a barrage of thorns in their direction. A second later there was the sound of broken glass. Sarah gasped.

Valerie turned around and saw that a large thorn was protruding out of Sarah's stomach. A trickle of blood seeped out of her mouth. She wrapped her hands around the thorn and fell over on her side.

Lieutenant Michael shouted, "We're surrounded!"

Valerie looked around and fully-grown Harvesters filled the streets in every direction. They were completely cut off. The Harvesters screamed as they stood there twitching their mandibles at them.

Jennifer's face morphed into Mary's face. Jennifer's wavy dark brown hair changed into Mary's straight black hair with twin tails. Mary said, "Don't worry, I'll stop them. You take care of Sarah, Valerie." Mary leapt toward a group of Harvesters.

One of the Harvesters caught hold of Mary in its mandibles. Two Harvesters began to play tug-of-war with Mary. She screamed. Her voice echoed in Valerie's ears, "Valerie, they're killing me! Help me!" Her screams were cut off as her mid-section split open and her innards fell onto the street below.

Valerie began to panic. Her heart beat faster and she began to breathe heavily. She looked over to Sarah who was still lying on the street as if she were dead. She looked to her other side to find Lieutenant Michael, but he was not there. She looked from side to side and could see Lieutenant Michael nowhere.

Valerie stood there next to Sarah. The Harvesters began to charge towards her. With nowhere to run, Valerie dropped to her knees and shut her eyes. She began to chant over and over again, "It's not real! It's not real! It's not real!"

Valerie woke up with a shock. She flung the blankets off of herself and rolled out of bed, landing on the floor with a thud. Her heart was still beating fast. Her breathing was still labored. Her pajamas were soaked in sweat. After a moment she began to calm down. She got on her hands and knees and then stood up. She moved through the darkness to the light switch by her door.

Valerie sat down on her bed and wiped her eyes. Tears had apparently slipped out as she was having her nightmare. She looked towards her alarm clock and saw that it was only two-thirty in the morning.

Valerie looked towards her pillow and grabbed the butterfly shaped pillow beside it. She held it close to her chest and hugged it tightly. "What a horrible dream," she said to herself.

Still hugging her butterfly pillow, she stood up and shuffled to the door. She turned off the light and opened her door. She quietly made her way to Lieutenant Michael's room. She gently opened the door and silently shuffled over to his bed. She carefully crawled onto it and slid under the blanket. As she slid under the blanket, Lieutenant Michael rolled over in his sleep. She shut her eyes and quickly went back to sleep.

The alarm went off at six-thirty and Lieutenant Michael rolled over. He turned off the alarm. He tossed the covers off of himself and sat up on the edge of his bed. He shook his head and yawned. He rubbed his eyes and then stood up.

A small cheery voice came from behind him, saying, "Good morning, Lieutenant!"

Surprised, Lieutenant Michael turned around to see Valerie sitting on his bed, holding her butterfly pillow. She smiled up at him.

Lieutenant Michael ran his hand through his hair and said, "Wow, Valerie, you're getting better at sneaking into my room, aren't you? I didn't feel you at all. Did you have another nightmare?"

Valerie clung to her butterfly pillow and nodded her head. Her smile faded away into gloominess. She said, "Yeah, I had a really, really bad dream. I was really scared."

Lieutenant Michael stepped towards the bed and reached his hand out to her. He rubbed the top of her head and said, "Do you want to talk about it?"

Valerie shook her head and said, "That's okay. I was just dreaming about what happened in Los Angeles. I'm over it now."

Lieutenant Michael nodded his head and said, "I understand. Go ahead and get ready for today, we've got a very busy day today."

Valerie nodded her head and said, "Okay, Lieutenant." She scooted over to the edge of the bed and slid off the side. Her small feet quickly moved across the floor as she lightly ran out of his room.

Lieutenant Michael walked over to the open door and closed it. He locked the door and began to change out of his sleepwear.

Valerie ran into her room and put her butterfly pillow on her bed. She then took off her pajamas and placed them on her bed. She reached into her closet and grabbed a uniform that was hanging from a hanger. She slid the dress over her head and pulled it down over her body. She took her yellow tie and slipped it over her head. She tightened it around her neck.

Valerie then pulled out a pair of socks from her dresser drawer and pulled them up to her knees. She put on her boots and tied them one by one. She reached for her dress jacket and put it on, buttoning the black buttons.

As she left her room, Jennifer was leaving her room too. Valerie saw her first and said, "Good Morning, Jennifer!"

Jennifer, still a little sluggish, said, "Good morning, Valerie."

Together, they went into the bathroom. Sarah was already standing at her sink, brushing her hair. When the door opened, Sarah turned and said, "Good morning, girls."

Valerie and Jennifer both said, "Good morning!" at the same time.

Valerie and Jennifer both walked up to their own mirrors and began to brush their hair too. Sarah took Mary's old hair band and put her hair into a pony tail. Sarah said, "I hope we don't have to fight today. I really don't feel up to it."

Valerie brushed her hair as she said, "Well, we have to check the outside of the wall everyday now. We'll probably run into some more Harvesters like Fourth squad did yesterday. The more we go out there, the more likely there are to be more Harvesters."

Jennifer, still brushing her hair, said, "I don't mind it. I want to kill every single Harvester there is."

Sarah, staring at her own reflection in the mirror, said, "That's the right attitude, but I've been doing this for so long and I'm starting to get tired of it." Her eye drifted to Jennifer's right wrist as she saw the scars on her wrist again.

Valerie took a cheap hair clip and pulled the hair on the right side of her head over her ear and clipped it up. She glanced at the butterfly clip that sat lonely in her drawer. She sighed and shut the drawer.

Jennifer turned to Valerie and said, "What's wrong, Valerie?"

Valerie sighed again and looked in the mirror at her reflection saying, "Oh, I just miss wearing my butterfly clip that my dad got me."

Jennifer said, "Why don't you wear it then?"

Valerie said, "If we're going into combat, I don't want to lose it in the field."

Jennifer separated the hair on her temples and pulled them behind her head. She took a hair band and tied the hair on the sides of her temples behind her head. She said, "Yeah, I can see that. If I had anything special like that, I wouldn't want to lose it either."

Valerie said, "That's the second lesson that I learned from Mary and Sarah when I first came here."

Jennifer said, "What was the first thing?"

Valerie looked at Sarah and smiled, she said, "The first thing they taught me was that it's okay to be scared. I was really scared at first and knowing that helped me a lot."

Valerie scooted herself towards Sarah and wrapped her arms around her. Sarah embraced her back and said, "That was the first lesson Mary and Susan taught me too."

Jennifer said, "I wish I could have gotten to know Mary. From your stories, she sounds like a fun person to be with."

Valerie smiled at her. She took Jennifer's hands into her own hands and said, "She was. I wish I could have gotten to know Annie and Julie too."

Jennifer nodded her head and said, "I know they would have really liked you too."

Sarah said, "We all lose so many of our friends in this war. We're going to keep on losing our friends till we win it."

Valerie turned to Sarah and said, "Do you really believe we can win the war?"

Sarah nodded her head and said, "We got to win or else losing all our friends in the war will mean nothing."

Sarah rested her hands on the countertop and leaned forward. She said, "I can't let myself believe we won't win. We will win. Mary's sacrifice will be worth it when we win."

Jennifer said, "Yes, we're going to win. This is our world after all. We've been here for a really long time. I'll make sure that Annie and Julie's deaths won't be for nothing too."

Sarah said, "I'm sorry, I didn't mean to sound so depressing. I'm sure the Lieutenant is starting to wonder why we're taking so long. Let's get ready for breakfast!"

Sarah put on a forced smile and raised her fist high into the air. Valerie and Jennifer nodded. They followed her out of the door and down the hall.

Lieutenant Michael was already in the kitchen, wearing his wine colored apron. He was mixing something in a mixing bowl. Sarah, Jennifer, and Valerie came into the opening of the kitchen.

Sarah said, "Good morning, Lieutenant. Do you want any help making breakfast?"

Lieutenant Michael smiled and said, "Sure, you girls can help if you want to. I'm making pancakes now."

Valerie grinned and started to jump for joy. She clapped her hands and said, "Yay! I love pancakes!"

Valerie started to spin in a circle as she chanted, "Pancakes! Pancakes!"

Jennifer smiled and said, "It's been a while since we had pancakes."

Sarah walked over to the stove and said, "I want to flip them."

Lieutenant Michael nodded his head and said, "Sure, Sarah. That's fine." He then turned to look straight at Valerie and said, "Valerie, why don't you crack open those eggs and mix them for us."

Valerie stopped spinning and nodded her head with a grin, saying, "Okay, I'll do it, Lieutenant!" She walked to the back of the kitchen and picked up her stepping stool. She brought it over to the counter where Lieutenant Michael had put the eggs and an empty bowl. She scooted the stool up to the edge and stepped up on top of it.

Jennifer stood in the doorway waiting for her assignment. As Lieutenant Michael continued to stir the pancake batter, she started to become a little anxious. She grabbed onto her right arm, tilted her head, and started to twist her body a little from side to side. She said, "Is there anything that I can do, Lieutenant?"

Lieutenant Michael looked up and said, "After Valerie is done getting the eggs ready, you can cook them. Okay?"

Jennifer's mood perked up. She let go of her arm and nodded with a grin. She said, "Okay, Lieutenant." She walked over to the stove and waited at the free heating coil next to Sarah.

Valerie stood on top of her stool and counted the eggs. As she counted each egg, she placed a finger on each one and counted its number out loud. She said, "Four eggs to a container. Lieutenant? Why do they only sell eggs in containers of four? Don't you think it would be better if they sold like eight eggs in one container?"

Lieutenant Michael handed the stirred batter to Sarah, who began pouring it into circles. He said, "Well, most people can only afford a little bit of eggs. This four pack carton of eggs costs sixteen dollars. We're lucky that we're in the Spirit Wielders since the government pays for our food we can get whatever we want without worrying about how much it costs."

Valerie's mouth dropped and her eyes went wide. She started counting on her fingers and she said, "Sixteen dollars! That's like four dollars an egg!"

Sarah flipped the pancakes in her pan and said, "Yeah. We're really lucky that we can get whatever we want."

Jennifer said, "Most of the food at my parent's house was rice and beans."

Lieutenant Michael said, "Yeah, that's the type of food that people with low incomes eat. It's much cheaper."

Valerie said, "Lieutenant, how come food is so expensive?"

Lieutenant Michael paused and looked to be deep in thought. He said, "It's because of two reasons. The first reason is a thing called scarcity. Do you know what scarcity is?"

Valerie looked confused and shook her head.

He continued, "Scarcity means that you don't have enough of something. When you don't have enough, the price goes up because that item becomes more valuable. The other reason is that the World Government has official prices for everything. They are the ones controlling all the resources so they are the ones that get to say what everything costs."

Valerie nodded with a smile and said, "I think I get it, Lieutenant!"

Lieutenant Michael smiled and rubbed her on top of the head. He said, "Go ahead and get those eggs ready. Jennifer is waiting for you."

Jennifer stood there with her arms folded across her chest and waited impatiently, saying, "Yeah, Valerie. Hurry up! I'm getting hungry."

Valerie picked up the first egg and said, "I'm sorry. I'll do it right now." She cracked the first egg and dropped it into the bowl. She took the second egg and cracked it. A small piece of the shell fell into the bowl as she did so. She said, "Oops" and began to dig around the egg whites to retrieve it. She then continued cracking the last two eggs into the bowl. Valerie stirred the bowl and started to sing the Magical Girl Squad theme song again.

Jennifer said, "You really like that song don't you, Valerie."

Valerie said, "Yep! I love everything about Magical Girl Squad. Plus, that song gives me hope."

Sarah asked, "Valerie, how does that song give you hope."

Valerie said, "Because ... because it makes me feel like I am one of the magical girls. Don't you think that we're like them?" She handed the bowl of mixed eggs to Jennifer. She hopped off of the stool and pushed it towards Jennifer with her foot. Jennifer took it and stood on top of the stool as she prepped the pan to make eggs.

Sarah shrugged her shoulders and said, "I guess I can see that."

Jennifer said, "I like Magical Girl Squad a lot. But, I think Lost Sword Saga is even better."

Valerie started to become defensive and said, "Why would you think Lost Sword Saga is better than Magical Girl Squad? It doesn't have magical girls."

Jennifer started to blush and acted shyly. She glanced towards Sarah and then glanced towards Lieutenant Michael. She looked toward the ground and said, "That's just the way I think. Why ... why does it matter to you so much?"

Sarah began to chuckle and said, "Is it because that boy Elric runs around in a loin cloth and without wearing a shirt?"

Jennifer's face turned beet red as she blushed heavily. She pouted her lips in embarrassment. She said nothing as she stared straight into the pan of eggs she was cooking.

Sarah put the last of the pancakes she cooked onto the platter and said, "I'm right, aren't I? Yes, he is cute."

Lieutenant Michael leaned his head over so he could better see Jennifer's face. She looked really embarrassed. He smiled and chuckled, saying, "Wow, Jennifer. So you're already starting to notice boys now, eh?"

Jennifer shook her head vigorously and said, "That's not why! I ... I just like the story better!"

Sarah smiled mischievously and said, "Yeah, the 'story' is pretty good." She made imaginary quotation marks with her fingers as she said 'story'. Sarah giggled at her.

Lieutenant Michael put a hand on Sarah and Jennifer's shoulder and said, "Okay, that's enough teasing. We have a busy day today. After breakfast, we'll do the dishes and then do our daily exercises. After that's done, we'll meet with everybody at the wall and check the outside perimeter."

Sarah groaned in exaggeration. She slumped forward and let her arms droop, saying, "We got to do it again?"

Lieutenant Michael put his hand on top of her head and said, "Yep, we have to do it every day now thanks to those terrorists. After we check our section of the wall, we'll do some grocery shopping."

Valerie brought her hands together and held them up underneath her chin as if in prayer. She looked up at Lieutenant Michael with hope in her eyes. She said, "Can we make pizza tonight for dinner?"

Lieutenant Michael patted her on the head and said, "I'll think about it."

Valerie tilted her head and looked up at him. She silently begged him with her face. She batted her eyes at him.

Lieutenant Michael said, "I said I'll think about it. Why don't you girls set the table now? Okay?"

The three of them began to set the table. Lieutenant Michael put the platter of pancakes and the bowl of eggs on the table. After the girls finished setting the table, Valerie approached Lieutenant Michael again. She clutched onto the sleeve of his jacket. She looked up at him with shaky eyes and a quivering lower lip. She cautiously said, "Lieutenant ..."

Lieutenant Michael looked down at her face and rolled his eyes, saying, "What is it now, Valerie?"

Valerie, still clutching onto his jacket said, "Lieutenant, did you think about it yet?"

Lieutenant Michael said, "Valerie, are you going to be doing this all day?"

Valerie strategically smiled. She gently twisted her body side to side and said, "That depends on how you answer my question."

Lieutenant Michael, defeated, sighed and said, "Do the rest of you girls want pizza tonight too?"

Sarah nodded her head with a smile and said, "Of course! What, are you new?"

Jennifer looked toward him out of the corner of her eye. She became subdued and lowered her head a little. She shyly said, "I wouldn't mind pizza."

Lieutenant Michael looked down towards Valerie and said, "Okay, Valerie. You win. If they have the stuff at the store than we'll make pizza for dinner tonight."

Valerie smiled in celebration and excitedly said, "Yay!   Thanks, Lieutenant!"

Lieutenant Michael pulled his chair out and plopped himself down in it. Valerie scooted out her own chair and sat down. She brought her palms together, lowered her head and closed her eyes in silent prayer.

Time passed quickly as they completed their assigned duties. There was only a little Harvester resistance outside the wall this time. The girls easily destroyed them without assistance.

After checking the wall, they returned to their apartment. They all took a quick shower to rinse off the dirt and sweat of today's mission. They got dressed in a new uniform and headed back out to the local store.

As they walked to the store, Sarah walked beside Lieutenant Michael. Valerie and Jennifer walked behind them. In the past Mary used to walk beside him and now Sarah was taking that role from her. He felt a small twinge of pain in his heart as he thought about Mary again. He pushed the feeling deep inside of himself.

As they walked, Sarah noticed that the people around them seemed different today. It was hard for her to fully understand it but there was a lot of tension in the air.

Lieutenant Michael noticed it too. He also saw the look of concern on Sarah's face. He said, "Looks like everyone is nervous about what happened yesterday."

Sarah nodded and said, "Yeah. It's really scary that there are people who want to blow up the walls."

A crowd had gathered around the store. The World Police Force in full gear helped to keep the crowd under control. There was a line for people who wanted to get inside the store.

Lieutenant Michael walked up to one of the officers of the World Police Force and said, "Is there any trouble here?"

The police officer shook his head and said, "Not yet, but there is another food shortage and on top of that they raised the prices again. We've got orders to help keep things calm here."

Lieutenant Michael said, "Does that mean we got to wait in line to get in?"

The police officer shook his head and said, "No, since you are in the Spirit Wielder Corps, you can bypass the crowd and just go straight in."

Lieutenant Michael nodded with a smile, saying, "Thanks, officer!"

The police officer lifted up a rope and allowed them in ahead of the line. As they went under the rope there were several cries of dissatisfaction from the crowd. A man shouted out, "Oh come on! I've been waiting in line for two hours!"

Another voice shouted out, "This is bug shit! They get to do whatever they want just because they fight Harvesters!"

Lieutenant Michael and the girls ignored the shouts of displeasure and walked into the store. There were several more police officers inside nearby the checkout stands. Valerie said, "Why are the people so angry at us."

Lieutenant Michael said, "They're not really angry at us. They're just frustrated because of the situation. They got to wait in line for a while and food prices just went up again. That's going to make it even harder to get the food they want."

They began to look around the nearby shelves and saw that there were hardly any products on the shelves left. Lieutenant Michael said, "It looks like the store is almost sold out of stuff. This means the World Government will be forced to distribute rations again soon."

Together, they began to look for the stuff that they would need to make a pizza, in addition to other supplies they needed. They walked into the baking section and looked for flour. There were two bags left on the shelf. Lieutenant Michael took one and looked at the price. It had gone up four times the amount from last week.

Lieutenant Michael stuck the bag of flour in his bag and said, "Geez. This price hike is ridiculous. We're lucky that we don't have to worry about it. But, I feel bad for the ordinary citizens. Looks like most people will be eating beans and rice again for a while."

Sarah shook her head and said, "Why do they make the prices so high, Lieutenant?"

Lieutenant Michael shrugged his shoulders and said, "It's probably because of scarcity. Also, yesterday's terrorist attack probably has the World Government all worried so they're probably trying to stockpile supplies. They know what's best though so we need to trust them. If they are stockpiling than that means something worse might be coming."

Next, they went to the pasta section. There was one last can of pizza sauce on the counter. He quickly snatched it up and stuck it in the bag. Again, the price of it was four times as much as last week.

They went to get mushrooms and olives next, but they were out of them. They were also out of cheese. They did manage to find some imitation pepperoni. They also took the last of the imitation milk and the last of the oatmeal.

With only half of the items they wanted, they went up to the checkout stand. As they checked out their items, they heard a voice through a megaphone outside, saying, "Attention. This store is now considered closed for the time being. Please disperse. Tomorrow morning, World Government Ration Stations will be set up in your designated area. Please disperse. This store is now closed."

Lieutenant Michael gave a sigh of relief and said, "We're lucky! Looks like we made it just in time."

As they left the store there was still a great commotion among the crowds of people. Some people were shouting at the police officers. Others were shouting, "Boo!" as well as some obscenities.

Lieutenant Michael and the girls started to walk through the crowds. Lieutenant Michael said, "I want you girls to stay extra close to me as we go home."

A man walked up to Lieutenant Michael and said, "It must be nice to be on the public payroll. You guys can get whatever the hell you want and we just pay for it." Lieutenant Michael ignored him and walked around him. The man followed them.

Another person, a woman, began to shout at them, saying, "When are you Spirit Wielders going to stop the Harvesters! You've had ten years and all I see is a whole lot of nothing!"

A crowd of people started to focus their attention on them. They began to gather around them. Another person shouted, "Yeah, when are you girls going to stop the Harvesters. If you stop them then we wouldn't have to live behind these damn walls!"

Valerie said, "Lieutenant, what's going on."

Lieutenant Michael said, "Don't worry. Just keep moving."

The crowd started to become thicker around them. Another person shouted, saying, "Thanks to you cutting in line, I wasn't able to get the food I need today!" More and more people started to shout so that their voices drowned each other out.

Sarah said, "Lieutenant, should we activate our powers?"

Lieutenant Michael shook his head and said, "No, we can't use those powers on people. We don't want them to get hurt."

Valerie said, "I'm getting scared, Lieutenant!"

A rock came hurling through the air. It struck Valerie on the side of her head. Valerie cried out in pain and a splash of blood sprayed out of the side of her head, showering Sarah, Jennifer, and Lieutenant Michael with her blood. Valerie grabbed the side of her head and fell down to her knees, crying out in pain.

Immediately, without hesitation, Sarah's eyes glowed blue. Her hands radiated with blue light. She brought her hands together and then threw them apart, causing a shield to expand around them. It pushed those who were too close away.

Instinctively, Jennifer activated her own power. Her eyes glowed with their red light. Lieutenant Michael dropped down to his knees, saying, "You'll be okay, Valerie. Activate your power and heal yourself."

Valerie, still sobbing from fear and pain, activated her own power. Her eyes glowed yellow and the wound on the side of her head began to quickly close. Even though the wound was gone, Valerie continued to cry. Blood stained her hair and her jacket. She said, "Why would they throw a rock at me?"

As she spoke, there was a sudden ringing of gunfire from the police officers. The crowd began to scream and run. People trampled each other to get away. A bullet hit a woman in the head in front of Squad three. She fell over dead instantly. Pieces of her skull were scattered on the ground and blood poured out of the wound.

Another man was shot in the back as he tried to flee. The bullet went right through his heart. He too, dropped dead instantly on the pavement.

Valerie, still crying, buried her face into Lieutenant Michael's chest. Jennifer clutched onto his shoulder and shut her eyes at the carnage. She leaned forward and buried her face into his shoulder. Lieutenant Michael wrapped an arm around Jennifer and held her too. Sarah stood there with her arms extended, maintaining the barrier. She watched the carnage unfold.

Several bullets ricocheted off of the barrier. There was another volley of gunfire and more people dropped to the ground. Some of them died instantly. Others were just injured.

Lieutenant Michael watched and waited till it was over. He continued to hold Valerie and Jennifer. A police officer walked over to them and said, "It's okay now Wielders. You don't have to worry anymore. You're safe now."

Lieutenant Michael nodded and said, "Okay, Sarah, let the barrier down." Sarah nodded and dropped her hands. The barrier shrunk back inside of her.

Lieutenant Michael pulled Valerie off of his chest. Jennifer stood up on her own. He said, "Valerie, I know you're scared, but there are people injured here so you've got to save them. Okay?" Valerie nodded her head in silence. He took her hand and began to observe the people around them.

Together, they walked past the first woman. They all saw the dead stare in her eyes that looked into nothingness. Several other men nearby were already dead with multiple bullet holes in their chests.

The next man was still breathing. Valerie let her hands radiate with yellow light. She put her hands on the man and the bullet wound closed up. He woke up and stared up at them. Before he could say anything, two police officers grabbed him, and flung him over. They cuffed his hands behind his back with plastic ties.

The next person was a woman. She was dead. She had died using her body as a shield to protect her young daughter, who appeared to be around six years old. The child was crying underneath her dead mother. They rolled the woman off of the child and checked her for injuries. The police took the child to see if there were any surviving family members to care for her.

They found another woman who was gasping for breath on the ground. A bullet had pierced her shoulder. Valerie healed her too. She was also arrested and dragged away by the police after being healed. The rest of the people appeared to be dead so there was no one else to save. Another team of police carried away the dead bodies for disposal.

Sarah, Jennifer, and Valerie looked around the area where they stood. Pools of blood stained the pavement in the places where dead bodies once lay. Valerie started to tremble again. She placed her hand over the spot on her head where the rock had hit her. She felt the wet blood that matted her hair.

Lieutenant Michael saw her in the corner of his eye. He turned to look at her. He placed his hand on her shoulder and gently squeezed it. Valerie started to cry again. She said, "Why ... I ... why did this have to happen? Why did they hit me with a rock? I didn't do anything to them."

Sarah, who was standing next to her, also put her hand on Valerie's other shoulder. Jennifer put her hand on Valerie's back. Lieutenant Michael said, "When people get together sometimes it's like a morality switch gets shut off. These people were angry and frustrated because of the food rationing and they decided to take it out on us."

Valerie, still crying, said, "They were bad ... but ... but ... they didn't deserve to die like this. I've never seen people killing other people before."

Jennifer said, "I've never seen people killing other people before either."

Lieutenant Michael said, "These things sometimes happen. It's horrible but that's just the way the government deals with situations like this. Let's get back home before something else happens."

Valerie looked up at Lieutenant Michael. She wiped the tears from her eyes and said, "Lieutenant, can I hold your hand?"

Lieutenant Michael nodded and held out his hand with a smile. She took his hand. Lieutenant Michael turned his face towards Jennifer and held out his hand to her, saying, "Do you want to hold my hand too?"

Jennifer stared at his hand. She hesitated for a moment but then took it. She looked away from him and her cheeks started to blush a little. She said, "O ... okay."

Lieutenant Michael felt Jennifer's hand tremble a little in the palm of his hand. She handled the incident better than Valerie but it still shook her up. What the police did was understandable from their perspective, but it was definitely overkill. It was probably an overreaction caused by the shadow of the terrorist that was still fresh in everyone's mind. The government is on edge and the citizens are stuck in between the government and the Harvesters.

They started to walk home. Jennifer and Valerie held onto Lieutenant Michael's hands. Sarah walked behind them holding the grocery bag. She held the bag with both of her hands in front of the skirt of her dress. Her face looked down toward the pavement. She saw the splatters of Valerie's blood that stained the arm of her jacket. A large splatter of blood streaked across Jennifer's jacket. Patches of blood stained Valerie's shoulder below the place where she was hit with a rock. Small specks of blood tarnished one of the legs of Lieutenant Michael's pants. His jacket was smeared with blood where Valerie had put her head.

Sarah started to feel her eyes burn. She wanted to cry like Valerie had done. The image of the dead stare of the first woman was burned into her mind. The splatters of brain matter and splintered bone spread out on the pavement. She held herself back. She looked over at Jennifer. The scars were still visible on her wrist. She started to remember all the blood on the bathroom floor. She remembered Jennifer sprawled on the floor. The dead eyes of the victims flashed into her mind again. Those dead eyes that stared into nothingness. Eyes void of light.

Sarah started to feel nauseous and weak. She stopped walking and dropped the grocery bag. Lieutenant Michael stopped and turned his head around to see what happened. He said, "Sarah, what's wrong?"

Sarah dropped to her knees and propped herself up with her arms. The ground below her started to spin. She started to gag. She lurched forward and began to vomit. Lieutenant Michael let go of Valerie's and Jennifer's hands and knelt down beside her. He put his hand on her back and began to rub it as she finished throwing up. She sucked on her tongue and spat out the taste of bile in her mouth. She sat up and said, "I don't feel so good."

Lieutenant Michael said, "Can you walk or do I need to carry you on my back?"

Sarah pouted her lips and looked up at him, saying, "Can I please ride on your back?"

Lieutenant Michael sighed and said, "I guess so, but you're getting big now." He turned around and allowed Sarah to crawl onto his back. When she was firmly planted, he stood up. Both Valerie and Jennifer took hold of one of his arms. Sarah held him tightly and rested her head on his shoulder. Jennifer picked up the bag of groceries and slung it over her shoulder. They walked like this the rest of the way home.

Lieutenant Michael let go of the girls' hands and then squatted down on the ground. Sarah slid off of his back. He stood back up and asked, "How are you feeling? Do you need to see Doctor Lovecraft?"

Sarah slowly shook her head. She looked down to the ground and said, "I feel much better now. Seeing all those people getting killed made me a little dizzy, I guess."

Lieutenant Michael nodded and said, "Yeah. We're not used to seeing people kill each other now, are we?"

Sarah shook her head again and said, "No. I hope we never get used to seeing people kill each other. I'm still not used to Harvesters killing people."

Valerie said, "I feel like this is all my fault because I wanted pizza tonight."

Jennifer shook her head and said, "No. It's not your fault. We were planning on going to the store before you asked for pizza."

Valerie thought for a moment. She glanced upward, tilted her head, and brought her right index finger to her lips. She said, "Yeah. Guess I forgot about that."

Lieutenant Michael opened the door to the Phoenix Guard complex and let the girls walk in first. Together they walked up the stairs. Their feet clanged against the metal steps. As they were walking up, Lieutenant Rachel and her team were walking down.

Lieutenant Rachel stopped in her tracks causing Giana to ram into her from behind. Elsa crashed into Giana, and Tina, who was always slower, gracefully stopped. Giana shouted, "Hey! Why'd you have to stop like that?" She leaned to the side to see what was going on. She saw Squad three. She then noticed all the blood on their uniforms.

Lieutenant Rachel said, "What the hell happened to you? I didn't know you were on a mission this afternoon."

Lieutenant Michael shook his head with a frown. He said, "We weren't on a mission. We were in the middle of a small food riot."

Elsa looked past Giana and said, "Whose blood is that on your uniforms?"

Valerie said, "It's mine. Someone threw a rock at me and it hit me in the head."

Tina spoke in her melancholy tone, saying, "Humans are not much different from Harvesters. Except the Harvesters are mindless brutes and humans are just brutes."

Lieutenant Rachel said, "Are you okay?"

Valerie said, "Yeah. I just healed myself but there was a lot of blood."

Lieutenant Michael said, "Yeah. Head wounds tend to bleed a lot. But everyone's okay. If you were planning on going to the store right now, don't bother. It's closed due to rationing."

Lieutenant Rachel sighed. She slumped her shoulders forward and drooped her arms, saying, "Great. Guess it's time for rice, beans, and field rations."

Lieutenant Rachel turned around and waved her hands upward, saying, "Alright, everyone. Back upstairs. We're having beans and rice tonight."

Giana sighed loudly and said angrily, "Geez … they certainly chose the perfect time to go to rations! I hate rice!"

Elsa said, "Well, at least we got food."

Jennifer said, "With some salsa, beans and rice taste really good."

Sarah said, "But we don't got any salsa."

Valerie said, "We got an old bottle of hot sauce."

Giana rolled her eyes and said, "No thanks. You can keep it."

Together, they walked back up the stairs and went into their apartments. Lieutenant Michael shut the door behind them and said, "You girls can take a shower and change into new uniforms. Make sure you put your spoiled uniforms in your basket."

The girls collectively said in a bored tone, "Okay."

They went into the bathroom to put their dirty clothes away. Lieutenant Michael stared at the small blood splatters on his pants and the smeared blood on his jacket. He shook his head and went into his own room to change into a new uniform.

- 4 -

Lieutenant Michael took what ingredients he had managed to get at the store and started to make what could be called a ration pizza. It would be nothing but dough, pizza sauce, and imitation pepperoni. He quickly assembled the dough, using the last of his yeast. He turned on the oven and let the dough sit on top of the stove to rise.

Valerie and Jennifer were watching the television. Sarah sat at the table by herself. Her arms were crossed and rested on the table top. Her head was buried in her arms.

Lieutenant Michael saw her sitting there, looking depressed. He took off his wine colored apron and gently tossed it on the counter. He walked over to her and began to run his hand over the back of her head. He said, "Are you okay Sarah?"

Sarah, not looking up, said, "People shouldn't kill other people."

Lieutenant Michael stopped stroking her head. He rested his hand on her shoulder and said, "Are you still worried about what happened earlier?"

Sarah sat up and stared into his face. Her eyes were moist as if she had been crying. She said, "It's bad enough that the Harvesters are trying to kill us, but people definitely shouldn't be killing each other. What's going to happen to that little girl who was shielded by her dead mom? I wish I could have protected her too."

Lieutenant Michael gently squeezed her shoulder and said, "You're right. People shouldn't kill people. If things were right, people would never have to kill people. But, all throughout our history, people have always made excuses to kill people. If it wasn't for the Hour of Despair and the Harvesters, we would probably still be at war with other people."

Sarah said sternly, "I'll never use my power to kill a person!"

Lieutenant Michael nodded with a smile and said, "Of course. I'd never ask you to kill someone. I know it's hard not to worry, but try not to think about what happened earlier."

Sarah nodded her head and looked down at the table top. She said, "Okay, Lieutenant. I'll try not to think about it. I hope I never have to see it again."

Lieutenant Michael patted her head and said, "If you need to talk about it some more, I'll be there for you. Okay?"

Sarah looked back up at him and tried to force a smile on her face. He started to turn and Sarah spoke up again, saying, "Lieutenant, if I didn't have to fight Harvesters, I think I'd like to be a chef so I could make all the yummy food I want for people."

Lieutenant Michael turned his head with a smile, saying, "Yeah, I'd bet you'd make a great chef. If you want, you can help me finish making this ration pizza."

Sarah smiled for real and slid her chair out, saying, "Sure, I'll help. But, we only got the crust, pizza sauce, and pepperoni."

Lieutenant Michael chuckled and said, "Well, that's why I called it a ration pizza because it's made with what rations we got left."

Together, they went into the kitchen. Lieutenant Michael lifted the towel that covered the bowl of rising pizza dough. "It's ready," he said.

As set the towel on the counter, a woman's voice came over the intercom system, saying, "Lieutenant Snyder, Third squad. Report to C.O.'s office." The voice repeated herself once more and then shut off.

Lieutenant Michael sighed and said, "Now what?" He put his hand on Sarah's shoulder and said, "Go ahead and make the pizza and put it in the oven. I'll come back as soon as I can."

Sarah saluted him with a huge grin, saying, "Aye, Lieutenant! Try not to take so long or else we'll eat it without you."

Lieutenant Michael pointed at her and said, "At least try to save me one piece."

She smiled mischievously and said, "I can't guarantee the safety of your dinner ..." She became somber again and said, "... so try to come back soon."

Lieutenant Michael heard the worry in her voice. He said, "It shouldn't take too long. It's probably about what happened at the store today." He walked out of the kitchen.

Valerie and Jennifer ran up to him. Valerie said, "Why did they call you, Lieutenant?" Is it because people hit me with a rock?"

Lieutenant Michael said, "I'm not sure, but it's probably related to that. Don't worry. I'll be back as soon as possible. Just keep enjoying your shows. Sarah is keeping an eye on dinner." He turned and walked out of the door and into the hallway that led to the stairs. They stood there watching him leave with concern on their faces.

Lieutenant Michael jogged down the hallway and down the stairs too. He stopped when he came to the first floor to quickly catch his breath. He brushed his uniform to clear any flour that had accidently dusted onto him through his apron. He opened the door and went into the foyer area.

The Captain's office was the first room on his left. He walked through the foyer and opened the door to the Captain's office. He walked past the secretary's desk. She smiled and nodded at him. He smiled back at her as he walked past her desk. He knocked on the Captain's door and a man's voice spoke through it, saying, "Come in, Lieutenant."

Lieutenant Michael opened the door and stepped in. Captain Faust sat at his desk. To his surprise there was another man, who had his back turned to him. The man wore a long black trench coat. It was the common uniform style worn among the Intelligence Division of the military. The man held his black-gloved hands behind his back. His hair was reddish-brown and was slicked back with gel to keep it in place. The man had a familiar air to him.

With sudden realization, Lieutenant Michael's eyes went wide. His jaw dropped and he said, "Jo ... Josh? Is that you?"

The man turned around dramatically with a stern gaze on his face. The sternness quickly disappeared and was replaced with a big grin. They quickly walked up to each other and wrapped their arms around each other in a large embrace. The man said, "It is good to see you Michael."

They let each other go and Lieutenant Michael, still in shock, said, "Josh. Wow, this was the last thing that I would have expected today."

Captain Faust cleared his throat. Lieutenant Michael remembered his station and saluted him, saying, "Sorry, Captain. Josh and I go a long way back."

Captain Faust said, "So I've heard. Josh, or rather, Major Josh O'Brian, is actually here to make a request of you, Lieutenant Snyder. Of course, this is not an order. You are free to turn it down if you wish."

Josh interrupted him and said, "I will take it from here, Captain Faust. Yes, Lieutenant Snyder. I have come here in my official capacity as a Major in the Intelligence Division to make a personal request of you. You can turn me down if you wish but I do not believe that you will."

Lieutenant Michael nodded his head and said, "Of course, brother. You know you can always count on me if it is something that I can do."

Major O'Brian said, "I know. That is why I am coming to you first, brother. It will be a very dangerous mission. I need to have a Wielder squad escort me through the Harvester Zone outside of Berlin Sector to a secret location. I am sorry, for security reasons I cannot divulge more information than that. Once I reach my intended destination, you may return to Berlin Sector on your own."

Major O'Brian took a black glove off of his right hand and held it up to Lieutenant Michael. He said, "Well, brother. What do you say?"

Lieutenant Michael took his friend's hand and said, "Well, I want to help you of course. But, since it is a voluntary mission, I feel I should ask my squad if they will be willing to risk their lives too. This isn't something I think I should force them to do."

Major O'Brian nodded and said, "Of course. Volunteers do better than people forced, so I completely agree with you."

Lieutenant Michael let go of his hand and said, "Why don't you come up and meet my squad. They might be more willing if they met you first."

Major O'Brian said, "Of course. I would be happy to meet them now. I have already read their files, but they know nothing about me so it is only fair that I introduce myself to them first."

Major O'Brian turned to the Captain and approached him with his hand outstretched, saying, "Thank you for your assistance Captain Faust. I will return to you after I meet with Squad three."

Major O'Brian turned to Lieutenant Michael and said, "I'm ready, Lieutenant Snyder. Lead the way to your squad."

Lieutenant Michael saluted Captain Faust. Captain Faust nodded and looked downward toward some papers on his desk. Lieutenant Michael turned toward the door and led the way out for his adopted brother.

As they walked toward the stairs, Lieutenant Michael asked, "Do you know that Rachel is the Lieutenant of Squad four here."

Major O'Brian held his hands behind his back as he walked beside Lieutenant Michael. He nodded and replied, "Of course, Michael. I am in the Intelligence Division after all. I keep tabs on all my friends."

Lieutenant Michael rolled his head back and said, "Yeah, I should have figured that out already. If my team says no, will you ask Rachel then?"

Major O'Brian nodded his head thoughtfully and said, "Yes, but she is my second choice. To be honest, I would rather have both your squad and her squad together. But, they would only authorize me to take one squad with me under the current circumstances."

Lieutenant Michael shrugged his shoulders and said, "Yeah. I'd probably feel better if she came with us too. But, thanks to that terrorist, the World Government has become really strict lately. In fact, earlier today we had to escape a food riot."

Major O'Brian's face went blank and he said, "Yes. I can only imagine. And, it is only going to get worse."

Lieutenant Michael jerked his head toward him and he said, "Worse? What do you mean by 'worse'?"

Major O'Brian said, "I am sorry Michael but that information is classified."

Lieutenant Michael sighed and said, "Yeah, figures.   Do they know anything about the terrorist group that blew up the wall yet?"

Major O'Brian nodded and said, "Of course they do."

Lieutenant Michael said, "But I guess you can't tell me that either, can you?"

Major O'Brian smiled and said, "That is right, brother. I wish I could tell you more but there is enough surveillance equipment surrounding us that would let my superiors know that I have spoken too much."

Lieutenant Michael nodded and said, "Yeah, I get it. We're so used to all the surveillance around here that we don't even think about it anymore. But, it's okay since we have nothing to hide."

Both of them went silent for a moment as they continued to walk up the stairs. Lieutenant Michael said, "I don't know what your schedule is like tonight but I think it'd be fun if Rachel, you, and me could sit and talk for a while. It's been a while since we three have spent time together."

Major O'Brian nodded his head and said, "Yeah, I have time for that. I am free in the evening for a couple of hours. If you say 'yes' to my proposal, we will leave first thing Monday morning. It will take three or four days to escort me and then you can return. After I get an answer from your squad, I will report to your Captain. Then I will return to spend time with you and Rachel."

Lieutenant Michael opened the door that led from the stairs to his hallway. He grinned and said, "Great! After you leave, I'll get Rachel. I'm sure she'll be both surprised and thrilled."

Lieutenant Michael opened the door to his apartment and said, "Girls, I've got a surprise for you. Come to the dinner table."

Sarah had already put the pizza in the oven and the smell of it was filling the room. She stepped out of the kitchen and smiled as she saw Lieutenant Michael standing in the doorway. She then noticed a man in a dark uniform standing behind him. Her face showed her confusion and she said, "Lieutenant? What's going on?"

Lieutenant Michael replied, "Give me a moment, Sarah. Sit at the table and I'll explain everything."

Valerie and Jennifer came running toward Lieutenant Michael with grins on their faces. As soon as they noticed the man in the dark uniform they stopped in their tracks and began to look worried.

Lieutenant Michael said, "Don't worry, girls. Everything is fine. Just sit at the table and I'll explain everything."

The girls sat down at the table. Lieutenant Michael stood in front of them with Major O'Brian beside him. He said, "This is my best friend, Josh O'Brian. He is a Major in the Intelligence Division."

Valerie tilted her head and blinked her eyes. She said, "What's a 'major'?"

Sarah leaned over and quietly said, "A Major is a rank in the military. It's the next rank above Captain."

Understanding fell upon Valerie. She said, "Oh, I get it. So he is the boss of Captain Faust, like Captain Faust is the boss of the Lieutenant."

Lieutenant Michael said, "Yeah, that's right. Major O'Brian is also my adopted brother. Remember the story I told you about that after my parents were killed, I lived with another family. He is the son of that family."

Sarah said, "Wow! It's a pleasure to meet you Major."

Major O'Brian said, "It is my pleasure to meet all three of you: Sarah, Jennifer, and Valerie. Please, you may call me Josh. There is no need to be so formal with me."

Valerie bounced forward in her chair and said, "Hello Josh. I'm glad to meet the Lieutenant's brother!"

Jennifer leaned back in her chair and crossed her arms across her chest. She said, "Hey, what's up."

Lieutenant Michael put his hand on Josh's shoulder and said, "My brother here has asked me for help. He wants us to escort him through the Harvester Zone outside of the Berlin Sector. He told me that it will take about three or four days to get there. Now, we are not being ordered to do this. We are volunteering, which means that we can say 'no' if we don't want to do it. I told him that I would talk to you about it before deciding. What do you girls think?"

Josh stepped forward and said, "Now girls, this will be a dangerous mission so I do not want you to think about it lightly. I am asking this of your Lieutenant because I trust him and he is my brother. I hope that you will agree to it."

Sarah leaned back in her chair and said, "Lieutenant, I'll do it just because it's you asking me. I'll go where ever you ask me to go."

Jennifer said, "I don't care what I do as long as I get to kill Harvesters."

Josh said, "Yes, since we are going into the Harvester Zone, I can assure you that you will get to kill Harvesters."

Jennifer shrugged her shoulders and said, "Sure, I'm in then."

Valerie shifted her eyes toward Sarah and then looked over to Jennifer. She next looked up toward Lieutenant Michael and said, "I'll help too, Lieutenant. I'm a little scared though."

Lieutenant Michael smiled in understanding and nodded his head, saying, "Thank you, girls. This means a lot to me." He then turned to Josh and said, "There you have it. We're in!"

Josh nodded his head and said, "I knew I could count on you, brother. I will take my leave then and report to your Captain. I shall then return as promised." He turned and walked out of the door without waiting for a response.

Sarah stood up from her chair and walked over to Lieutenant Michael. She stopped in front of him and looked up into his face saying, "So, Lieutenant. When are we leaving?"

Lieutenant Michael replied, "Well, I don't know all the details yet. But, he told me that we will leave on Monday morning."

Valerie suddenly gave a sigh of relief and said, "Oh, guess that means I'm going to miss the new episode of Magical Girl Squad this Friday."

Jennifer said, "You'll get to see it next Wednesday though."

Valerie raised a finger up and said, "Yeah, I know. But it's still hard knowing that I'll have to go a whole week without watching Magical Girl Squad."

Jennifer said, "Is that what you were afraid of?"

Valerie nodded her head and said, "Of course. It scares me when I think that I might miss a new episode."

Jennifer rolled her eyes and shook her head, saying, "Geez, talk about melo ... melodratic."

Sarah chuckled and said, "I think you mean melodramatic."

Jennifer crossed her arms over her chest. She scrunched her face and said, "Whatever ... melodramatic."

Valerie pointed her finger at Jennifer and said, "You're just trying to act older than me. Instead, you're just making yourself look young and adorable."

Sarah stepped up beside Jennifer and began to rub the top of her head. She spoke in baby talk, saying, "Awe! Look at the little girl trying to speak like a grown up. You're so cute!"

Jennifer batted Sarah's hand away and said, "Knock it off! You suck!"

Lieutenant Michael held up his hands and said, "Okay now. Let's stop goofing off and get dinner started." He pointed at Sarah and said, "Okay, Sarah, go ahead and get that pizza out of the oven and get it served. I'm going to tell Lieutenant Rachel that Josh is here."

Without waiting for a reply, Lieutenant Michael rushed out of the room. Sarah squared her arms on her hips and said, "Okay. Val and Jennifer, you two set the table. I'll get the food out and then you little girls can eat your num-nums."

Jennifer rolled her eyes and shook her head. Valerie giggled and said, "She's making fun of you."

Jennifer flicked her hand toward Valerie and said, "She's making fun of you too, idjit!"

Sarah spun both of them towards the kitchen and said, "Okay, no more teasing. Just get the table set."

Jennifer said, "You're the only one teasing anybody here."

Valerie said, "I thought it was funny."

Together they went into the kitchen and began pulling out the dinnerware. Sarah took the pizza out of the oven and cut it up into eight slices and put it on the table.

Valerie stared at the pizza. Her face became sullen and she sighed, saying, "It's not a real pizza if it doesn't have any cheese on it."

Sarah said, "Well, it's all we've got so you got to live with it."

Valerie, still depressed, said, "I know. I know." She place her hands together, lowered her head, and closed her eyes in silent prayer.

Lieutenant Michael stood in front of Squad four's door with a big grin on his face. He knocked on the door and waited. After a moment the door opened and Tina stood there glaring at him with her emotionless face. She said, "Yeah?"

Lieutenant Michael looked down toward her and said, "Hey, Tina, how're you doing?"

Tina shrugged her shoulders and spoke in her melancholy tone, saying, "I'm one day closer to oblivion. How are you--not that it matters much."

Lieutenant Michael rolled his eyes. He ignored her sarcastic jesting and said, "I'm doing fine. Is Lieutenant Rachel available?"

Tina, in her same tone of voice, said, "Just one moment." She turned her head and shouted loudly, "Lieutenant! Your boyfriend is at the door."

Lieutenant Michael started to stutter and tried to correct her but Tina had already walked away from the door. He heard Lieutenant Rachel argue with Tina, saying, "Tina, why'd you do that? He's not my boyfriend. That's very rude of you!"

After a moment he heard Tina reply to her, saying, "Is he a boy?"

Lieutenant Rachel said, "Yes, but you ..."

Tina interrupted her, saying, "Is he your friend?"

Lieutenant Rachel replied, Yes, but I ..."

Tina, sounding a little annoyed, interrupted her again and said, "Well, then doesn't that make him your boyfriend? Get used to it."

Tina then flung open the door and pointed at Lieutenant Michael. She glared at him and said, "And you, why don't you stop being so stupid and take Lieutenant Rachel out on a date already!"

Without waiting for an answer, Tina turned around and stormed off leaving both Lieutenant Michael and Lieutenant Rachel standing there stunned. Lieutenant Michael looked at Rachel. His eyes glanced at her embarrassed expression. His eyes darted from her face to her ample chest and then back to her face. He stroked his chin and said, "Well, you are cute."

Lieutenant Rachel started to blush. Her mouth formed into an embarrassed smile. She looked down to the ground and said, "I'm sorry about that, I don't ..."

Lieutenant Michael stopped her and said, "Don't worry about it. I'm already used to little girls making fun of me. It just kind of blows over me now. We can talk about that later. I got even bigger news."

Lieutenant Rachel gained control of her embarrassment and tried to push it down inside of herself. She crossed her arms over her chest and leaned her back along the door post, saying, "What's going on?"

Lieutenant Michael placed both of his hands on her biceps and firmly squeezed them. He smiled again and said, "Guess who just showed up?"

Surprised, she shrugged her shoulders and slightly shook her head, saying, "Who?"

Lieutenant Michael excitedly replied, "Josh!"

Realization fell upon Rachel's face and she said, "Josh? Josh O'Brian? Your brother, Josh?"

Lieutenant Michael nodded his head and said, "Yeah! He's with the Captain right now. As soon as he's done down there, he's going to come back up. We were both hoping that you'd like to come on over and join us for a little reunion."

Lieutenant Rachel nodded and said, "Yeah, of course. I was just finishing dinner now. I'll drop on by after I'm done with that. Okay?"

Lieutenant Michael excitedly nodded and said, "Yeah, yeah! Come as soon as you can. I'll be waiting for you."

Lieutenant Rachel nodded and slipped back inside her apartment. She shut the door behind herself and leaned her back against the door. She sighed deeply and then glared at Tina, who was sitting back at the dinner table. Tina glared back at her.

Lieutenant Rachel sat back down at the table and pushed her anger down inside of herself before saying, "Tina, I really can't believe you did all that. That's something I'd expect from Giana, but not you."

Tina shrugged her shoulders and said, "What? I was just trying to help. I'm sick of all this beating around the bush. You know you're not getting any younger. Do you want a younger girl to come along and steal your man away?"

Giana nodded her head and said, "Yeah, I agree. All you two do is a little flirting that leads to nowhere. The purpose of flirting is to get you two hooked up. Like, you need to take it to the next level, or something, anything. If I were you, I'd walk up to him and wrap my arms around his arm so that his arm was squeezed between my boobs. Then, I'd lean over to his ear and whisper into it, saying, 'Why don't we go someplace where we could be alone?' Or, something like that."

Elsa nodded and said, "Yeah, or you can use your arms to squeeze your ..."

Lieutenant Rachel waved her hand toward Elsa and said, "Okay, that's enough out you three. Please, just don't do anything like that again girls. Okay?"

Lieutenant Michael went back into his apartment and sat down at the table. The girls were already stuffing their faces with ration pizza. He looked down at the pizza plate and saw that there were still two slices left. He happily took the two slices and put them on his own plate. He thought to himself, *I wonder if I really should ask Rachel out? Well, we got this mission coming up in a couple of days. Maybe after that?*

Lieutenant Michael's thought was interrupted by Valerie, who seemingly read his mind, saying, "Lieutenant?"

Lieutenant Michael focused his attention on Valerie, saying, "Yes, Valerie. What is it?"

Valerie said, "I think you and Lieutenant Rachel would make a good couple."

Lieutenant Michael darted his eyes back and forth to Sarah and Jennifer, whose eyes were fixed on him. They were smiling at him. They must have heard what Tina said in the hallway. He said, "So, did you girls hear the conversation that I had outside in the hallway just now?"

Sarah nodded and said, "Yep, we all heard it."

Lieutenant Michael leaned forward and rested an elbow on the table. He propped his head up with his hand and said, "So ... do you three think I should ask Lieutenant Rachel out on a date?"

Valerie nodded and said, "Yeah. We already know she loves you because she likes to make cookies for you. My mom says that you make cookies for the people you love."

Jennifer shrugged her shoulders and blushed saying, "I ... I guess. It doesn't matter to me though. It's not like I care about that kind of stuff."

Sarah leaned over and started to pat him on the back, saying, "Come on, Lieutenant. Just admit it that you like her. What's holding you back?"

Lieutenant Michael shrugged his shoulders and said, "Well, we've been friends for so long. I guess I'm afraid that if something goes wrong then I'd lose one of my best friends."

Sarah said, "I know I'm only eleven and don't understand complicated adult stuff. But, aren't relationships supposed to be with the people who are your best friends? You might lose something but you also might gain something instead of losing."

Lieutenant Michael contemplated for a moment and said, "Yeah, I can see that. It's also hard to be in a relationship in the military since we're always going out on missions. Always worrying about whether the other person is safe or not."

Sarah stopped patting his back and said, "Any one of us can die at any moment. When I woke up that morning we went to Los Angeles, I didn't think that Mary would be dead before I went back to sleep. I'm sure Jennifer didn't think that she'd be the last survivor and end up here. I guess I can live my life worrying if I'm going to hurt someone or be hurt. Or, I can live each moment the best I can and find what happiness I can."

Lieutenant Michael sat up and nodded, saying, "I see your point. I guess my thoughts are pretty ridiculous. Guess I'll have to rethink about it." He leaned back in his seat and took a bite out of his now cold ration pizza.

Lieutenant Rachel came in first. Giana, Elsa, and Tina came with her. Giana flopped down on one of the recliners in the sitting room. She lifted the foot rest up on the recliner, crossed her legs, and rested her hands behind her head. She gave a sigh of relief and said, "Almost time to watch my boy Elric on Saturday's re-run."

Sarah took residence in the other recliner and lifted her feet up too, saying, "You mean my boy, Elric? Did you notice on Thursday that his loincloth slipped a little and you could almost see his butt?"

Giana chuckled and said, "Uh, yeah. Like I wouldn't notice that. I wanted to take a quick bite." She started flexing her fingers and imitated taking a bite out of the air.

Giana and Sarah started to laugh. Lieutenant Michael yelled from the dinner table, saying, "Girls, watch your language! Geez!"

Giana rolled her eyes and said, "What? I didn't say anything bad. I was just speakin' what we were all thinkin' over here."

Jennifer, who was sitting on the far side of the couch, next to Sarah, started to blush.

Valerie, who was sitting right next to her noticed it and said, "How come you're blushing, Jennifer?"

Jennifer shook her head vigorously and denied it saying, "I'm not blushing!"

Sarah leaned over to get a better look at her face and said, "You are blushing."

Jennifer began to blush even more and she firmly stated, "I'm not blushing!"

Sarah chuckled and said, "It's okay, Jennifer. Just admit that you have a crush on Elric too and you'll feel better about it. We all do so it's okay to admit it."

Jennifer became subdued and she crossed her arms across her chest, saying, "I ... I ... why does it matter so much to you!"

Giana rolled her eyes and dropped her arms onto the armrests with a thud, saying, "Geez, Jennifer, it seems to me that you are the only one who cares. It's okay to like boys, you know."

Elsa, who was sitting next to Valerie, said, "Come on, stop teasing Jennifer. She's still too young to deal with her emotions right now. Just let her pretend that she's not interested in boys yet, even though it's obvious that she is." She went quiet for a moment. She tried to suppress laughter that wanted to come. She brought her hand to her mouth and held it shut as giggles started to slip out.

Jennifer rolled her eyes and leaned back on the couch with her arms crossed over her chest.

Giana sat up and said, "Trust me, girls I know all there is to know about boys and how to trap them."

Tina, sitting next to Elsa on the edge of the couch, with her arm supporting her head, said, "And what exactly do you know about boys? All I've ever seen you do is hit on Lieutenant Michael with Mary."

Giana shrugged her shoulders and said, "What? He's a boy. I only hit on him to tease Mary though. It's not like I was actually trying to trap him for real."

Tina said, "So, you claim to be an expert, yet you've only ever tried it on Lieutenant Michael?"

Giana scooted off of the recliner and said, "I know what to do, just watch."

All five girls turned their heads and watched as Giana walked up to Lieutenant Michael casually. As she walked up to him, she pretended to trip. Out of reflex, Lieutenant Michael caught her and said, "What do you think you're doing?" He set her back on her feet.

Giana wrapped her arms around Lieutenant Michaels arm and looked up at him with a look of pure innocence. She tilted her head and said, "I don't feel so good, Lieutenant." She then dropped to the floor and scooted her legs over to her side as she sat on her behind.

Lieutenant Michael squatted down and felt her forehead saying, "Well, I guess you do feel a little warm."

Giana tilted her head and batted her eyes at him. After realizing what was going on, he rolled his eyes as he stood back up with a sigh. She unbuttoned the top two buttons on her jacket and slid the jacket off of her left shoulder and let it hang, as she said suggestively, "Only you can make me better, Lieutenant."

Lieutenant Rachel walked over to her and picked her up from off the floor. She then smacked Giana upside the back of her head, saying, "Knock it off!"

Giana caressed the back of her head, saying, "Ow, Lieutenant! That hurt. Geez, I was just playing around. I wouldn't really try to steal your man."

Lieutenant Rachel pushed her toward the sitting room, saying, "Just go over there and quit being stupid."

As Giana dejectedly walked back toward the recliner, a knock came at the door. Lieutenant Michael opened the door and Josh stood there waiting on the other side. Lieutenant Michael stepped aside and waved him toward the table where Lieutenant Rachel sat. He said, "Make yourself at home, brother."

Josh stepped inside and said, "Thank you, brother! I believe I shall." He looked towards the table and saw Lieutenant Rachel sitting there. He smiled at her and said, "Hello, Rachel. Long time no see. I hope you are doing well."

Lieutenant Rachel stood up and walked towards him with outstretched arms, saying, "I'm good, Josh. How are you?"

They embraced each other in a hug and Josh said, "I am glad. I am doing very well too!"

With the greetings out of the way, the three of them sat at the table. The noise from the theme song of the re-run episode of the Lost Sword Saga started to fill the apartment. The three of them sat there silently as they looked back and forth at each other.

Josh started to chuckle and he said, "You know, I have been keeping an eye on you two. As a friend, of course, not as a government agent."

Michael said, "Yeah, well I guess our reports must be pretty boring though."

Josh shook his head and said, "Not at all. The reports surrounding you two have been well above average. Especially since the evacuation of Los Angeles. Your squad particularly, Michael. Thanks to Mary's sacrifice, your sector had the most civilians saved."

A memory of Mary returned to Lieutenant Michael's mind. He hadn't thought about her in a while. The hole that was in his heart since her death had been temporarily plugged by Jennifer. The difficulty surrounding Jennifer's transfer had forced him to focus a lot of attention on her. This left him with little time to mourn for Mary as he tried to help Jennifer.

The look on Michael's face must have changed because Josh suddenly spoke, bringing him out of his thoughts of Mary. He said, "I am sorry, Michael. I did not mean to bring up a subject that is probably very sore for you."

Michael shrugged his shoulders and said, "Don't worry about it. I'm sorry. It was just that when you mentioned Mary, I realized that I hadn't thought about her in a while. We had a lot of difficulty in getting Jennifer situated that it took up all my attention. I found myself thinking about Mary less, and thinking more about Jennifer. I suppose that's a good thing. It's not good to dwell on the past so much. It's just that ... I guess Mary was such a big part of my life here. I haven't forgotten her, I just have other things to think about. She was afraid that I'd forget about her."

Josh nodded his head in understanding and said, "Yes, I can only imagine the heartache that comes with both of your positions. I know this will not make up for it. But, please, believe me that there are big changes that are coming. I cannot tell you about it because it is classified, but there are big changes coming. All the pain that you two have been forced to endure will not be for nothing."

Rachel leaned forward in her chair and said, "I hate it when you say everything and nothing at the exact same time."

Josh chuckled and said, "I know, darling. But, as a person in my position, I need to be discreet in what I say."

Michael said, "I get it that military intelligence needs to be secretive, but come on. Does it have to be so secret? Our only enemy is the Harvesters and they don't have any intelligence as far as I can gather. They're basically animals so why do we have to worry so much about keeping our own secrets?"

Rachel said, "Yeah, I thought about that too. They're animals so it's not like they have any formal units or anything."

Josh leaned back in his chair. He brought his hands up and connected them together at the finger tips. He said, "Well, those are certainly good points. But, let us say that … and I mean that this is just speculation. I am not saying this is how it actually is. This is merely speculation on my part. Do you understand?"

Both Michael and Rachel nodded their heads. Rachel said, "Yeah, I get it. Keep going."

Michael, sounding annoyed said, "Yeah, yeah. I got you."

Josh continued saying, "We know that the Harvesters are stupid brute animals. But, what if there was a higher intelligence behind the Harvesters? What if the same aliens that initiated the Hour of Despair, are the same aliens that sent the Harvesters as a second wave of an invasion? What if they were using the Harvesters to clear out the earth before their final invasion?"

Michael thought about it for a moment. It made sense to him. There never has been a connection found between the first aliens and the Harvesters. But, then again, they knew so little about the first aliens except for their ships and their main weapon. He said, "I see your point. We know so little about the first aliens that they might as well be behind the Harvesters and we would never know."

Rachel sighed and said, "I suppose we'll never know the truth. But, I see your point now. We don't have enough information so we have got to be careful. I'll keep that in mind."

Josh changed the subject and said, "Just so you know, Rachel. The reason I have come here is to have Michael and his squad escort me through the Harvester Zone outside Berlin Sector. It should take a week, but then I will send him back to you."

Rachel started to look nervous. She glimpsed at Michael and then focused her attention back on Josh, saying, "Berlin Sector Harvester Zone? That … that sounds dangerous."

Josh nodded and stated as a matter of fact, "It is."

Rachel said, "Don't you think that maybe my squad should go with you too?"

Josh said, "Well, to be honest, I did want both of your squads but they told me that I could only take one. I chose to ask Michael first. If he had said 'no', you would have been my second choice."

Rachel replied, "Don't worry, I understand. Michael can handle it. He's always been the stronger one."

Josh nodded in agreement, saying, "Yes, he has always been the stronger one. Even stronger than me too. That is why I need him for this mission. I cannot give you the details of course. But, this mission is very important. If it was not, I would not have asked him to risk his life."

Rachel slouched in her chair and stared at her hands. Michael, seeing her attitude change, put his hand over her hands and said, "Don't worry, I'll be back before you know I'm gone."

Rachel nodded and tried to smile, saying, "Yeah. I'll be waiting."

After the Lost Sword Saga was over, the girls began to talk among themselves as Michael, Rachel and Josh continued to do so as well. An hour later, Josh looked at his watch and stood up, saying, "I ought to get back now. I will return Monday morning when it is time for us to depart for Berlin Sector so please be ready to deploy by eight hundred hours."

Michael and Rachel stood up after him. Michael said, "Yeah, okay. We'll be ready to deploy by eight hundred hours. And it's getting late, so I should get my team to bed."

Rachel said, "Yeah, same."

Josh had already made it to the door. He stopped in the doorway and said, "Thank you again, Michael for helping me. This is something really important to me and I am glad that you will be at my side on this. Have a good night then." He turned back around and walked out of the room without waiting for any reply.

As Josh left, Giana, Elsa, and Tina slowly got up out of their seats. They all said their goodbyes and followed Lieutenant Rachel to their apartment across the hall.

After Squad four left, Lieutenant Michael stood in front of Sarah, Jennifer, and Valerie, saying, "Okay, girls, it's time for bed."

Sarah said, "Did you have fun with your brother?"

Lieutenant Michael nodded and smiled, saying, "Of course. It has been a few years since I last saw him."

Valerie said, "He talks kind of funny too."

Lieutenant Michael ran his hand through his hair and said, "Yeah, well. He does sound kind of pompous. And, it's only gotten worse since he joined the Intelligence Division."

Valerie ran up to Lieutenant Michael and wrapped her arms around his right arm. She looked up and smiled at him, saying, "Don't worry, Lieutenant. He seems like a very nice man. I look forward to working with him."

Jennifer said, "Yeah, I bet he can tell us some embarrassing stories about the Lieutenant when he was younger."

Lieutenant Michael chuckled and said, "Yeah, he probably can."

As the girls moved to go to their rooms, they each gave him a quick hug as they passed by him. As they entered the hallway, Lieutenant Michael said to them, "Thanks again girls for agreeing to help me help my brother."

The three of them stopped and turned their heads to face him and gave him a big smile. They nodded and Sarah said, "We're a family. So, we got to help our family." They then continued on down the hall and disappeared into their rooms for the night.

- 5 -

The alarm clock rang at six-thirty hundred hours in the morning. Lieutenant Rachel sighed as she was forced awake. She reached out and tried to silence the alarm. With her vision still blurry, she misjudged the distance and fell short. She tried again the second time and managed to hit it. She rolled over on her back and felt pain in her lower stomach. It was that time of the month again. She slid herself to the edge of her bed and struggled to stand up.

The door flung open and Giana stood there with a big grin on her face, shouting, "Wakey, wakey, Lieutenant! It's morning!"

Lieutenant Rachel glared at her, annoyed, saying, "Knock it off. I feel like crap."

Giana chuckled, saying, "Oh, I guess it's that time of the month already. You were a little late so I beat you to it. I guess that's why you've been so moody lately. I was beginning to think that maybe you got yourself pregnant."

Lieutenant Rachel grabbed a pillow and flung it towards Giana's face. Giana quickly reacted by shutting the door as the pillow smashed into it. She then opened the door again, and said with a big smile, "Don't worry, Lieutenant.

I'll make breakfast this morning. Take your time. Do you want rice or beans? I know, I'll make rice porridge."

Giana shut the door without waiting for an answer. Lieutenant Rachel sighed and shook her head. She ran her hands over her lower stomach. To make things worse, she was still thinking about the secret mission that Michael had agreed to go on. In addition to her physical pain, there was a gnawing dread in the pit of her stomach. She trusted Josh, but still, the idea of Michael not coming back worried her.

Lieutenant Rachel got dressed and stepped out into the hallway. Elsa and Tina were already sitting at the table. Elsa was twirling a spoon with her fingers as it rotated on the table surface. Tina sat there looking depressed, so it seemed to be a normal day for her. She held her head up by leaning on her own hand. With her other hand, she pressed on the head of a spoon causing it to go up and clank on the table.

When Lieutenant Rachel stepped into the area, Tina stopped clanking the spoon and looked right at her. She spoke in her melancholy tone, saying, "I hear you got your period finally. So … you're not pregnant then?"

Annoyed Lieutenant Rachel rolled her eyes, saying, "No, I'm not pregnant. I don't have that kind of relationship."

Tina, not changing her tone, replied, "Really? I thought maybe your baser instincts finally took over and you snuck into Lieutenant Michael's bed. Then you ripped off …"

Lieutenant Rachel waved her hands back and forth, shouting, "Okay, missy. That's enough out of your mouth. I'm an adult, you know. You should treat me with more respect! Geez, now I'm starting to understand how Lieutenant Michael feels. Who the hell taught you to speak like that!"

Tina, shrugged her shoulders and replied in her melancholy tone, "I learned it from Giana and Mary."

Giana, who was in the kitchen standing over the stove, twirled around and pointed a dirty serving spoon at Tina, shouting, "Hey now, don't get me involved in your stupid business!" As she shook the spoon at her, rice porridge that was stuck to the spoon started to fling off.

A splatter of rice porridge hit Lieutenant Rachel in the face. She wiped it off and then glared at Giana. Giana backed away, saying, "Hey, I didn't mean to do that!"

Lieutenant Rachel ignored her and glared at Tina again. She shook her head and sat down at her place at the dinner table.

Giana came out of the kitchen holding a pot of rice porridge, saying, "Tina's joking aside, what are you going to do about Lieutenant Michael leaving? You don't want him to leave right? Why don't you ask him to stay?"

Lieutenant Rachel sighed and stared at her empty bowl on the table. She said, "I ... I can't do that. I don't have the right to ask him that. This is something he needs to do with his brother."

Elsa stopped twirling her spoon and she looked up at Lieutenant Rachel with a smile. She innocently said, "Tina may have been joking, but, it is a good idea. You can always sneak into his room and do that thing that will put a baby in your belly."

Elsa rubbed her own stomach with both of her hands. She continued, "Then you can tell Lieutenant Michael that you're pregnant with his baby and that baby will need a daddy. He'll have to stay then."

Lieutenant Rachel was shocked by Elsa's statement. Elsa, who never joined into adult conversations like this before had finally joined in. Sure, Giana and Mary were the worst so it was expected from them, but this was a first for Elsa.

Lieutenant Rachel stared at her in shock as she tried to process what she said. She tilted her head and looked upward as she started to seriously think about that suggestion. A sly smile broke out on her face as she thought about it, but then she shook her head, saying, "No, it's too late for that. I would have had to have done that a few months ago for it to work."

Giana plopped a giant spoonful of rice porridge into Lieutenant Rachel's bowl, saying, "You know, Lieutenant. Elsa might be on to something, though in the wrong way. It's too late to convince him to stay, but you can still get pregnant and have a love child. It might give him a reason to work harder at coming back. Besides, you got to give it a shot. You are a woman you know. Lieutenant Michael is a good man. You got to fulfill your duty to humanity during humanities greatest struggle and make sure that Lieutenant Michael has someone to continue the struggle when he dies."

Lieutenant Rachel shook her head and said, "Even if I went through with your stupid idea, I can't get pregnant right now because I'm on my period."

Giana tilted her head and brought a finger to her lips as she thought for a moment. She shrugged her shoulders and said, "Oh yeah, I forgot about that little detail. Well I guess you're just out of luck then. Don't worry, Lieutenant. I'll think of something."

Lieutenant Michael stood in front of the door as he waited for the girls to get out of the bathroom. He looked at the clock and began to feel agitated since the girls were taking so long. He calmed himself and waited patiently. The outer wall check could wait. After all this time there had not been any sign of any other terrorist activities. Hopefully it was only a one-time thing. The one who planted the bombs did blow himself up with the wall.

Lieutenant Michael heard the bathroom door open. The quietness in the air was replaced by little girls giggling. Sarah, Jennifer and Valerie came around the corner and when they saw him, they stopped their idle chatter.

Lieutenant Michael sternly said, "You girls took really long in there today."

Sarah waved her hand in dismissal and said, "Don't worry, Lieutenant. We had to make sure we were all empty so we don't get distracted during today's wall check."

Lieutenant Michael sighed and said, "Yeah, yeah. I get it. Let's go and get this over with."

Valerie raised her right arm high in the air and said, "Yeah, let's get this done in time for dinner so we can watch the special Magical Girl Squad movie that is being shown tonight!"

Sarah stuck her hand out. Valerie put her hand on top of Sarah's hand. Jennifer put her own hand on top of Valerie's hand. Sarah said, "Let's go out there and keep each other safe!"

Jennifer nodded and said, "You know I'll do my best!"

Valerie nodded too and said, "Yeah, I'll do my best too!"

They broke their hands apart and Sarah turned to Lieutenant Michael, saying, "Okay, Lieutenant. We're ready to go!"

Lieutenant Michael gave them all their com units and equipment. They checked their gear to make sure it was working and then Lieutenant Michael opened the door. As they began to leave, Squad four's door opened.

Lieutenant Rachel stumbled out into the hallway. Her face showed signs that she was having a bad morning. She stopped abruptly as she realized that Lieutenant Michael was there. She looked up at him. She felt her heart begin to race. Her face started to feel warm. She started to worry that she was blushing so she looked down to the ground.

Giana accidently rammed into Lieutenant Rachel's backside and she said, "What's the big ..." She stopped as soon as she noticed Squad three standing there.

Giana pushed Lieutenant Rachel out of the way and walked over to Sarah, saying, "Hey Squad three. Since the Magical Girl Squad movie is finally coming out tonight, why don't we all watch it together?"

Valerie cut into the conversation, saying, "Yeah, more people means more fun! You girls can come over to our place if you want."

Giana gave her a thumbs up and then looked at Lieutenant Michael with a big grin for conformation. Lieutenant Michael nodded his head and said, "That's fine with me." He then looked at Lieutenant Rachel and said, "If that is okay with you?"

Lieutenant Rachel nodded her head and said, "Yeah, that's fine with me."

Giana then said, "Great! While we're watching the movie, you two can go have your own kind of fun."

Lieutenant Michael nodded his head and said, "Of course, that's what we always do. It's not like we want to watch your kiddie shows. Alright, let's get going. We're already late as it is." He then started walking down the hall so Sarah, Jennifer and Valerie followed behind him.

As they went Valerie started to sing the Magical Girl Squad theme song in preparation for tonight's special episode. She skipped and danced down the hallway.

Lieutenant Rachel waited till they went through the hallway door and closed it behind them. She said, "Giana, what ..."

Giana held up her hand and said, "Hold on, Lieutenant. I told you that I'd take care of it. I'll make sure that you have some alone time with Lieutenant Michael. I don't care what you do, but whatever you do, just make sure that you won't have any regrets later. Okay."

Lieutenant Rachel paused in silence. She then put her hand on top of Giana's head and gave it a gentle rub, saying, "Thanks, Giana, for looking out for me."

Giana grinned and gave her a thumbs up, saying, "Of course, Lieutenant. We're a team so we help each other out."

As Squad three walked down the stairs, Valerie said, "It's a good thing that you get to see Lieutenant Rachel tonight. Now you can tell her that you want to go out with her."

Lieutenant Michael's face went downcast and he scratched the top of his head, saying, "I don't know about that."

Sarah said, "Why not, Lieutenant? Seems to me that it would be a perfect opportunity since we're going on that mission with your brother."

Lieutenant Michael went silent for a moment as they continued to walk down the stairs. He sighed and said, "That seems too much of a cliché to me. You know, those movies where you have the couple make all these promises to each other, only to have them die before they can fulfill them."

Sarah stopped in her tracks. She turned around with an intense look on her face that he interpreted to mean 'are you serious?'

Lieutenant Michael stopped walking down the stairs and responded to her silent response by saying, "Look, I don't want to not come back and leave Rachel with a bunch of unfulfilled promises."

Sarah rolled her eyes and turned back around, saying, "I can see your point, I guess."

Jennifer crossed her arms over her chest and shyly said, "I ... I agree with the Lieutenant. I think it would be worse to make a promise you couldn't keep."

Valerie, who was hoping from step to step as she went down the stairs, added her own voice, saying, "You just need to make sure you come back then. Don't worry, Lieutenant. With my abilities, I'll be much better at keeping every one safe so we can all come back home."

Lieutenant Michael nodded and said, "I know you'll do your best, Valerie. Don't worry, girls. I'll make sure to talk to Lieutenant Rachel tonight when we get together."

All the squads returned to their headquarters after the wall check. It was a pretty normal day. A few roving packs of Harvesters were encountered, which were easily dealt with. Again, there was no sign that the walls had been sabotaged.

Later that night, after a dinner of rice and beans, Squad three did the dishes together. Sarah stood at the sink and was scrubbing the dirty dishes. She handed the scrubbed dish to Jennifer, who rinsed it. Jennifer then handed the dish to Valerie, who wiped it dry. Valerie would then grin and hand the dish to Lieutenant Michael who placed it in its proper place.

As Sarah started scrubbing the final dish, someone started pounding on the other side of the door. Giana's voice echoed from the other side of the door, shouting, "Hey! The Magical Girl Squad movie is about to start soon! Let me in!"

Lieutenant Michael rolled his eyes and shouted back at her, yelling, "Geez, just wait a minute! You still got like ten minutes."

Lieutenant Michael opened the door and Giana stood there with her arms squared on her hips and she was tapping her right foot. The image of her posture brought a memory of Mary back into his mind. He pushed the thought aside.

Giana pointed at him and said loudly, "Took you long enough!"

Lieutenant Michael stepped aside and directed them toward the sitting area with his hand. He dispassionately said, "Yeah, yeah. Come on in."

Valerie moved into the entranceway of the kitchen holding the last dish in her hand as she dried it with a towel. She grinned and said, "We're almost done here so just wait a moment."

Valerie handed the dish to Lieutenant Michael and said, "Here you go, Lieutenant."

Lieutenant Michael accepted the dish but said, "You know, Valerie, you could have put the dish away too."

Valerie tilted her head in confusion and stared at him blankly. She replied, "But ... but that's your job, Lieutenant."

Lieutenant Michael rolled his eyes and said, "Okay, whatever. You three go have fun with Squad four now."

Valerie quickly turned and tossed the towel on to the countertop. She ran passed him toward the sitting area. Jennifer hopped off of the stool and shyly slid past him. Sarah rinsed her hands, dried them off on a towel, and went out of the kitchen. As she passed Lieutenant Michael she gave him a thumbs up. She joined the others in the sitting area.

Lieutenant Rachel continued to stand silently in the doorway. Lieutenant Michael turned to her and said, "Come on in." She smiled and nodded, saying, "Okay."

The two of them headed for the table to sit. Lieutenant Michael put his hand on a chair and began pulling it out. Giana, standing in the sitting area, pointed at them and shouted, saying, "What do you two think you're doing?"

Lieutenant Michael looked at her annoyed, saying, "Uh ... we're just going to sit here and talk like we normally do?"

Giana shouted again, saying, "Uh ... no you're not! You can't have real adult time if you just sit there like that."

Lieutenant Michael chuckled and replied, "Just where are we supposed to go then?"

Giana pointed toward the hallway and said, "Geez! You can like go into your room. Or, if you can't handle that, just go to our apartment across the way. Geez ... why do I got to think of everything around here?"

Lieutenant Michael paused for a moment in deep thought. Lieutenant Rachel saw the look on his face and began to raise her hand. She stepped forward and was about to yell at Giana. Suddenly, Lieutenant Michael grabbed her wrist and sternly said, "Fine!" He gave a slight bow and said in imitation of high class society, "We shall be in my room then if you need us."

Before, Lieutenant Rachel could say anything, he began to pull her toward his room. She looked in shock at Giana. Giana gave her a big grin and a wink.

Lieutenant Michael opened his door and pulled her into his room. Her heart began to beat faster and faster with excitement. She was too nervous to say anything. When they entered the room, he shut the door behind them. They stood there awkwardly and stared at the bed.

Lieutenant Michael watched her face out of the corner of his eye. She looked down toward the ground, her face was flushed with red. She looked embarrassed. She was clasping her hands together in front of her waist.

Lieutenant Rachel tilted her head and glanced at Lieutenant Michael out of the corner of her eye. Their eyes inadvertently met. In embarrassment, they both looked away from each other. Lieutenant Michael, trying to calm things down, said, "Uh ... this is new for us."

Lieutenant Rachel chuckled and said, "Uh ... yeah."

A noise came from the other side of the door. It was Giana shouting at someone, saying, "Don't go over there! Just leave them alone!"

Another voice, possibly Valerie, said, "But I want to know what they're doing."

Giana shouted back, "They're making babies, that's what they're doing?"

The girl replied, "Oh so that's what you mean by adult time."

Lieutenant Rachel's face turned a shade of red that he had never seen on her face before. She covered her face with her hands. Lieutenant Michael looked upward and sighed deeply, saying, "Geez ... why does she always do that."

Lieutenant Rachel dropped her hands and started to speak, saying, "I'm sorry about ..."

Lieutenant Michael waved his hand in dismissal and said, "Don't worry about it." He moved toward the bed. Instead of sitting on the bed, he slid onto the floor and leaned his back against the side of the bed. He motioned with his hand for her to sit down beside him. He said, "I'm used to Giana joking around like that so it doesn't really bother me anymore."

Lieutenant Rachel composed herself. The red color of her face disappeared. She nodded her head and moved to sit down next to him. When she sat down next to him, they both sat there in silence again.

After a moment they both started talking at once. Lieutenant Michael stopped and motioned for her to continue. She shook her head and said, "No, you start."

Lieutenant Michael accepted this and said, "Well, we've been friends for so long that it feels natural to be with you. It feels unnatural to me to think of being apart from you. Well, I ... uh, well ..."

Lieutenant Rachel excitedly nodded her head and urged him to keep going. He said, "Well, as you know I'm going on that mission with my brother. I ... I don't want to leave you with any promises before I go. But ... after I get back, I ... I want to talk to you about our future together. If that is something you want to talk about too."

She nodded and disappointingly said, "I see. Michael I ... I ... I lo- ..." She started to blush again. She composed herself and said, "I'm going to ask you something really selfish of me."

Lieutenant Michael nodded and said, "Okay."

Lieutenant Rachel paused for a moment, closed her eyes and said, "Please don't go on that mission. I have a really bad feeling about it. Just stay here with me. I ... I need you." She dropped her head onto his chest. She turned herself and placed her hand on the other side of his chest. She gripped the fabric of his jacket and said, "There's something different about Josh. I feel that he has an ulterior motive."

Lieutenant Michael said, "Woman's intuition huh? Yeah, I see a change in Josh too. He definitely feels different to me."

Lieutenant Rachel said, "There's just too many unknowns and I don't want to lose you." She tried to hold herself back but tears started to roll down her cheeks, staining his jacket.

Lieutenant Michael draped his arm over her back and said, "You know I have to help my brother."

Lieutenant Rachel sighed and said, "Yeah, I know. That's one of the reasons I like you. Promise me that you'll do everything that you can to come back to me. Would you at least do that?"

Lieutenant Michael squeezed her tightly and said, "Yeah, I'll do everything I can to come back to you. I can promise you that much right now."

They continued to sit like that for a few minutes in silence. Suddenly, in the silence, the emergency siren began to wail. They both sat up and waited for the deployment announcement. A woman's voice rang over the loud speaker, saying, "Squad four, Squad Five, prepare for deployment, ten minutes." It repeated the statement.

The noise of the announcement went silent and there was a sudden loud and drawn out yell of, "Noooooo!" from a bunch of girls in the other room.

Lieutenant Michael sighed and stood up. He reached his hand toward Rachel. She took it and he lifted her up from off the floor. She stared deeply into his eyes. He reached out to her and pulled her close to him. He wrapped his arms around her and embraced her. He said, "You come back safe too."

Lieutenant Rachel nodded and said, "Yeah."

Lieutenant Michael let her go and opened the door of his room. Together they went out into the sitting room where Giana and Elsa sat collapsed on the floor as they pretended to cry. Tina sat motionless on the couch with her hands held together in her lap. He had seen this look on her face before. It was taking all her energy to not express her emotions.

When Lieutenant Rachel entered, Giana lamented, "Why now of all times, Lieutenant?"

Tina, in her melancholy tone, said, "How vexing."

Lieutenant Rachel said, "Come on, girls. You know we got to go."

Sarah arrogantly smiled and said, "Yeah, you girls got a job to do so you got to do it."

Giana, Elsa, and Tina reluctantly stood up and started to follow Lieutenant Rachel. Jennifer waved good bye with a huge grin and said, "Don't worry, Giana. I'll tell you what you missed when you get back."

Giana, stopped in her tracks, turned around aggressively, and pointed at her, shouting, "Don't you dare spoil it you bitch!"

Jennifer responded with a fake smile and waved, saying, "Buh-bye, cow!"

Giana balled her fists and threw them down along the side of her body. She stomped her foot and groaned in annoyance. She twirled around and followed her team out of the door.

As they left, Valerie balled her fists and brought them to her mouth. Her eyes started to get watery and she said, "You girls shouldn't make fun of someone who has to miss Magical Girl Squad. If that happened to me, I'd just die."

When Squad four entered their own apartment, Giana crossed her arms and said, "Well this really sucks. Couldn't have had worse timing. Did you confess your feelings to Lieutenant Michael?"

Lieutenant Rachel began to pull their equipment out of the storage locker and began to distribute it. In response to Giana, she said, "Sort of. I guess we're planning to talk about it more when they get back." She handed Giana her com unit ear piece

Giana took it, stuck it in her ear while turning it on, and said, "I see."

Lieutenant Michael stood there in silence as he stared at the door that Lieutenant Rachel had just left out of. Sarah watched him and said, "Are you okay, Lieutenant?"

Lieutenant Michael sighed and turned around to face her. He said, "Yeah, I'm fine. I just seem to have some bad luck today."

Valerie, kneeling on the couch as she rested her upper body on the back, said with a smile, "Are you a daddy now? Did you make a baby with Lieutenant Rachel?"

Lieutenant Michael chuckled and said, "No, not today."

The commercial ended and Valerie twirled around in her seat and focused her attention on the television. Lieutenant Michael shook his head and thought to himself, *I need to have a chat with Giana about what she's teaching them.*

- 6 -

Squad four did not come back that evening. They did not come back in the morning either. That morning was Monday, the same day that Squad three were to go on their secret mission. Lieutenant Michael and Rachel would have to wait to see each other when they both come back from their missions.

Lieutenant Michael tried to put his worry for Rachel out of his mind and focused on preparing for the mission. As they were getting ready, a knock came to the door. Sarah opened the door for him and Major Josh stood there on the other side. Sarah looked up at him and said, "You're early."

Major Josh smiled with a nod and said, "I know, my dear. May I come in anyway?"

Lieutenant Michael spoke loudly from the dining area and said, "Sure, come on in."

Sarah stepped to the side and waved him in. Major Josh entered and stood at ease in the dining area entrance. He smiled as he patiently waited for Lieutenant Michael to finish putting their gear together.

Lieutenant Michael finished preparing the last of the backpacks for the girls. He helped them put them on. He handed Sarah her belt with the two scabbards for her metal sticks. He handed Valerie her cattle prod and holster. He helped her to attach it to the side of her backpack. He then handed them their com units and they all tested them out to make sure that they were working properly.

With preparations completed, Lieutenant Michael approached Major Josh. He saluted him and said, "We're ready to go, Major."

Major Josh nodded and said, "Excellent, Lieutenant. Now, this is your last chance to back out. Once we get onto the helicopter, then you are pretty much committed to assisting me."

Lieutenant Michael shook his head and said, "Don't worry, sir. We're already committed to helping you."

Major Josh nodded again and said, "Very well then. Let us depart for the roof and we shall begin with our mission."

Together they made their way to the roof. Once they reached the top of the stairs, Valerie saw that it was not a normal helicopter. She exclaimed, "Wow! I've never seen a helicopter like that before! It's huge and there are no propellers on it."

Major Josh chuckled and said, "I apologize, I misspoke. I called it a helicopter, but, it is actually a VTOL jet called a Sparrow Hawk. I did not think that you would know what I meant so I used a term I knew you were familiar with."

Valerie said, "Yeah, I've never heard of that before."

Major Josh said, "Yes, I am aware. These types of craft are reserved for specialized units. For this mission, you are a specialized unit so you are going to be allowed to use this craft."

Lieutenant Michael said, "Instead of propellers it has those huge jet engines that have the ability to rotate so that it can fly in any direction. I hear that they are super-fast too."

Major Josh said, "Yes, brother. They are super-fast. We shall arrive in the Berlin Sector in only a matter of five hours."

Major Josh walked up the ramp of the Sparrow Hawk and turned around. He held his hand out towards them and said, "If you are ready to go, please come on into the craft. If you are going to back out, this is your last chance."

Lieutenant Michael walked up the ramp, followed by the girls. The inside of the Sparrow Hawk was small. Unlike the transport helicopters, the Sparrow Hawk had only eight seats. Each seat was separate and came with a special harness.

Major Josh directed them all to sit. He then personally strapped each person into their seat. When he was done, he said, "Do not, for any reason, remove that harness while we are in flight. We will be traveling at speeds so fast that if you were thrown from your chair, your body would be plastered against the wall."

The girls collectively saluted and said, "Aye, sir!"

Major Josh sat down in his own seat and strapped himself in. He then clicked a small communicator on his shoulder and said, "You may depart."

A voice echoed through his communicator, saying, "Aye, sir." The lights in the cabin switched to red and a loud explosion rung throughout the air around them. The girls screamed in shock and covered their ears.

Major Josh spoke loudly over the roaring noise and said, "Do not worry, my dears. The explosion that you heard is nothing more than the engines turning on."

Sarah shouted, "Jeez, you trying to give me a heart attack?"

Jennifer crossed her arms over her chest and shouted, "You could have given us a warning at least."

Valerie gripped the harness straps and said, "I hope we don't explode."

Josh smiled at her and said, "Do not worry, these Sparrow Hawks are quite safe, as long as you are strapped in."

The upward lift of the Sparrow Hawk ceased. The engines rotated and then roared again as the air craft surged forward at incredible speeds. Everyone in the craft was pushed against their seats as the craft rocketed forward.

Lieutenant Michael said, "I see what you mean when you said we'd be going really fast."

Major Josh said, "I did give you a warning."

Jennifer sighed and said, "Is this really going to take five hours? I should have brought my book to read."

Sarah said, "It's probably better that you didn't. That's just one more thing you'd have to carry in the field. Plus you might lose it too."

Jennifer looked downcast and said, "I know, but five hours is a long time just sitting here."

Valerie said, "When I get bored I like to sing!"

Jennifer said, "Yeah, we know that Valerie."

Valerie sat there motionless. Lieutenant Michael could see the look of agitation on her face. She started to look around the cabin. She then took a deep breath and started to sing the theme song to Magical Girl Squad:

"When evil covers the land,
It's time for girls to take a stand!
Deep inside you a power is sleeping.

Magical power to illuminate the world!
Fight the darkness that surrounds you.
When girls combine nothing can stop you.
With your friends by your side,
You transcend above the darkness below.
With a shot of love your powers flow,
You've tasted the fruit that fell from the tree.
Rise up and fight the foe, it is your destiny!
The Path of the Future calls you!
You are Magical Girls!
Your destiny is calling you!"

Jennifer covered her ears with her hands and said, "Do I got to listen to this for five freaking hours?"

Major Josh chuckled and waited for Valerie to finish singing. When she was done, he said, "Valerie, do you know what that song means?"

Valerie thought for a moment and said, "I've thought about it before. To me, it sounds like they are saying that girls have all the power so they should work together as friends to fight evil. Lieutenant Michael told me that he thinks it is about getting us ready to be Spirit Wielders."

Major Josh grinned slyly at her. He said, "How perceptive of you, little Valerie. Yes, girls definitely have great power, which you can wield to fight against evil. Your Lieutenant is also correct that your favorite show was created by the World Government to get girls with your power ready to join the Spirit Wielder Corp."

Lieutenant Michael couldn't help but notice that when Josh said 'World Government' his face revealed a momentary sneer. It was a look that he had only seen on his face when Josh really despised someone. Rachel's words came back to his memory saying that Josh felt different. He wondered if this is what caused him to seem different. He decided to let it go and see what would happen. He trusted Josh and doubted that he would do anything that would harm him.

Major Josh continued to talk to Valerie, saying, "You see, Valerie, those who are in the World Government have a weird rule that they must follow. In this rule, they must reveal to the public the things that they do in secret. To accomplish this they create themes and concepts in television shows, movies, and books based on their secret goals. This way they tell the people what they are doing while, at the same time, making regular people think that if they learn about their secret goals it is just from a television show, movie or book so they will not believe that it is real."

Valerie thought for a moment and said, "So ... what you are saying is that Magical Girl Squad is based on real life?"

Major Josh chuckled and said, "In a sense, yes."

Valerie tilted her head and brought her finger to her lips as she tried to process this new information. She said, "So ... what you are saying is that I am really a Magical Girl like in the show?"

Major Josh nodded his head and said, "In a sense, yes."

Valerie started to grin and clap her hands, she raised her hands high in the air and said, "I knew it! I knew it! I knew it! I really am a Magical Girl!"

Lieutenant Michael scratched his head. A look of confusion fell on his face. He said, "Is that really true? They hide stuff like that in what we watch on the television? How can we know what is the secret stuff and what is just make believe for fun?"

Major Josh nodded his head and said, "Yes, it is true. The only way to know what is the secret stuff and what is the made up stuff is if you already know the plan."

Lieutenant Michael said, "Do you know the plan?"

Major Josh smiled coyly at him, he then turned to Valerie to speak to her again.

Lieutenant Michael thought, *I guess he's not willing to tell me.*

Major Josh said, "Valerie, do you know that there are two World Governments?"

Valerie shook her head and said, "I don't know too much about that kind of stuff."

Major Josh said, "There are two World Governments: there is the open World Government that everybody sees and there is a secret World Government that only certain people know about. We call the open World Government the World Government, this is the same government that everybody knows about. The secret World Government is known by a different name. It is called the Path of the Future."

The name didn't seem to mean anything to anybody so Major Josh said, "Valerie, why don't you sing that song again."

Valerie nodded her head with a smile and started to sing. When she was near the end she sang the line that says, "The Path of the Future calls you!" She stopped singing and gasped, saying, "The Path of the Future. Just like in the song!"

Major Josh nodded his head and said, "That is right, Valerie. The Path of the Future is calling you, it is your destiny! This line in your song is trying to show you that it is this secret World Government that hides in the shadows that is calling you to perform your task as a Spirit Wielder, a Magical Girl."

Sarah grabbed the sides of her own head and said, "Geez, all this information is starting to hurt my brain. I'm getting a headache."

Major Josh said, "Try not to worry about it. I probably told you too much, but what I told you is part of the truth."

Lieutenant Michael said, "So, are you not going to answer my question then?"

Major Josh said, "Brother, I have told you as much as I could at the moment. We are not under audio surveillance at the moment, which is why I told you as much as I did. The time is coming when I can tell you more, but that time is not right now. Please be patient and trust me. I know what I am doing."

Lieutenant Michael shook his head and said, "I trust you, brother. But, I don't like being kept in the dark like this."

Major Josh nodded and said, "I know, brother. I do not like keeping you in the dark either. But, please, trust me anyway. I will give you the opportunity to know everything when the time is right if you still want to know it."

Lieutenant Michael sighed and readjusted his positioning in his chair as best he could. He said, "Alright, I'll let this go for now and wait."

Major Josh nodded his head and kept quiet.

For the next two hours, everybody stayed silent. Valerie appeared to be in deep thought as she thought about what Major Josh said. Jennifer had fallen asleep. Sarah kicked her feet in the air as she stared at the ceiling, bored.

Valerie kept staring at Major Josh, the look on her face said that she wanted to ask him a question. Lieutenant Michael noticed it and said, "Valerie, is there something you want to say?"

Valerie looked to Lieutenant Michael and said, "I got a question for Major Josh."

Major Josh said, "Yes, Valerie. What is it?"

Valerie said, "Well, I've been thinking about what you said so I've been going over the lyrics to the Magical Girl song in my head. I don't understand too much but there is another line in there that makes me think. It sounds familiar to me."

Major Josh said, "Which line is it?"

Valerie said, "You've tasted the fruit that fell from the tree."

Josh said, "And how does it sound familiar to you? What does it make you think of?"

Valerie thought for a moment in silence and said, "Well, when I lived with my mom and dad, they would read the Bible to me."

Major Josh nodded his head and said, "Yes."

Valerie continued, saying, "In the beginning of the Bible it says that God had a tree with fruit that gave people knowledge."

Josh said, "Ah, yes. I remember that. So you think the two are connected?"

Valerie nodded and said, "I'm not too sure, but I think they are."

Major Josh nodded his head and said, "You are certainly an intelligent little girl. I agree with you that the two are connected."

Valerie said, "Can you tell me how?"

Major Josh said, "I could tell you how, but where is the fun in that. Give it some more thought and you just might figure it out on your own. I will tell you if you have come to the correct conclusion."

Valerie's face scrunched in annoyance and she sighed as she went back into deep thought.

Both Sarah and Valerie fell asleep too. Jennifer woke up to find them sleeping. Lieutenant Michael saw that she had woken up and he said, "Did you have a good nap?"

Jennifer tried to stretch in her seat but the harness made it difficult to do so. She yawned and said, "I guess so." She sighed and shook the sleep off of her face and said, "Are we there yet?"

Major Josh said, "We should be approaching our destination soon."

The noise of the conversation caused Sarah to stir. She opened her eyes and looked around confused. She said, "Oh yeah, we're in an aircraft." She looked at Valerie, who was still sleeping, and then at Jennifer, who was now awake. She said to Jennifer, "What's going on?"

Jennifer shrugged her shoulders and said, "Nothing much, just sitting here board out of my mind."

Sarah held out a fist and said, "You wanna play rock, paper, scissors?"

Jennifer shrugged her shoulders and said, "I guess so." She then held out her own fist and the two of them began to play rock, paper, scissors.

Valerie continued to sleep soundly as the two girls played. Lieutenant Michael watched her sleep and hoped that she was having good dreams. He knew that she had a lot of nightmares and those nightmares were centered on the death of Mary. Again, he felt the pain of her loss in the depths of his heart. He felt his own worthlessness for not having any power to fight for and protect them. *If only I could be stronger for them,* he thought to himself.

Suddenly the Sparrow Hawk came to a stop and the force of the movement caused everyone to be shaken in their seats. Valerie, who had been forcibly awoken from her deep sleep, began to flail her arms and legs. She began to scream in the confusion and then stopped as she began to remember that she was in an air craft.

Major Josh chuckled at the sight and said, "Do not worry, little Valerie, it appears that we have arrived at our destination."

The Sparrow Hawk began to descend. Without any windows in the passenger compartment, they could not see what was going on outside, but they could feel the descending motion as their bodies began to unnaturally fall toward the ground. The Sparrow Hawk descended and then gently touched the ground with a large clank.

The ramp began to lower. A wave of fresh, cool air began to rush in replacing the stale warm air of the interior of the Sparrow Hawk. Beyond the ramp, the whole area was kept artificially lit by large flood lights.

Major Josh unhooked his own harness and said, "Alright, everybody, unharness yourself and let us depart."

Lieutenant Michael unhooked himself and cautiously stood up. His arms and legs felt tight from being forced to sit without motion for so long.

Sarah unhooked herself first and slid out of her chair. She raised her arms over her head and began to stretch as she stumbled towards the ramp.

Valerie tried to figure out how to unhook herself but couldn't manage it. Lieutenant Michael saw her struggling with it so he walked over to her and said, "You need a hand?"

Valerie pouted and said, "Yes, please."

Lieutenant Michael smiled at her and unhooked her harness. He picked her up by her armpits and set her feet on the ground. She smiled but then began to yawn and stretch from the long ride. Her feet seemed unstable as she moved toward the ramp.

Lieutenant Michael turned his head to see how Jennifer was doing. She was also struggling with the complex harness. He walked over to her seat and said, "Do you need some help too?"

Jennifer shook her head and said, "No, I can do it."

She continued to struggle and then sighed in frustration saying, "Lieutenant, I can't do it."

Lieutenant Michael reached over and undid her harness. She pouted and embarrassingly said, "Thanks." She slid out of her seat and also stretched.

They walked down the ramp and onto the pavement of what appeared to be a military air field. The wall of the Berlin Sector was on the other side of a runway or street. It towered over the area ominously. It was the only barrier preventing an onslaught of Harvesters from slaughtering the people of this city.

Valerie tugged onto Lieutenant Michael's jacket and quietly said, "I've got to pee, Lieutenant."

Sarah nodded and said, "Yeah, I got to pee too."

Jennifer, who still seemed embarrassed, crossed her arms over her chest and nodded her head, saying, "Me too."

Lieutenant Michael turned to Major Josh and said, "Is there a bathroom around here?"

Major Josh pointed to a row of portable toilets and said, "Right over there."

Sarah drooped her shoulders and said, "Great. Old, stinky, portable toilets." She sighed and began to walk towards them. Jennifer and Valerie followed her.

As Valerie caught up with her, she said, "Well, at least we got some toilets now. After this we're going to have to go in the field."

Sarah said, "Yeah, I know. But, still. Old, stinky, portable toilets."

Jennifer said, "I hope nobody peed on the seat this time."

There was a row of four portable toilets and they were all empty, so they did not have to wait. Sarah put her hand on the door handle and pulled it open. As she did so a wave of damp, warm, stale air, rushed over her face. She scrunched her face in disgust and went in to do her business.

Altogether, they stood on top of the wall of the Berlin Sector. The darkness of the night was chased away by a sea of lights that revealed the old city of Berlin. The twinkling of the lights proved that life went on even on the other side of the planet. Jennifer stood there watching over the old city. There was a look of disappointment on her face. Her arms were crossed over her chest. She sighed and said, "I wish we had time to explore the city."

Sarah, who was standing next to her, put her right hand on Jennifer's shoulder and replied, "Yeah, the buildings kind of look different than they do in Sacramento Sector. I bet there'd be some interesting stuff."

Lieutenant Michael nodded and said, "Yeah, I wouldn't mind taking a peek around there at least once." He scratched his chin and said, "Well, maybe when we get back we might have some time to look around."

Jennifer dropped her arms from her chest and began to grin. She nodded her head and said, "Yeah! Let's do that, Lieutenant!"

In contrast, the Harvester Zone on the other side of the wall was pitch black. A cold wind blew from the east as autumn approached.

Valerie said, "I wonder what the Harvester Zone looks like in the light?"

Major Josh said, "Most of the area outside of the wall here is scorched earth. Nuclear bombs were used out there to slow the Harvester advance. When you get to see it, it will look even more devastated then in the areas in North America."

Valerie frowned and said, "That makes me sad."

Lieutenant Michael pulled a pair of goggles out of a pocket on his backpack and said, "Alright, team, let's put on our night vision gear." He put the goggles over his head and flipped a switch on them.

The girls in unison said, "Aye, Lieutenant!" They pulled their own night vision goggles out of their own backpacks and put them on. With their night vision goggles on, they could begin to see the devastation outside the wall.

Major Josh pulled a small black bottle out of one of his pockets and handed it to Lieutenant Michael. Lieutenant Michael took it and looked at it in his hand, saying, "What's this for?"

Major Josh replied, "It will take us three days to get to where I need to go. We don't have any time for sleep on this mission. Those are special pills designed to keep soldiers awake for several days at a time. There is enough to keep you all awake for a week in there."

Lieutenant Michael shook his head and said, "Josh, I don't think it'd be right to give these to little girls."

Major Josh nodded in understanding. He said, "I understand, but there is no safe place to sleep in the Harvester Zone. We also do not want them to get sluggish out there. It might just save their lives."

Lieutenant Michael tightened his grip around the bottle and sighed. He said, "You're right. I understand, but I get to determine when to give it to them."

Major Josh replied, "Of course. That is why I gave them to you."

Valerie tugged on Lieutenant Michael's jacket sleeve and said, "Are those pills bad, Lieutenant?"

Lieutenant Michael said, "Sort of. But Major Josh is right. These pills will help us keep awake and alert in the field." He then spoke authoritatively to the girls, saying, "I want you to tell me the moment you start getting sleepy. Okay?"

The girls in unison said, "Aye, Lieutenant."

Major Josh squared his shoulders and placed his arms behind his back. He said sternly, "Alright, Squad three. At this moment, we will head into the Harvester Zone to our destination. There is an abandoned air field three days in that direction. You will escort me to this air field and then we will part ways. Your primary purpose is not to engage the Harvesters, but to see to it that I am able to get to this abandoned air field. You will only engage in combat on these two conditions: One, if we are in an immediate threat, or, two, when I give you an order to engage. Is that understood?"

The girls saluted in their childish manner and said in unison, "Aye, Major!"

Major Josh pointed toward the ladder that led down the side of the wall, saying, "Alright, I want Jennifer to go down first, then Sarah. Valerie will follow Sarah down, then your Lieutenant and myself will follow."

Sarah saluted him again and said, "Aye, Major!" She looked toward Jennifer and then to Valerie. There was a slight hesitation in her.

Lieutenant Michael noticed it and said, "It's alright, girls, you can do it."

Sarah nodded with a smile. She extended her hand outward with her palm facing down. Jennifer put her own hand on top of Sarah's hand. Valerie put her hand on top of Jennifer's hand. Sarah said, "Let's keep each other safe!"

Jennifer said, "I'll do my best to protect you!"

Valerie said, "I'll do my best to heal you!"

They then broke their hands apart and Sarah said, "We're ready to go now, Lieutenant!"

Lieutenant Michael nodded and said, "Alright, girls! Activate your powers and deploy, Sarah first, Jennifer, then Valerie."

The girls activated their powers. Blue, red, and yellow light started to glow around the edges of their goggles. One by one they started to descend down the ladder.

As they descended, Major Josh spoke quietly to Lieutenant Michael, saying, "I hope that I did not confuse them."

Lieutenant Michael waved his hand in dismissal and said, "Don't worry, they're not used to your style and I know more about their own styles then you do. They like to do that ritual before they go; it helps them feel better."

Major Josh said, "I will rely on your guidance in leading your team."

Lieutenant Michael said, "Don't worry, brother. I got you covered." He then looked to Valerie as she went down the ladder. She stopped for a moment and grinned at him and then continued downward. Lieutenant Michael followed behind her down the ladder.

- 7 -

Major Josh hopped off of the ladder and onto the ground. Lieutenant Michael and the girls stood there in a circle waiting for him to lead them. Major Josh gripped his hands behind his back and said, "Alright, team. Follow me." He started walking in a direction that Lieutenant Michael assumed was east.

Lieutenant Michael pointed at Jennifer and said, "Jennifer, go on point behind the Major."

Jennifer replied, "Aye, Lieutenant." She moved to follow behind Major Josh.

Lieutenant Michael then pointed at Sarah and said, "Sarah, take the rear."

Sarah replied, "Aye, Lieutenant."

Lieutenant Michael started following Jennifer. Valerie instinctively walked alongside him as she always did. Sarah followed behind him several paces.

The view through the night vision goggles were in shades of gray. The ground below their feet looked to be pitch black. It crunched underneath their combat boots. There was no doubt that the ground was littered with charcoaled remains of vegetation from past fire bombings to clear the undergrowth of vegetation.

The night vision goggles revealed a large opening of cleared ground surrounding the wall. Beyond the large opening of ground, there seemed to be what looked like little hills pushing out of the horizon.

As if he had read their minds, Major Josh pointed toward the little hills and said, "See those little hills?"

Lieutenant Michael replied, "Yeah, I see them."

Major Josh said, "That was once a city. Now it is scorched earth. You cannot really see it now, but when we get there, you will see the true devastation of the Harvesters."

Lieutenant Michael looked toward the ruins of the dead city. Most of the Harvester Zone in North of America were abandoned areas since they had time to build the walls before the Harvesters reached them. Abandoned cities were mostly intact except for the decay of time. In the rest of the world, most cities were devastated from weapons of war.

Lieutenant Michael called out, saying, "Josh, not that it matters, but why can't we just fly to your destination? Don't you think that would be better?"

Without changing his stride, Josh replied, "Normally, I would agree with you. But, the location I am going to needs to remain secret. The pilot cannot know where I am going, otherwise I would have to kill him. And I would like to avoid killing people if possible."

Lieutenant Michael heard the sincerity in his voice and said, "That didn't sound like you were joking."

Major Josh replied, "That is because I am not joking. By the time you get back to civilization, it will not matter if you tell anybody where I am going. So, it is much better to have you take me, then to have a pilot take me and then have to kill that person."

Sarah, listening in on their conversation, began to remember the people who were killed right in front of her. She spoke up and said, "People shouldn't kill people."

Major Josh stopped and turned around to look at her. He nodded and said, "That is right, Sarah. People should not kill people." He then turned back around and continued walking.

In addition to the veil of darkness that shrouded them from sight, there was great benefit to walking in the open in the middle of the night. The Harvesters were mostly night sleepers so during the night they would hunker down underneath their shells and sleep. Of course this did not mean that you could move through their territory loudly, as even small noises caused them to wake up and attack. They also woke up well before sunrise so the darkness did not offer complete security.

In the distance, they saw a pack of mounds rising from the ground. The mounds were no doubt Harvesters sleeping out in the open. Major Josh began to walk in a curved path around their location to avoid causing them to awaken from their slumber. The girls understood already how important it was to be quiet when they were close to them like this.

The sun began to rise early in the morning and they were very close to the ruins. As the sunlight peaked over the earth, the need for their night vision goggles disappeared. They took them off and returned them to their backpacks.

The ruins were masses of concrete and rebar sticking out of them. Beside the piles of broken concrete lay the square-ish foundations of what used to be buildings. The last remnants of human artifacts lay scattered throughout the rubble. The ground looked burnt from what was most likely repeated nuclear detonations. Unlike the ruins around Sacramento area, these ruins seemed not to contain any plant life. Or, it was so small and sparse that it was not noticeable from this distance.

Jennifer looked over the ruins and said, "How depressing." She looked to the ground and saw a half burnt doll in front of her feet. She picked it up and examined it in her hands.

Valerie noticed her and wrapped an arm around Jennifer's arm. She looked at the scorched features of the doll and said, "I hope the girl who owned that doll is safe."

Sarah rested an arm on top of Valerie's head and said, "I hope so too."

Jennifer dropped the doll on the ground. It bounced once and then settled back into the rubbish.

Major Josh pulled a small device out of one of his pockets and said, "The scenery is only going to get worse from here, so I hope you have prepared your minds for it. We are approaching the Last Defense Line."

Valerie tugged on Lieutenant Michael's jacket sleeve and said, "Lieutenant, what's the Last Defense Line?"

Lieutenant Michael gazed at the ruins in amazement and said, "That is where the United Earth Forces gathered to hold the line against the Harvesters. Because of their sacrifice, the local sectors were able to finish constructing their walls."

Valerie said, "What happened to them?"

Lieutenant Michael said, "They all died."

Jennifer grasped at the scars on her wrist as she began to remember the pain of losing all her friends in Los Angeles. Sarah noticed her and wrapped an arm around her shoulders. Jennifer released the grasp on her wrist and took hold of Sarah's hand.

Major Josh held up the device, which ended up being a type of advanced compass, which he was not at liberty to discuss. They made their way toward the ruins and entered in through what looked like the remnant of a street.

Sarah tugged on Lieutenant Michael's sleeve and said, "Lieutenant, I'm getting sleepy."

Valerie joined in and said, "Yeah, me too."

Jennifer nodded her head and said, "Yeah, it's probably our bed time back home."

Lieutenant Michael nodded and said, "Yeah, I'm feeling it too. Guess we'll have to take those pills now."

Lieutenant Michael pulled the small bottle out of his pocket and opened it. He pulled out four little white pills and handed one to each one of the girls.

Major Josh said, "It is okay to just put it in your mouth and chew and swallow it."

Valerie stuck the pill in her mouth and started to chew it. In surprise, her eyes opened wide and a look of deep satisfaction fell upon her face. It was very sweet to the taste. She said, "Wow! That tastes just like candy!"

Jennifer and Sarah stuck the pill in their mouth and chewed it too. As Valerie had said, it was very sweet like candy.

They continued to go through the ruins. The sun was now fully exposed in the sky. Valerie suddenly tripped and crashed into Lieutenant Michael. She grasped onto his jacket to stop herself from falling. She said, "I'm sorry, Lieutenant. I tripped over something hard."

Sarah pointed from behind them saying, "You tripped over that."

Together, they all looked at what Sarah was pointing at. A human skull laid rolled over on its side. The hollowed out cavities of the skull stared menacingly at Valerie. She gave a small shriek and she grasped on to Lieutenant Michael's jacket again as she buried her face in his jacket.

All around them lay scattered bones of dead humans. The skeletons were not intact, no doubt they were torn apart by Harvesters and scattered throughout the area as the Harvesters feasted on them.

In addition to the remains of the soldiers, there were tanks, riffles, and other military equipment that laid about rusting in the open air. This was the Last Defense Line where brave men and women laid down their lives so that what remained of humanity in this continent could survive.

Valerie's shriek was answered by the loud screech of a Harvester. In the distance another Harvester screeched in response to the first.

A look of guilt fell upon Valerie as she lowered her head in submission and raised her shoulders in embarrassment. Her lips pouted as she realized that she had made the Harvesters aware of their presence.

Jennifer pointed her finger at Valerie and in a hushed tone, angrily said, "Good job, Valerie! You called some Harvesters over!"

Valerie quietly replied, "I'm sorry, I didn't mean to. I just got scared by the skull."

Lieutenant Michael said, "Don't worry, they can't see us yet so let's just keep going forward. We can deal with any Harvesters that come across our path if we have to."

They began to jog out of the area, but it was in vain. A fully-grown Harvester crawled on top of a large mound of rubble and spotted them. It let out a loud screech, which was answered by several other Harvesters. Soon this area would be overrun by the local Harvesters.

Major Josh said, "You have permission to engage."

The girls responded in unison, "Aye, sir!" Their hands began to glow with the light of their eye color.

Lieutenant Michael watched as the Harvester that stood on the mound began to quiver in agitation. Clear drool began to spill from its mouth as its mandibles opened and shut at them.

A second fully-grown Harvester appeared in a gap between two heaps of rubble and a collapsed overpass. It screeched and shook its mandibles side to side.

The first Harvester began to charge at them. Jennifer leapt toward it, landing to the side of it. She pulled her fist back and swung it with all her might. She landed a hit right across the side of its face between two of its eyes. Its head was tilted from the blow.

The Harvester ceased running straight and ran in the direction that its head was now pointing at. It stopped and shook its body and clicked its mandibles, which was a sign of anger.

The second Harvester, following the first ones example, began to charge at them as well. Sarah pointed her palms at it and began to fire her blue spear of light out of her hands. The Harvester began to spin in a circle as it tried to avoid the painful bursts of energy.

A third fully-grown Harvester climbed up another pile of rubble and focused its attention on Jennifer. It screeched and then ran at her with all of its strength.

Valerie saw it and yelled out, "Jennifer! Behind you!"

Without hesitating or even looking, Jennifer jumped straight up into the air narrowly missing a direct charge from a Harvester.

The third Harvester ran right underneath Jennifer as she leapt into the air. It crashed into the first Harvester, causing it to roll over on its side. The first Harvester kicked its legs and managed to roll back onto its feet.

Jennifer now stared down two fully-grown Harvesters. She leapt at the first one and smashed a fist into its face. She then leapt toward the third Harvester and did a power kick into the side of its head, damaging one of its four eyes. The Harvester screeched from the pain.

Valerie watched on as Jennifer continued to hop from the first to the third Harvester as she tried to fight both at the same time. Sarah continued to distract the second Harvester with her spear of light ability.

Valerie turned to Lieutenant Michael and said, "Lieutenant, let me go out there and help Jennifer."

Lieutenant Michael shook his head and said, "No, it's too dangerous."

Valerie threw her fists down alongside of her body and angrily said, "Lieutenant, I can help with my special ability! Just let me go and help!"

Lieutenant Michael shook his head and said, "No, not yet."

Valerie sighed in frustration.

Major Josh put his hand on Lieutenant Michael's shoulder and said, "Valerie, I am ordering you to assist Jennifer."

Valerie looked to Lieutenant Michael, who now looked annoyed. He gave a slight nod. Valerie grinned and ran toward Jennifer. She held up her palms and caused them to glow with yellow light. She yelled out, "I'm not afraid of you, stupid bug!"

Valerie ran up to the third Harvester and grabbed onto one of its mandibles. As she grabbed onto one of the mandibles, she yelled to Jennifer, "Distract that Harvester while I kill this one."

Jennifer replied, "Got it!"

Valerie's hands began to grow brighter as she held onto one of the Harvesters mandibles. The Harvester screeched as it felt the pain of its life being slowly drained. It began to shake its head in the hope of getting away from the pain.

Valerie tried to hold on but was violently thrown from the Harvester. She landed in a pile of concrete rubble. There was a gash in her head from the impact and a gash in her arm where it was cut from the mandible of the Harvester.

Lieutenant Michael looked on in horror as Valerie was thrown from the Harvester. Major Josh quickly grabbed onto his shoulder to stop him from running to her. He said, "I know you care about them deeply and you do not want them to get hurt. But, you need to let them do their job. You cannot take it all on yourself you know."

Instead of crying, Valerie grinned and stood up from the pile of rubble. Her eyes glowed brighter and the wound on her head and arm started to close on their own. She wiped the trickle of blood on her face with her sleeve and dusted off the back of her dress. She ran back to the Harvester and grabbed onto its mandibles again. The life force of the Harvester began to drain out of it. Again, she got thrown from the Harvester into a pile of rubble.

Sarah managed to kill off the second Harvester. She called out to Jennifer, saying, "I'll distract that Harvester, Jennifer. Hold down the other one for Valerie."

Jennifer replied, "Got it!"

She leapt toward the third Harvester and grabbed onto both of its mandibles and then braced her feet as she held it in place.

Sarah ran towards the first Harvester and began to fire her spear of light at it.

Valerie picked herself up out of the rubble. More cuts began to heal automatically. She ran up again to the third Harvester and placed her hands on top of its head as Jennifer held it in place.

Life flowed out of the Harvester and into Valerie's tiny body. It screeched in protest and tried to escape from Jennifer's grip, but it became weaker as its energy was drained out of it. Finally, it stopped moving and collapsed under the weight of its own body.

Jennifer let go and said to Valerie, "Let's get the last one together."

Valerie nodded with a grin and said, "Yeah!"

Sarah stopped firing at it and Jennifer grabbed onto its mandibles. Sarah pulled out her two metal sticks and covered them in her blue light energy. She ran alongside the Harvester and hacked off each of its legs, one by one. Valerie approached its head and placed her hands on it. She began to absorb its energy till it stopped squirming.

Valerie and Jennifer began to jump for joy as they celebrated their victory. Sarah walked around the dead Harvester and kicked it on the side of its head. She pumped her fist in victory and said, "That's what you get for messing with the wrong squad!"

Sarah held up her palm and gave Jennifer and Valerie a high-five. Valerie and Jennifer then gave each other a high-five.

The girls walked back with their arms linked together to where Lieutenant Michael and Major Josh stood.

Valerie's excitement went away as she approached them. She let go of Sarah's arm and stood in front of Lieutenant Michael. She placed her hands on top of each other and dropped them in front of the skirt of her dress. Her body began to twist side to side and she tilted her head to the side, looking downward. She said, "Are ... are you mad Lieutenant that I used my power."

Lieutenant Michael shook his head and placed his hand on top of her head, saying, "No, I'm not mad. I just get worried that you'll hurt yourself if you use that power too much. You girls worked together very well so I'm very happy with all of you."

Valerie returned to her cheerful self and she gave Lieutenant Michael a huge grin.

Sarah put her hands on her stomach and said, "Lieutenant, all that fighting made me hungry. Can we take a food break?"

Lieutenant Michael looked to Major Josh. Major Josh nodded his head and said, "Sure, that sounds like a good idea."

They all took off their backpacks and pulled out one of the ration bars. They sat and ate it together amidst the piles of concrete rubble and human remains.

The sun went down and the dark veil of the night covered them. Lieutenant Michael distributed another pill to everyone from the black bottle that he kept in his pocket. It energized them and would let them stay awake for another twelve hours.

Since it was night, they knew that the Harvesters would be most likely sleeping so they could relax a little as long as they were quiet. Unfortunately, their field of vision was obscured by the ruins around them.

Valerie sighed from boredom, she wanted to break out into song but knew that, if she was loud, she could attract local Harvesters. The pills made her feel twitchy but she managed to control it.

Jennifer kept glancing back at Lieutenant Michael who was behind her. At times she seemed embarrassed by him and he didn't understand why or if that was really the case. She also felt an increase of energy from the pills.

Sarah, being more mature, tried to focus on the mission. The pills that she took made her feel alert. Her mind drifted though as she thought that, if Mary had taken the pills, she would be bouncing all over the place. A small chuckle escaped from her lips as she imagined Mary jumping all over the place.

Lieutenant Michael turned his head and glanced at her. She covered her mouth with her hand and then whispered into the com unit, saying, "Sorry, Lieutenant. I was just thinking that, if Mary took one of those stay-awake pills, she'd be bouncing all over the place."

Valerie whispered into her own com unit, saying, "Yeah, I can see that."

With Sarah's words fresh in his mind, Lieutenant Michael imagined Mary taking one of those pills. He also felt the buzz from the pills. He could definitely see Mary jumping around because of it. Mary's voice whispered into his mind as if she was speaking from the grave. The memory of her brought sadness to his heart again. *She could have been on this mission with us*, he thought to himself.

Lieutenant Michael tried to push the pain out of his mind. He turned his attention to Jennifer. She was glancing back at him again. When their eyes met, she quickly thrust her face forward to avoid looking at him again. He rolled his eyes and wondered why she was acting like this lately.

The sun began to rise again. As the sun rose, it was greeted by the screeches of Harvesters. Fortunately, the Harvesters did not see them going through that region.

As the sun rose fully in the sky, they had made it through the old metropolitan area that surrounded old Berlin. In front of them was a barren wasteland that had once been a forest. Now, there was nothing but burnt down stumps and flattened charcoal trunks scattered about the land.

The ground was blackened with soot and charcoal. The ground crunched underneath their combat boots. The smell of fire had long since dispersed.

Unlike the Harvester Zone in North America, the whole region seemed dead. There were no birds chirping. There were no rats scurrying over the abandoned ruins of humanity. Except for their own movements, the only sounds that could be heard were the sounds of wind rushing over the desolate land and the screeches of Harvesters.

Being in the open, they could see if there were Harvesters around more easily. The drawback was that the Harvesters could see them more easily as well. A large pack of baby Harvesters and junior-sized Harvesters intercepted them, but they were easily dealt with.

Since they were in the open and could see all around them, they relaxed their discipline. Valerie, who had been itching to sing for a while started to sing in a soft tone. Instead of being annoying, it brought some feeling of life back to the desolate region. It was a welcome sound even to Jennifer.

Much to Lieutenant Michael's surprise, Jennifer started to sing along with her. It was a welcomed sight. He thought back on their first experiences with Jennifer. Her extreme depression and guilt caused her to wall herself off from everybody. Now, she had fully integrated herself into the group and was joining in during fun activates instead of sitting alone and reading her books.

As they continued their journey, they encountered a small group of mid-sized and a couple of fully grown Harvesters. It was a little more difficult, but they managed to dispose of them.

The sun began to set again. This was their second day in the field. Major Josh told them that they would definitely reach their objective soon. He had become strangely quiet since they left the Berlin Sector. He even stopped talking to Lieutenant Michael, except to convey some needed information. Lieutenant Michael wondered at this but decided that it was because of the stress of this mission.

They left the desolated forest region and entered into another metropolitan area. Again, the cities that once stood there were nothing but collapsed and burnt ruins.

The girls started to yawn as the sun went down. Lieutenant Michael took the little black container out of his pocket and distributed a little pill to every one again.

In one of the rare moments of communication, Major Josh started clapping his hands and said, "Congratulations! We have left what was once Germany and have now entered what was once called Poland."

The girls uncaringly raised their right fist into the air and said in an unimpressed tone, "Yay."

Valerie said, "How come there used to be so many different countries? They were always fighting each other too, weren't they?"

Sarah said, "Yeah, people have always fought wars with each other. For the first time in our history, the Harvesters gave us a reason to stop fighting each other and unite as a people. I hate to say it but it might have been a good thing that the aliens came. If it wasn't for them, we'd still be a bunch of different countries fighting each other."

Major Josh, who avoided unnecessary conversation, decided to join in and said, "So, Sarah. Do you really think that it was good that the aliens came in their ships and murdered half of the world's population?"

Sarah shook her head and said, "No, I don't think it was good, but since it happened anyway, it ended up doing some good for us since we now have the World Government and one people. We don't fight wars with each other anymore."

Major Josh replied, "Now Sarah, do you know why we do not fight wars with each other anymore?"

Sarah said, "Yeah, because we're one people now."

Major Josh said, "How did we get to be one people?"

Sarah shook her head in frustration and said, "I don't get what you're asking me, Major."

Major Josh said, "Okay, I apologize. Let me be more direct if you will. The World Government confiscated all the world's weapons so now they are the only ones with the weapons. Using those weapons, they forcefully disbanded all national governments. Nations that resisted were devastated by those same weapons. In addition to this, they eliminated all cultures and artificially created a new culture, which they forced the people to accept on penalty of death or imprisonment. I guess what I am trying to say is that the World Government has used a constant state of war to force all the people in the world to be under them."

Sarah said, "Well, when you put it that way, I can see that. I know the World Government can be harsh. I don't think that it is good to kill people. But, since we are always living under the threat of the Harvesters, I can understand why they do all those harsh things."

Valerie butted into the conversation and said, "Major Josh, you don't like the World Government, do you?"

Major Josh shook his head and said, "You are right, Valerie. I do not like the World Government. For now, we are forced to endure it. Soon this war will be over though."

Lieutenant Michael said, "I know you mentioned that before but you said you couldn't talk about it. We're out here all alone now, can't you at least give me a hint? I promise not to tell anyone."

Major Josh sighed and stopped walking. He turned to Lieutenant Michael and said, "I want to tell you. I cannot tell you right now. If I tell you now, it might endanger your life in the future and I do not want to do that to you."

Lieutenant Michael nodded and said, "Alright, alright. I won't push you. I just wish that I could be a part of it. If we could bring this war to an end ... I'd ... I'd do whatever I could to end it so that the girls don't have to fight anymore."

Major Josh nodded with a smile and turned back around. He continued to walk toward their destination in silence.

The sun rose and climbed high in the sky. It was now the third day. It was the day that Major Josh had promised that they would reach their destination. During the night they had made it through the next metropolitan area and had entered another devastated forest region.

Major Josh pulled out his mapping instrument again and took a quick reading. He then turned in a sharp angle and started walking straight.

Lieutenant Michael said, "Are we getting close, Josh?"

Major Josh replied, "Yes, we are getting close. We should make it to our destination before the sun sets."

Lieutenant Michael sighed.

Valerie quietly said, "Lieutenant, are you worried about your brother?"

Lieutenant Michael nodded and said, "Yeah."

Valerie said, "Maybe you should talk to him about it. That is what I would do."

Lieutenant Michael glanced over at Josh and thought about her suggestion. He had tried to talk to him before but it had gotten him nowhere. He stopped walking. Valerie stopped beside him. Sarah, standing a little ways behind him walked up to the other side of him and stood next to him.

Jennifer heard their footsteps cease. She looked behind herself and saw that they were just standing there. She stopped and turned around completely, saying, "Is something wrong, Lieutenant?"

Major Josh stopped in his own tracks and turned around. His eyes met with Michael's eyes. He said, "Is there a problem, Michael?"

Lieutenant Michael just stood there and continued staring at him.

Major Josh said, "Michael?"

Lieutenant Michael finally opened his mouth and said, "Josh, I need you to tell me what's going on, please."

Major Josh said, "I am sorry, brother. I cannot do that at this time."

Lieutenant Michael became angry and started walking aggressively towards Major Josh. Josh stood there unintimidated.

Lieutenant Michael stopped a few paces from him and said, "I can't accept that as an answer anymore. Since we've been out here, you've barely spoken to me. When you do speak, it's in cryptic remarks that mean nothing to us. I need you to tell me what's going on right now. Or, we're going back right now. My first priority is to protect these girls."

Major Josh frowned and looked down toward the ground. He said, "Do you really believe that I would do something to harm either you or your team?"

Lieutenant Michael looked him straight in his eyes, trying to read his intentions. He said, "I ... I don't want to believe that you would. But ..."

Lieutenant Michael reached his hands out and grasped onto Josh's jacket and started to shake him. Major Josh grabbed onto Lieutenant Michael's wrists.

Lieutenant Michael stopped shaking him and said, "You ask me to trust you, but you don't trust me?"

Tears started to form in Josh's eyes. He said, "What I know is so horrible that you would not believe me if I just told you. I ... I would not believe it till I saw it with my own eyes."

Much to Michael's surprise, Josh started crying. Lieutenant Michael let go of his jacket. Major Josh covered his face with his hands.

Lieutenant Michael put his right hand on Josh's shoulder and said, "What's going on? What are you holding onto that is eating you up inside? I'm right here with you. You can trust me."

Major Josh composed himself and said, "Come with me, Michael and I'll show you. I'll show you everything that I saw. I know that every fiber of your being is telling you to not trust me, but, trust me, and I will show you what I cannot speak."

Major Josh held his hand out toward him. Lieutenant Michael took it and said, "Alright. I'll trust you. Show me what you want to show me."

Major Josh smiled and gave a quick nod. He said, "Alright, let us keep going then."

For the rest of the day neither Michael nor Josh spoke to each other. They barely said anything to anybody except to respond to one of the girls if they asked a question.

The sun started to set and the sky turned orange. Major Josh stopped in his tracks and pointed toward the horizon, saying, "There is our destination."

In the distance there was what looked like a broken up runway. Several small metal shacks, surprisingly, were still standing beside the runway. In the middle of the broken runway there was what looked like a small single engine helicopter.

Lieutenant Michael glared at the sight and said, "So, is this what you wanted to show me?"

Major Josh shook his head and said, "No, no, brother. If you are willing to come with me. We will take this helicopter to the thing that I want to show you."

They walked up to the helicopter. It looked to be really old. It looked like it was built before the first alien attack on earth. It was white and, if it was marked with any identifiers, they had been sanded off leaving a bare metal patch.

Jennifer looked at the helicopter and said, "Geez, can that thing even fly?"

Major Josh chuckled and said, "I hope so because we have to use that thing to get to our next destination."

Major Josh opened the side door to the helicopter. It creaked and seemed like it was going to snap off. He said, "Alright, my friends. Either you will come with me now or you will go back to your home and not worry about a thing. If you do come with me, I can promise you that you will learn the truth of everything in this world and how we can stop this war. But, if you come with me, you will be dead to the world where you are from.

Lieutenant Michael shook his head and said, "There you go being all cryptic again. Can't you just speak normally and not sound like a pompous ass?"

Major Josh chuckled and replied, "My apologies, brother. What I mean to say is that, if you come with me, the World Government will think that you were killed in action. They will not think that you are still alive. If you come with me, you will never be able to go back to the life you have been living. The only thing I can promise you is that, if you agree to come with me, you will know the truth to this world. You will know why your girls have their power. You will know why the Harvesters are here. I know how to stop them. I will stop them."

Lieutenant Michael looked dumbfounded. He started to stutter and said, "What? What? You know why these girls have this power? You know how to stop the Harvesters? You're right. I don't think I would have believed you if you just told me."

Major Josh held his hand open towards them and said, "But, it is true. Will you come with me or will you return to your normal life?"

Lieutenant Michael stood there in silence. His own thoughts raced in his own mind. He knew his brother wouldn't lie to him but the whole thing just seemed so crazy. If he knew how to stop this war, wouldn't the World Government be behind him? Rachel's face flashed in his mind. If he went with his brother, would he be able to see her again?

Lieutenant Michael put his hands on top of his head and sighed loudly in frustration. He looked down at the girls who were standing beside him. Sarah stood on his left. Valerie and Jennifer stood on his right.

He spread out his arms and pulled all three of the girls into an embrace and said, "Okay, girls. What do you think about this? If just one of you wants to go back home, we'll all go back together. If you all want to learn this truth that my brother claims to know about, then we'll all go with him together."

Jennifer looked up at him. She looked a little embarrassed in his embrace. She said, "If we can stop all the Harvesters, I'll vote that we go with Major Josh."

Sarah rested her head on his chest and said, "I want to know why we have this power. I vote that we go with Major Josh too."

Valerie hesitated to speak. They all looked at her. She looked up at Lieutenant Michael and said, "Since I learned about this power that I have, I always felt that I was special. I want to know why I was given this power. I vote that we go with Major Josh too."

Lieutenant Michael tightened his embrace around them and said, "Okay. We'll go and learn the truth together."

Valerie sighed in his embrace and said, "We're going to miss Magical Girl Squad, aren't we?"

Lieutenant Michael chuckled and said, "Probably."

- 8 -

Lieutenant Michael released his hold on the girls and said, "Alright, brother. I'm putting my trust in you. We've decided that we'll go with you."

Major Josh nodded with a smile and said, "I just knew that you would come. That is the real reason why I asked for you to escort me here. I wanted you to come see what I have seen. I promise you all that you will not regret it."

Major Josh reached inside the helicopter and pulled out an olive drab colored duffle bag. He tossed it on the ground in front of their feet. He said, "I need you all to take off your clothing."

Lieutenant Michael chuckled and said, "Take off our clothes? Are you joking?"

Major Josh shook his head and sighed in frustration, saying, "Your clothing has a small locator chip woven into the fabric. If you do not take off your clothing, then the World Government will be able to locate where you are."

Realization fell upon his face. He had never thought about it before but Josh was right. Everything they had as far as clothing and equipment was tagged with a small tracking chip so that they knew who had what and where it was.

Lieutenant Michael looked at the duffle bag and pointed at it, saying, "Are there at least spare clothes in the bag that aren't tagged?"

Major Josh shrugged his shoulders and said, "Not exactly." He bent over and sat the duffle bag upright. He opened the top and pulled out a large white towel. He held it up with both hands with a grin on his face.

Lieutenant Michael looked at Josh. The look on his face seemed to be saying, "Really?" Lieutenant Michael took the towel with a sigh and shook his head.

Major Josh chuckled nervously and said, "Sorry, it was the best they could do. I promise we will get you some new clothes at our next destination."

Lieutenant Michael turned around and said, "I hope so."

He then turned to the girls and said, "I'm going to change into this towel so cover your eyes and don't look."

Lieutenant Michael started to walk till he was twenty paces away. He did not want to move too far away in case Harvesters showed up. He stopped, looked behind himself and saw that the girls were covering their faces. He took off his jacket and let it drop to the ground. He loosened his tie and slipped it off over his head. He kicked his shoes off and pulled off his socks. He undid his combat belt and then took off his shirt and his pants.

Lieutenant Michael stood there in his underwear. He glanced over his shoulder to make sure that the girls were still covering their faces. They were. So he quickly slipped his underwear off and strapped the towel around his waist.

While Lieutenant Michael was changing, the girls stood there with their hands covering their faces. Or, so it would seem. As he changed the girls slid open their fingers to see through the cracks in their hands.

Sarah tilted her head slightly to look at Jennifer, one of her eyes could be seen through a crack in the fingers. Jennifer noticed that Sarah saw what she was doing so. She started to blush and quickly snapped her fingers shut. Sarah started to giggle.

Lieutenant Michael walked back to them and said, "Okay, girls you can open your eyes now."

They took their hands off of their faces, both Sarah and Jennifer avoided looking at each other. They both started to blush a little.

To their surprise, Valerie brought her hands together and started to fiddle with her thumbs. She looked downward, embarrassed and said, "I'm sorry, Lieutenant. I was curious about what a boy looks like so I peeked and saw your butt."

Lieutenant Michael crossed his arms over his naked chest and said, "Really? Well, thank you for being honest." He then pointed to Sarah and Jennifer, saying, "I suppose by the look of embarrassment on both of your faces, you two peeked as well?"

Sarah twisted her body side to side. She looked towards the ground and blushed again, saying, "I guess so."

Jennifer crossed her arms across her chest and said defensively, "I heard a noise and I was worried about a Harvester attacking so I looked and it was just an accident that I saw your butt."

Lieutenant Michael rolled his eyes and said, "Yeah, okay. Now it's your turn to change into these towels."

Lieutenant Michael went next to Josh and the two of them turned away to look in the opposite direction of where the girls were to give them some form of privacy out in the open.

Sarah was the first to start taking off her clothes. She took off her jacket and let it fall to the ground. She undid her combat belt and dropped it to her feet. She loosened the tie from around her neck and slid it over her head. She then lifted her dress off and dropped it on top of her jacket. She loosed her combat boots and kicked them off one by one. Then she pulled off her socks, her underwear and her bra. She wrapped the towel around her naked body.

As soon as Sarah started to change, Valerie followed suite. After completely changing out of her uniform, she wrapped the towel around her body. A cold wind was blowing and it started to make her skin get goosebumps all over. She started to shiver.

Jennifer stood there and watched Sarah and Valerie change out of their clothes. She crossed her arms over her chest again and waited clinging onto the white towel.

After Sarah was done changing, she looked at Jennifer and said, "Come on, Jennifer. Get out of your clothes so we can get going. It's cold out here."

Jennifer shook her head and said, "I don't want to change because I'm afraid the Lieutenant is going to peek at me."

Sarah shook her head and chuckled, saying, "Don't worry, He ain't going to peek at you."

Jennifer looked shyly at Lieutenant Michael and said, "I don't want him to see me naked."

Sarah rolled her eyes and said, "Jennifer, he's already seen you naked. Remember?"

Jennifer replied, "I don't want him to see me naked again!"

Valerie ripped the towel from Jennifer's grip and said, "What if Sarah and I held your towel up so that it can act as a cover for you?"

Jennifer nodded and said, "That's okay, I guess."

Lieutenant Michael shook his head and muttered to himself in annoyance. Major Josh laughed.

Valerie and Sarah held the towel up like a curtain. Jennifer hid behind it and took a quick look at Lieutenant Michael and Major Josh. She said, "No peeking!"

Lieutenant Michael wanted to respond to her by saying, "You don't have anything I want to see." But, decided that it would be better to just let it go and keep his mouth shut.

Jennifer quickly changed out of her uniform and allowed Valerie and Sarah to wrap the towel around her naked body.

When they were done, Sarah poked Lieutenant Michael in the back and said, "We're ready, Lieutenant."

Lieutenant Michael and Major Josh turned around and the three girls were standing there, shivering in their bath towels.

Valerie said, "Doesn't Major Josh need to take off his clothing too?"

Major Josh smiled slyly and said, "Nope, as a member of Intelligence, I have the option of not having tracking devices on me, for obvious reasons."

Valerie tilted her head and looked at him questioningly, saying, "What reasons?"

Major Josh fixed his collar, took off his hat, and ran his hand through his hair. He said, "It is because I am in the Intelligence Division and I act as a spy. I need to be able to hide sometimes without being able to be tracked, so I do not have to have the locator chip on me."

Valerie nodded and said, "Oh, I see."

Major Josh turned to Michael and pointed at his ear piece, saying, "Do not forget your com unit."

Remembrance fell on Lieutenant Michael's face. He pulled the com unit out of his ear and placed it in the palm of his hand. He held his hand out and the three girls pulled their own com units out of their ears and placed it in Lieutenant Michael's waiting palm. He closed his fist over them and then turned his hand over, dropping them on the ground.

Major Josh said, "Are you ready to go? This is your last chance to go back and forget about all this."

Lieutenant Michael shook his head and said, "No, we want to know what's going on."

Major Josh nodded and stepped inside the helicopter. He went into the pilot's seat and said, "Alright, take a seat. I know it is crowded so do the best you can."

Lieutenant Michael crawled into the back of the helicopter. There was only one bench that ran along the back of the helicopter. He sat down in the middle and realized that there was only room for himself and two others.

Lieutenant Michael said, "Looks like one of you are going to have to sit on my lap."

Valerie raised her hand and said, "I'll do it! That sounds like the warmest seat."

Lieutenant Michael shrugged his shoulders and said, "I guess so."

Sarah sat down to the right of him. Jennifer sat down on the left of him. Valerie hopped onto his lap and leaned back against his chest. Lieutenant Michael wrapped his arms around her waist to keep her steady.

Major Josh looked behind himself at them and said, "Okay, looks like we are ready to go. This is an old helicopter so it will not be as fast as you are used to. We are probably going to have a four hour journey ahead of us so feel free to rest and relax back there."

Major Josh started the engine and the rotors started to spin above them. It was louder than they were expecting. The helicopter started to rise in the air. There were large windows along the side of the helicopter so they could easily see around them.

In the distance, Sarah noticed a large pack of fully-grown Harvesters. She pointed at them and spoke over the noise of the rotor, saying, "Looks like we got out of here just in time." She counted the Harvesters and there was around thirty-three of them; all of them fully-grown.

Sarah sighed and rested her head on Lieutenant Michael's arm. The stay awake pills were starting to wear off so she was starting to feel tired again. She said, "I wish I could take a bath." She closed her eyes and quickly fell asleep on his arm.

Jennifer tried to sit up but she too quickly passed out. She unconsciously leaned over and rested her head on Lieutenant Michael's other arm.

Valerie looked over at Sarah and Jennifer and saw that they had both fallen asleep. She looked up at Lieutenant Michael and smiled. He looked down at her and smiled back.

Valerie shifted her weight and twisted herself so that she was now sitting sideways on his lap. She brought her mouth closer to his ear and said, "I hope we can really stop the Harvesters." She then yawned and cuddled herself against his chest. She closed her eyes.

Lieutenant Michael kissed her on top of the head and said, "Me too."

The sun had fully set and the region was overtaken in a veil of darkness. Lieutenant Michael tried to force himself to stay awake but he kept dozing off and on again and again.

Suddenly, he felt a hand grab him and shake him. He forced himself awake to see Josh standing in the doorway, reaching out to him. Despite his best effort, he had managed to fall asleep deeply.

Major Josh quietly spoke, saying, "We have made it to our first destination. We need to abandon this helicopter in favor of the helicopter waiting there."

Lieutenant Michael pushed Sarah so that she was now leaning against the window on her side. She continued to sleep soundly. He then started to push Jennifer but she wrapped her arms around his arm and held on tightly. She spoke unconsciously in her sleep, saying, "Don't leave me alone."

Lieutenant Michael carefully slid his arm out of her grip and he stood up holding Valerie, who was still sleeping in his arms. He stepped out of the helicopter and saw a new helicopter not too far away. It was hard to see in the dark but it looked to be bigger than the current helicopter.

Lieutenant Michael carried Valerie to the new helicopter and put her on the bench with her head leaning against the window.

Major Josh came up behind him, carrying Jennifer. He set Jennifer next to Valerie and then got into the pilot's seat to check over things. He turned on the light inside the back of the helicopter.

Lieutenant Michael ran back to the first helicopter and picked up Sarah. As he picked her up, Sarah started to groan and said, "Let me sleep longer, dad." She went back to sleep in his arms.

Lieutenant Michael brought her into the new helicopter and placed her on the bench. Jennifer was leaning on Valerie, Valerie was now leaning back on Jennifer as they both continued to sleep. He set Sarah on the bench and leaned her against the window.

The cabin was roomier so there was actually room for him to sit on the bench as well. He was about to sit down but noticed four black backpacks leaning against the side of the cabin. He picked one up and said, "What are these?"

Major Josh looked back to see what Michael was talking about. He saw the black backpack in his hand and said, "I am guessing that those are your new clothes and equipment."

Lieutenant Michael opened the backpack and it had girls' clothing in it. He closed it back up and proceeded to open each backpack until he found one that had men's clothing in it.

He looked back to the girls to make sure they were asleep still. They looked to be passed out. He dropped his towel and quickly changed into some old jeans and a plain white tee shirt. He put on some new socks and a pair of tennis shoes. He hadn't worn civilian clothing in a long time. It felt old and stale against his skin.

At the bottom of the backpack there was a belt with a gun holster. There was an old Glock-seventeen pistol sitting in the holster.

Lieutenant Michael picked up the belt and strapped it around his waist. He pulled out the pistol and checked it over. It seemed to be in working order. He pulled the magazine out and saw that it was fully loaded. He snapped it back in and returned the pistol to its holster. He said, "You really planned on having me come, didn't you?"

Major Josh replied, "Yeah, I did. I truly believed that I would be able to convince you to come. I am glad that it was easier than I thought. I do not think that I could do this on my own without you."

Lieutenant Michael put his hand on Josh's shoulder and said, "I want to believe in you. If you really do have a way to end this war. I'll see it through to the end."

Major Josh smiled and turned his head forward to look at the controls. He said, "This next trip should take five or six hours. We are going to meet a man I met. It is this man who showed me what I want to show you. I told him all about you. That is where this helicopter and clothing come from."

Lieutenant Michael nodded and said, "Alright then. Let's get going so I can meet him."

Major Josh nodded and said, "Yeah." He turned on the helicopter and the rotors started to spin.

Lieutenant Michael sat down between Jennifer and Sarah. As he sat down, Jennifer repositioned herself and leaned back against Lieutenant Michael's arm. Valerie slid down and laid her head on Jennifer's lap. Sarah followed suite and leaned back onto his arm. He closed his eyes and tried to go back to sleep.

The sun started to rise and they had been in the air again for about five hours. Valerie woke up first among the girls and realized that she was sleeping on Jennifer's lap. She sat up and looked around confused. She said, "How'd I get here?"

Lieutenant Michael, who had woken up just before sunrise, said, "While you were sleeping we got into another helicopter."

Valerie looked surprised and said, "Wow, I must have been sleeping really deep."

Lieutenant Michael nodded with a smile, saying, "Well, you have been up for three days straight."

Lieutenant Michael pointed at one of the black backpacks on the floor and said, "That first backpack is yours. It has some clothing in it for you."

Valerie perked up and said, "Oh, that's great!" She slid off of the bench and took the backpack and opened it to see what was inside. There was a yellow short-sleeved dress in it with socks and shoes and underwear.

Valerie put the backpack down and then dropped the towel on the floor. Lieutenant Michael was surprised and quickly covered his eyes with his hand, saying, "Valerie, you know I'm right here."

Valerie shrugged her shoulders and said, "I don't really care about that." She quickly got dressed and sat back down on the bench.

Sarah woke up next and saw that she was in a completely different place.

Lieutenant Michael saw the confusion on her face and said, "We changed helicopters while you were asleep."

Sarah didn't reply to him. Her face showed that she was still pretty groggy. He pointed at the backpacks and said, "That backpack on the left has clothes in it for you."

Sarah slid off the bench and stretched, saying, "Ah, good morning, Lieutenant. Guess I'll get dressed too."

Sarah opened the backpack and pulled out a blue short-sleeved dress. She held it up in the rising sun light and said, "Cute, but a little obvious that it's for me."

Valerie said, "What do you mean?"

Sarah replied, "It's blue. I'm a blue wielder. Your dress is yellow. You're a yellow wielder."

Realization fell on Valerie's face and she said, "Oh, I didn't notice that."

Sarah slid the blue dress over her head and let it fall over her body. She then reached underneath the dress and pulled the towel off of her body and let it drop to the floor of the helicopter. She then put on the underwear, socks and shoes. She then sat back down on the bench.

Jennifer continued to sleep. Lieutenant Michael started to shake her. Slowly she sat up and looked around. As with the others, she was confused about where she was. Again, Lieutenant Michael explained to her what had happened.

Jennifer picked up the back pack and pulled out a red short-sleeved dress. She held it in front of her body and looked back to Lieutenant Michael with a depressed look on her face. She said, "You mean I got to change out in the open again?"

Lieutenant Michael said, "All you need to do is put the dress on over your body and then take the towel off. That's what Sarah did."

Sarah nodded her head and said, "Yep, that's what I did."

Jennifer looked suspiciously at Lieutenant Michael and then put the dress on over her towel. She then pulled the towel off and continued to dress herself. When she was done, she sat back down on the bench.

Lieutenant Michael said, "We're going to meet a friend of Josh soon. He's supposed to be the one who will show us what Josh is talking about."

Major Josh spoke up and said, "Yeah, we are just about there."

They looked out of the window and saw the ruins of a city. Most of the buildings had fallen apart. There was what looked like an old church building where half of the roof had caved in. Beside the old church, there was an empty parking lot.

Major Josh set the helicopter down in the old parking lot and said, "We are here!"

Lieutenant Michael stood up and opened the door of the helicopter. The cool morning air rushed in to fill the stale air in the cabin. Sarah jumped out first and stretched. She breathed in the cool morning air and looked around at the scenery.

Jennifer came out next. She stretched and yawned. She looked over the horizon at all the ruins around them.

Valerie hopped out of the helicopter and said, "I'm hungry. I hope we can eat soon."

Major Josh nodded and said, "I am sure my friend has some food for you."

Lieutenant Michael looked around and said, "I hope all this noise doesn't attract some Harvesters."

Major Josh shook his head and said, "I would not worry about that, brother."

Lieutenant Michael looked at him questioningly, and said, "Why not?"

Major Josh smiled and paused for a moment. He said, "Because ... he has technology that can keep the Harvesters away from an area."

Lieutenant Michael's eyes opened wide and his jaw dropped. He shook his head and said, "No way! Really? He'd make a fortune off of that."

Major Josh nodded and said, "Yeah, he really does. The World Government already has this technology but they are not willing to use it. Let us go and meet my friend now. I am sure he is waiting for us."

Together, they walked up the old stairs that were in front of the abandoned church. The front door was large and made out of wood. It appeared to be rotting away. Josh pushed the door open. It creaked loudly. They stepped inside.

Most of the left side of the ceiling had collapsed onto the rows of pews beneath them. On the right side, spiders had woven a covering of webs over the pews that were not crushed by the ceiling. The morning sun shone through the open ceiling, bringing light into the abandoned church.

A dust covered red rug led from the doorway to the front of the church where an old podium stood. It too was covered in dust and cobwebs. Behind the podium was a large wooden cross.

Lieutenant Michael noticed a strange man with his back turned to them. He wore what looked like a navy blue trench coat and a black three-cornered hat. The mysterious man held his hands behind his back and looked up at the cross in front of him.

The man didn't seem to notice them. Josh started walking toward him. Michael followed him and the girls trailed behind. They got half way to the podium when the man finally turned around.

The man's face was covered with a mask. The mask was divided into two colors: on the left side it was black and on the right side it was white. The mask projected a wide sinister smile that alternated its color on each side of the mask. On the right side the mouth was black and on the left side it was white. Around the right eye hole there was the shape of a black sun and to the side of the left eye hole there was a white crescent moon. From the front, the trench coat that he wore looked more like an eighteenth century style frock coat. It was navy blue on the outside and had a red lining on the inside. He also wore a white waist coat with a white silk cravat.

Josh and the others took a few more steps closer to the podium. The man threw his arms wide open and said, "Greetings, Mr. O'Brian and Mr. Snyder! I have heard so much about you, Mr. Snyder."

As the man talked, the eyes behind the mask seemed off, like they were missing color or something. Michael couldn't tell what exactly was wrong. It was just a feeling he had.

In addition to this, the man seemed familiar to him. He knew that he had seen him before but couldn't quite place him in his mind.

The strange man walked out from behind the podium. He wore white breeches and black knee-length boots. His arms were still stretched out wide. The man said, "I am so glad that you have decided to join us. Mr. O'Brian told me that you could be depended on, Mr. Snyder."

Michael took another few steps forward.

The man put his arms down and said, "Mr. Snyder, my name is Justice."

Suddenly Michael had a flash back. He remembered a man standing on the Denver Sector wall. The man had on the same outfit and mask as the terrorist who blew up the Denver Sector wall.

Immediately, Michael pulled the pistol out of its holster, flung out his arm toward the man, and pointed the pistol towards the man's mask. He said, "You're that psycho that blew up the Denver Sector wall! How the hell are you still alive after that explosion?"

The man started laughing maniacally, he threw up his hands again and said, "I'm alive because I hold the power of God!"

The man put his hands behind his back and leaned forward a little. He took a few steps forward toward Michael.

Michael yelled at him, "Don't move, or I'll shoot!"

The man took a few more steps forward and said, "Are you afraid of me, Mr. Snyder?" He took a few more steps forward. His mask seemed focused entirely on Michael. He said, "You shouldn't fear me, Mr. Snyder." He took a few more steps forward. He then stopped and leaned forward till his mask was touching the barrel of Michael's gun in the middle of his forehead. He said, "You shouldn't fear me, a servant of God, Mr. Snyder. You should fear the government that thinks it is God."

Michael continued to hold the barrel of the pistol against the man's mask. He tried to stare into the man's eyes. Being closer, he could better see them through the eye holes of the mask. They looked wrong. They seemed to be just white. There were no pupil or iris as far as he could tell.

Michael said, "My brother tells me that you are the man who can show me the truth of this world. Is that really true?"

The man, still leaning his mask on Michael's gun said, "Yes, I can show you everything if you are willing to come with me and see."

Michael said, "Why did you blow up the Denver Sector wall?"

The man, not moving, said, "It was the only way I could obtain certain secret files that we needed from the World Government capitol."

Michael said, "You murdered millions of people just to get your hands on some secret files?"

The man stood up straight and spread out his arms wide, he looked toward the roof and shouted, "Fiat Justitia ruat caelum! Let justice be done though the heaven's fall!"

Michael said, "So, you're willing to do whatever you want to obtain your so-called justice?"

The man dropped his hands and held them behind his back again. The never changing expression of the mask was disturbing. It lacked true emotion.

Michael lowered his arm, dropping the gun to his side. He said, "How can I know that your so called justice won't get me or my girls killed?"

The man replied, "You can't. I may be killed myself. I didn't kill those people just to kill people. I sacrificed a few million people to save a billion people. If we don't stop the coming tragedy, all of humanity will be extinguished because of the delusions of the insane."

Michael stuck his gun in his holster and said, "Delusions of the insane? You sound pretty insane to me."

The man, Justice, laughed maniacally again. He said, "Oh, I am insane, but just because I am insane does not mean that I am wrong."

Michael turned to Josh and said, "Do you really trust this psycho?"

Josh nodded his head and said, "Yeah, I do."

Michael sighed heavily and said, "Alright, Justice. If my brother trusts you, then so will I for the moment. But, if I think you are going to do something that will harm one of my girls, I'll shoot you myself."

Justice bowed and said with a chuckle, "Agreed!"

Michael looked at the girls. They met his gaze. They could tell by the look on his face that he was unsure about the situation. They looked back at him with the same look.

Michael turned towards Justice again and said, "Alright, what do you want to show me first?"

Justice took off his hat and placed it over his heart and said, "First, let me introduce you to my lovely daughters."

He spun around to face the back of the church again. He stretched out his right arm towards a door located in the back and shouted, "Come forth, my darling angels!"

The door opened up in the back and three teenage looking girls stepped out of the back room. They wore Victorian-esque style dresses that went down to their knees. Their dresses were white triple-layered underneath with another colored layer of red, blue or yellow on the outside that opened in the front to reveal the white layered dress in front. The front of the dress was tied with a ribbon that ascended from the waist to the top of the bust. Along the hem of the dress in the front were two gothic crosses in the same red, blue, or yellow color.

The girl in the yellow dress had a pale complexion and platinum hair like Valerie's hair. She had it in twin tails with yellow ribbons tying them in place.

She stared at Michael and the girls with her yellow glowing eyes and a sinister smile.

The girl in the blue dress had red hair and a light colored complexion with freckles all over her cheeks. She wore a blue bonnet with white lace that held her hair back. She smiled nervously as she cautiously stepped out of the back room. Her eyes glowed blue. She glared nervously at Michael.

The last girl, in the red dress, had brown hair and a very light olive colored complexion. Her hair was down but was held back by a red colored head band with white lace that was tied underneath her chin with a ribbon. She looked at the little girls with a menacing smile and said, "Papa, are we going to kill them?" Her eyes glowed with red light.

Justice said, "No, my dear, they are going to join us. They're friends not foes."

The three young women walked over to Justice and surrounded him.

The girl in yellow wrapped her arms around his left arm and said, "Papa, the girls look so tiny."

The girl in blue hid behind his right arm. She peeked and glared at them from behind his arm.

The girl in red walked around Justice and stood in front of him. She squared her arms on her hips and glared at Michael. She said, "I won't let you hurt our papa! Papa saved us!"

Justice spoke up, saying, "Calm down, my angel. I know what I'm doing. They're going to help us stop the bad men."

Justice pointed to the girl in red and said, "This is Michelle, a red Wielder."

Michelle flared her dress with her hands and gave them a curtsy, saying, "It is a pleasure to meet you." She then walked over to Michael and looked him up and down. She walked around him while tracing her finger around his shoulders, saying, "You, Mr. Snyder, are a very handsome man."

Justice pointed to the girl in blue and said, "This is Gabrielle, a blue wielder."

Gabrielle, still hiding behind his arm, bowed her head in silence. Justice said, "Do forgive her, she's a little shy around strange men."

Justice then pointed to the girl in yellow and said, "This is Raphael, a yellow wilder."

Raphael let go of his arm and flared out her dress with her hands and did a curtsy, saying, "Welcome to our group. I hope that we can become good friends."

Michael shook his head and said, "Wait up, wait up, wait a minute. These three girls are Wielders, right? I can see their eye colors but they look too old. Just how old are they?

Michelle curtsied again and said, "I'm eighteen. I'm of legal age."

Raphael said, "I'm sixteen."

Gabrielle continued to hide her face behind her father's arm. Justice nudged her with his elbow and said, "Come on, my darling angel, tell the nice man how old you are."

Gabrielle shyly looked towards Michael and muttered, "I ... I ... I'm seventeen." She then hid her face behind his shoulder and went silent again.

Michael covered his face with his hands and said, "How is this even possible?"

Sarah looked at them and said, "Did you not have your period yet?"

Michelle laughed and said, "Of course I did. I was twelve when I got mine."

Sarah looked to Michael and tugged on his shirt, saying, "What does this mean? Is there a way to stop us from dying a year after our period?"

Michael looked over at them again. He shook his head and said, "How? How? How did you manage to stop their bodies from self-destructing from their powers?"

Justice freed himself from his daughters' grasp and walked over in front of Michael. He offered up his hand as if to shake it and said, "If you want to know, come with me and I'll show you everything that is hidden from you."

Michael stared at Justice's open hand. He knew that if there was a way to stop their self-destruction he had to find out no matter the cost. He grasped onto Justice's hand and shook it firmly, saying, "Alright, Justice. I'll go along with you. Count me in for now."

Afterword

I am so grateful to the people who supported me in my first book and told me they loved it. I am very happy to present to all of you who loved my first book with this second book. I hope that is was as enjoyable to read as the first one. I am also very thankful to Veronica, my niece, who drew the artwork for this volume as well. I am also grateful for the people who helped me to edit my story.

In this volume, I hoped to draw out that there is a very deep mystery in the world of Tears of Darkness. This mystery will be unraveled in the third volume that will be coming out. I haven't fully decided if Volume 3 will be divided into two Volumes or if I will release an expanded Volume 3 that will be the conclusion. I will see how much material I have when I get to a certain point.

Anyway, I hope that you will look forward to the third volume. I have already begun it. For now you will have to ponder how Michelle, Gabrielle, and Raphael managed to live for so long. Will Lieutenant Michael and Rachel ever get together? Will Valerie get to watch the next episode of Magical Girl Squad? Find out all the answers to those most important questions in the next volume.

If you want to stay updated on my projects please visit my blog @: sophialiddellbooks.webs.com

You can also find me on Crunchyroll: www.crunchyroll.com/user/SophiaLiddell

You can also join the TEARS OF DARKNESS Group on Crunchyroll: www.crunchyroll.com/group/Tears_of_Darkness

See you next time in,
TEARS OF DARKNESS, Volume 3:
Fallen Angels

www.ingramcontent.com/pod-product-compliance
Lightning Source LLC
Chambersburg PA
CBHW031956170626
46807CB00006B/2514